A FOOL'S CIRCLE

SUZANNE SEDDON

A WALLACE PUBLISHING BOOK

ISBN: 978-1-9996136-3-1

First published in 2019 by Wallace Publishing, United
Kingdom.

Cover Design: Hammad Khalid
Interior Layout: Luca Funari

sueseddon33@hotmail.com

www.facebook.com/AFOOLSCIRCLE

@suzseddon @AFOOLSCIRCLE

@suzseddon

ACKNOWLEDGEMENTS

I would like to thank a few people. Firstly, Ken Scott, for the help and advice he gave me. Also, my dear friend Emma Keast, who encouraged me and helped me more than she knows, always giving me that kick up the backside when I needed it. And my daughter, Poppy, for putting up with her mother and the endless amounts of paper she leaves everywhere.

Thank you x

CONTENTS

DEDICATION

For my mum, who always gave me love, strength and encouragement. I miss you every day.

For my beautiful daughter Poppy, for the joy and love you give me each day. I'm truly blessed.

For the strongest person I know, who has fought many battles. Me!

CHAPTER 1

A blonde head bounced on the floor in time to the yelling. Rays of the early morning sun caught her golden hair, and motes of dust hung in the air. Sophie Saunders was eight years old. Kneeling down on the floor, she played with her dolls, drumming Ken and Barbie against the carpet, her body bent forward, almost as if she were praying in her immaculately clean and pressed school uniform. But today her school uniform was the last thing on her mind. She bashed the dolls' heads off the pink floor in unison.

'Ring-a-Ring-a-Rosie,' she sang aloud to herself as she tried to drown out the voices that rose up through the floorboards.

The noises from downstairs were a regular occurrence, and fast becoming the norm. Sophie felt her dad's anger, ever-present in his voice as it vibrated through her bedroom, positioned over the kitchen. Scared, she dropped her dolls, raising her arms and clasping her small hands over her ears. Sophie closed her eyes. Blinded, she felt for Barbie and Ken and gripped the toys by the legs. With one in each hand, she remained still for a moment, and as the voices intensified beneath her, she sensed them possessing the dolls.

'You're an old bag. I hate you!'

Sophie's voice was deep and rough, as she rammed Ken's head into Barbie's chest.

'Why are you always so nasty to me?'

She raised the pitch of her voice as she shook the dolls hard.

'Because you make me want to vomit when I look at your fat ugly face,' she growled.

'Please stop being so cruel to me,' she enunciated.

'Who do you think you are? Don't you dare tell me what to do, bitch!'

With each word, she struck Ken against Barbie, again and again, until finally Barbie's head popped off and rolled across the carpet.

That hadn't been her intention. She didn't mean to decapitate the poor doll. Shocked, she stood up as she searched for the missing head. She found it under the bedside cabinet at the back, by the wall. She crouched down, stretched out her arm and grabbed it. Sophie sat up on her knees, struggling to reattach the plastic head to its body.

'Bloody shit! Why won't it go on?' The racket from below grew ever louder. 'Bloody shit.' Frustrated, she gave up, and flung the dolls across the room.

Downstairs, her father, Alan, almost lost his head. He shouted louder as his wife, Kate, persisted as the peacemaker.

'As useless as a one-legged woman in an arse-kicking contest.'

His voice echoed around the large stark white room, drowning out the soothing music from the old radio sitting on the window ledge.

'You're one useless bastard!'

The barrage of abuse had just hit average level.

'Fucking useless.'

The kitchen had seen better days, as had their marriage, but Kate worked hard to keep both spotless and functional.

'Can you hear me?'

She strived hard at everything, as she had for a lifetime.

'Hello? Is there anyone home?'

However, her efforts now went unnoticed or

drew heavy criticism for no reason.

'I'm fucking talking to you, whore.'

She knew only too well what was about to come her way, as she moved the blonde strand of hair out of her blue eyes and concentrated. She placed the boiled egg safely into its cup.

'Where's this fucking breakfast, for fuck's sake?'

She reached out her arm, picked up the knife and, clenching it tight in her hand, she decapitated the top of the egg.

'I can hear you, Alan.' The toast was the light side of brown, just as he liked it, but who knew these days? 'There's no point keeping on at me, shouting. I can't go any faster.'

She set the breakfast plate before Alan. His face was dark and menacing—the antithesis of the light sense of fun that had been knocked out of her.

'About fucking time. Talk about slow. You're like a human fucking sloth.'

After ten years together, she found it more of a challenge to stay positive. Alan had turned negativity into a vocation.

'What the flying fuck is this?'

She stared at the top of his head, bristling with the military-style haircut he'd had since he was a child, raised by an army commander who gave no quarter.

'Do you seriously expect me to eat this fucking lot of shite?' Alan had adopted the same rank in the family, but hadn't served a moment in the services. 'All these years, and you still can't boil a fucking egg? I mean, it's not fucking rocket science.' She watched him as he snarled at her. 'You've got to be having some sort of a laugh.'

He pushed the plate away with such force, it shot forward and hit the condiment pots. Kate flinched as the sharp noise pierced her ears. 'Why, what's wrong with it now?' She clenched her fists as her body shook. Her nerves were all on the surface, as he mocked her and revelled in her fear.

'What's bloody wrong with it? It's the wrong colour, undercooked and looks like my fucking snot. You really are a fucking retard!'

She watched as his sneer took what used to be a pleasantly rugged face – a lifetime ago – and warped it monstrously.

'Well, I can do another for you, if you like. It won't take me a minute!'

She tried her hardest to stay calm, fearful of what might come next.

'That's how long I think you boiled that one for, a fucking minute, so what's the bloody point? You'll only mess it up again, you thick tart.'

Kate, petrified, noticed the pure evil as it manifested once again across his face.

'You're miles away these days. Maybe you should go see a doctor and get some happy pills from him. For fuck's sake, you can't even time an egg.'

Once again defeated, she bit her lip and her voice broke.

'Well, I did boil it for three minutes.'

She watched his face as it reddened. She knew the inevitable was about to happen, and wished it over and done with.

'Yeah, yeah. Let's face it, darling, you're no good at cooking, no good in bed — in fact, you're no good at fucking anything really. I bloody dread mealtimes in this house.'

The victorious grin that had taken residence across his smug face frightened her.

'I try my best, Alan, I really do.'

Kate's voice sounded weak. Alan fed off her vulnerability as he chipped away at her. He cranked up the volume another notch.

'You really are a fucking retard. You're trying

to poison me with salmonella.' Alan stretched out his arm, picking up the boiled egg. Terrified, she eyed him as he gripped it tightly in his hand. 'Trying to do me in with food poisoning, are you?'

Kate jerked as he lobbed the egg towards her, raising her arm, shielding it from her face as it side-swiped her head. She tried to pick fragments of sticky shell out of her hair.

'That's what I think about your boiled eggs. Now go and fucking clean it up!'

She decided the best defence was to stay silent. Terrified, she turned her back on him, and tried to disappear into the background.

'Don't turn your back on me, I'm fucking talking to you! You're one ignorant bitch. Don't you dare fucking ignore me!'

She closed her eyes tight and gritted her teeth, trying hard to remain calm.

'I'm not ignoring you. I'm trying to get Sophie's breakfast ready or she'll be late for school.'

Her smooth tone stoked his fury more.

'I don't even know why I fucking married you. I could've done so much better. My parents were right on the money when they said I married down. An army bigwig and a doctor they were, and what are you? A washed-up failed actress, a shit teacher, and a poor excuse for a fucking wife.'

She ignored him as the vile comments became more and more aggressive.

'I mean, have you taken a fucking good look at yourself lately?'

He rotated his chair towards her. She watched him in terror as he looked her up and down like he'd just stepped in a massive turd.

'Please don't, Alan. Please don't start again today.'

She arranged the plate of food as fast as she could. Jumpy and exasperated, she picked up the tea towel from the draining board and wiped the edges clean, as he continued to mock her.

'"Please don't, Alan – please don't, Alan." Can you hear yourself, Kate?'

The onslaught continued towards danger point.

'You've really let yourself go over the years. You need to get yourself to the fucking gym and start exercising. I married a woman, not a lard arse. Just look at you!'

She was tall and well-proportioned. If Alan wanted an anorexic model, he was living in cloud cuckoo land – and the wrong neighbourhood.

'Oh, for crying out loud, Alan.' Her adrenalin kicked in, and she snapped out of her former resignation. She threw down the tea towel on the worktop. 'I do exercise, Alan, when I have the time!'

'Ha! Are you having a fucking bubble? You keep telling yourself that. You're a silly stupid fat tart. You should take a leaf out of your friend Jill's book. Now she looks great. Perfect little figure, and a great pair of tits!'

He did nothing to hide the wicked grin that was plastered across his face, or his semi-erection. Watching him, repulsed, she tried logic.

'Well, Jill hasn't got any children to worry about, or a husband for that matter, so she has more time on her hands than I bloody well do.'

She continued to busy herself, reaching into the cupboard next to her and removing a plate.

'Excuses, Kate, always bloody excuses with you! Don't you know the truth always comes out? Mind you, you wouldn't know the truth if it jumped up and took a bite-sized chunk out of your big fat fucking arse, you thick bitch.'

Her stomach churned. She didn't want another fight. Against her better judgement, she apologised. 'I'm sorry about the egg, Alan, I really am, but do you have to do this now? Sophie will be down for her breakfast any minute.'

She showed him Sophie's plate. Desperate, she reminded him of their daughter's existence. Kate was taken aback as she heard the almighty roar that bellowed out of his mouth.

'Who the fuck do you think you are? You think you can tell me what I can and cannot do in my own house!'

The house belonged to both of them, a wedding gift from his parents, but she wasn't about to argue the toss about that now.

'Please, Alan, Sophie will hear you. It's not fair she has to listen to this day in, day out. Do you not think about what this is doing to her? She's your daughter, for heaven's sake.'

She hated the sound of her weak voice.

'Well, that's fucking debatable.'

Sickened, Kate watched him as he swayed in his chair like a hypnotised cobra. A dreary Coldplay song rang out on the radio.

'I don't give a toss about you or your fucking daughter.'

The saliva flew in all directions across the kitchen, as he continued to spit more venom in her direction.

'It's my fucking house, my rules. Anyway, look at you. And what's that on your face? Is that make-up and lipstick you're wearing? Where do you think you're going today with all that crap on your face? You look like a washed-up old whore!'

She was frozen to the spot, and the colour drained fast from her face.

'It's just pink lip gloss, for goodness sake. What the hell's wrong with you?'

His eyes bulged from their sockets like a bullfrog's, his tongue sharp like a flickering whip, as he leapt from his chair and grabbed her firmly by the hair. 'Lip gloss, my arse.' She fought hard to hold on to Sophie's plate as he ground his thumb into her mouth and smeared the tacky pink gloss across her cheek.

'Ha! That's more like it! As if lipstick or lip gloss is going to help you.'

She felt the sting as the palm of his hand connected hard against her cheek. He picked up the dirty tea towel.

'Please, Alan, stop this.'

He rubbed it hard across her flushed skin. Kate, struggling to breathe, heard crash as the plate fell to the floor.

'Look at the tea towel, cunt. It's fucking make-up. Stop fucking lying to me!'

She could smell the remnants of the stale booze on his breath, which made her heave. 'I'm not lying.' She struggled hard to pull away from him, her eyes drawn towards the doorway. She noticed Sophie standing there, her perfect angelic face pale and in shock.

'Go away!' Kate mouthed to her terrified daughter.

'What was that, bitch? Are you talking back to me again?'

She felt the sharp pain hit, as he punched her hard in the stomach. As Kate fell to her knees, she heard Sophie's voice.

'Leave my mummy alone!'

Kate looked up at him, and at the same time his expressive dark eyes narrowed. Alan turned around and faced his daughter.

'Oh, it's you! Have you seen your mother? Doesn't she look like a cheap whore? This is what you'll look like one day if you let yourself turn into a sack of shit like her!'

He hoisted Kate up from the floor by her hair, on to her feet, and slapped her viciously again across her cheek.

She screamed. 'Get out, Sophie! Get out!'

Kate watched Sophie as she turned around

and raced from the kitchen in floods of tears. She pleaded with him:

'Alan, please stop this! Please!'

She stumbled as he pushed her hard into the side of the Formica worktop. Unsteady on her feet, she reached out with both hands and gripped on to it.

'You're lucky I've got things to do today and that I don't have to spend another minute looking at your gormless fucking mug!'

She watched as he grabbed his jacket off the back of the kitchen chair and threw it across his right shoulder.

'What have I told you about lying, Kate?'

She saw the triumphant expression on his face as he left the kitchen and whistled down the hallway. Kate listened out as he opened the front door, and jumped as she heard his voice again.

'Make sure you clean up all the mess and scrape all that raw egg off those bloody tiles.'

She closed her eyes for a split second and there came another almighty loud bang as the front door slammed shut behind him. Kate's whole body trembled with this aftershock.

'God help me,' she said to herself.

She crawled across the kitchen floor, picked up the newspaper off the chair and gathered the food and shards of broken plate onto it as she chanted to herself.

'Come on, Kate, come on, Kate, you can do this.'

She eased herself up, grabbed a cloth from the sink and rubbed away at the mess as she spoke to herself again. 'What did I do to deserve this bloody life?' Her thoughts turned to her daughter and she made her way out of the kitchen, calling out her name: 'Sophie.' Kate stood in the hallway and listened, but got no answer from her daughter. She spotted the photograph of Alan on the floor and was distracted for a moment. She looked at his sadistic face staring back at her through the cracked glass. She hung it slapdash back in its pride of place on the wall, and made her way back into the kitchen. Kate started once again on Sophie's breakfast, calling out to her again.

'Sophie darling, I'm making your breakfast. He's gone out. Please come down.'

Unable to stop the massive flow of tears that streamed fast down her sore, swollen cheeks, she placed another piece of bread in the toaster. She pulled a tissue from the box on top of the fridge as Sophie called out to her. Kate dabbed her swollen eyes.

'I'm coming now, Mummy, I won't be long, I'm just putting my toys away.'

Kate always worried at how much the arguments and fights her daughter had witnessed throughout her parents' volatile relationship had affected her and it made the anger inside her rise when she looked at him.

'Okay, Sophie, hurry up.'

She blamed him for being such a nasty, horrible bastard, a terrible father to their daughter. She had to get away from this monster somehow, but where would they go?

'I'm here, Mummy.'

The bread popped out of the toaster as Sophie's voice broke her from her reverie. 'Oh, good. I timed that just right.'

Surprised by Sophie's small arms around her waist, the intimate contact made Kate cry. Sophie's tears leaked out of her and soaked through her blouse as they sobbed together.

'Are you okay, Mummy?'

Sophie's angelic face was so wan and she worried so much for her. Determined, Kate pulled herself together for the sake of her daughter.

'Mummy, please don't cry. Are you okay?' She knew Sophie worried about her also.

Sophie continued to cry. Kate reached out for her face and kissed her flushed cheeks.

'I'm fine, Sophie. Don't you fret about me, Daddy is just in a bad mood, what with him losing his job.'

She held Sophie close. As she felt the small girl's heartbeat close to hers, she regretted the day she set eyes on Alan, and married the heartless bastard.

'Daddy is always in a bad mood, Mummy.'

The emotionless statement of fact chilled her to the bone.

'That job meant the world to Daddy. It'll be okay, Sophie, he's just upset.'

She didn't believe it but felt she had to say it anyway.

'But, Mummy, it's not your fault Daddy lost his job, is it? Why does he hit you all the time and say nasty things to you?'

She knew Sophie wouldn't understand the reasoning.

'Daddy doesn't mean to act like that, baby, he's just frustrated, and he feels upset a lot. He'll be fine once he gets another job, you'll see. Come on, Sophie, no more crying now please,'

She wiped away her daughter's tears with the sleeve of her blouse as she faked a smile.

Resolute as she got back to the job at hand, she busied herself once again.

'Well, I don't like it, Mummy.'

She removed the lightly toasted bread from the toaster, buttered it and popped it onto another plate, as Sophie continued to talk. 'He's a big bully.' Kate didn't feel the need to answer as she removed a glass from the cupboard, picked up the fresh orange juice carton and poured her daughter a drink.

'But Mummy, Daddy was mean to you even when he had a job. Why does he talk and smell funny when he drinks that stinky brown stuff? Children notice everything you know.'

Kate carried on regardless as she placed the toast and orange juice down in front of Sophie on the table.

'It'll be okay, Sophie, we just have to be a little bit more patient with him, that's all, and –'

The sound of the doorbell echoed off the kitchen walls and caused them both to jump. Kate, on tenterhooks, panicked. Had Alan forgotten his keys?

'Sophie, just sit there properly and eat your breakfast, love, let me go and get the door, okay?' Her heart pounded in her chest.

'It might be Daddy back again, Mummy.'

Unruffled, she pushed the hair out of her eyes, and snagged the dishcloth by the sink as she tried to wipe the rest of the sticky lip gloss from her face.

'Did I get it all?'

She watched Sophie; as she looked up at Kate's face she smiled.

'Come here, Mummy, you can't go to the door like that, let me help you.'

Kate perched herself on the kitchen chair as she handed Sophie the cloth, and with a delicate hand, she finished the job.

'All done, Mummy.'

Kate kissed her on the cheek, and smiled at her daughter. She knew Sophie was the only person that kept her going every day.

'What would I do without you? You eat up now like the good girl you are, Sophie.'

She stood up, as she stroked Sophie's hair, as fine as silk. It was the same burnished blonde as hers.

'I love you, Sophie.'

Sophie picked up her glass and sipped the tart soft drink. Kate watched her as she stared miserably at the cold toast on her plate, unimpressed.

'I love you too, Mummy.'

She breathed a sigh of relief as she recognised the voice that shouted through the letterbox.

'Sophie, Sophie, it's Megan. Are you ready for school?'

Kate started as Sophie gulped the rest of her orange juice, threw the cold toast back on its plate, and jumped up from her chair like she had just undergone an electric shock.

'It's okay. It's Megan and her mum. I've got to go or I'm going to be late for school, Mummy.'

Sophie picked up her school bag and kissed her on the cheek. Kate was captivated as Sophie raced towards the front door and shouted back to her.

'See you tonight, Mum. I love you.'

Relieved, Kate collapsed onto the kitchen chair, and tried to collect her thoughts. As she heard the doorbell again she spoke to herself as it echoed through the kitchen. 'I wonder what she's forgotten this time.' On her feet again, she walked along the hallway as Alan's father's Army headshot stared back at her. Ahead, through the glass in the door, she could see a silhouette of someone, as she called out.

'Sophie, is that you?'

Kate stood still, surrounded by the photographs in the hallway; a complete record of Alan's life from a Boy Scout bully armoured in badges, whistle and toggle to one of him with his distant half-brother, Barry, made her feel uneasy as she spoke to herself.

'What have you forgotten this time? I bet it's your pencil case again.'

Her brain was flooded by childhood photos of her first time on stage as an angel in the school nativity play and on a family holiday, as well as Christmas shots that once hung there. Saddened, she pushed them from her mind as she called out. 'Hold on a minute, Sophie, I'm coming.'

Kate knew nothing survived the passage of Alan. Like a slow-motion tsunami, he'd sluiced through their shared lives and swept them entirely from the landscape.

She smiled as she heard the voice from the other side of the door.

'It's not Sophie, it's me. Open the bloody door, Kate, I'm bloody freezing my tits off out here.'

Little did Alan know, right there, on the second step up against the skirting board, years ago, Kate had carefully raised the carpet and slipped the photo of her and Sophie underneath. So, now each time she walked past, or mounted the stairs, she'd know that no matter how much

Alan battered and pounded her, a part of her would always survive and that part had so many plans. But right now, all Kate had was uncertainty.

CHAPTER 2

Kate walked towards the door and pulled it open. She reeled backwards at the sight that stood before her.

'What took you so long?' She looked like the bride of Chuckie in a white braless dress. Her bleached blonde curly hair and scarlet red lips made Kate blink hard.

'Bloody hell, Kate, are you going to let me in or what? I'm starting to turn blue.'

Kate managed to raise a smile at her friend as she spoke. 'Where the hell have you been?' It was obvious she hadn't been home the evening before. Kate wondered what on earth had possessed Jill to do the walk of shame.

'Never mind that, let me in.'

Kate looked her up and down in a deliberate manner. As Jill stood in the doorway, she shivered in her flimsy dress.

'Did you get dressed in the dark or have you been out all night again?' Kate was almost flattened as Jill's large chest knocked her out the way as she stumbled down the hallway towards the kitchen. 'Bloody hell, Jill, careful.' Kate closed the front door and shook her head as she followed behind her friend. Jill was already sitting at the kitchen table as she caught up with her.

'Stick the kettle on, Kate. I'm spitting feathers here. It's that vodka I drank last night. Gives me a mouth like Gandhi's flip-flop.'

Confused at her friend's arrival, Kate did what she was told and studied her only confidante in the world. All dolled up like a back-street whore. Mesmerised, Kate forced a smile as she listened to her.

'I'm sorry for turning up unannounced, but I heard about your Aunt Beth passing away. As I was around the corner staying with my new man friend last night, I thought I would come and see how you're doing, but by the look of you, not so good!'

Kate, distracted by her sympathetic face, wondered if she was aware she only had on one false eyelash caked in thick black mascara. 'That's good of you. Thank you, Jill.' She decided not to mention Jill's latest conquest. She was touched that her best friend had tottered through the streets like an extra from *A Clockwork Orange* just to come and console her.

'I'm bearing up, Jill. It's been awful. I can't believe I'm not going to see her again. I'm really going to miss her, and Sophie is heartbroken. I just find myself bursting into tears all the time. I'm so glad you popped in.'

She appreciated her friend's kind, selfless act.

'Oh Kate, I can't imagine what you've been going through. You know I'm always here for you — you're my best friend, for heaven's sake. Just pick the phone up and call me; don't matter what time it is.'

Kate watched as Jill opened and reached into her handbag.

'Oh, and before I forget, these are for Sophie, I know she likes them, but that's all I could get this morning, and don't forget to give her a kiss from her Auntie Jill.'

Kate smiled as she watched her pull out four large bags of sweets and place them on the table. 'You didn't have to do that! Sophie will be pleased.' She felt blessed Jill was always there during the good times and the bad, although the latter had taken precedence these days.

'I'm so sorry, Kate, I know it must have been a big shock to you and Sophie. Wasn't Aunt Beth the one that was well off? The artist? I don't want to sound heartless but she might have left you and Sophie a few quid.' Kate raised a half smile. 'You never know. You and Sophie might be able to get away from that bastard of a husband, Alan, sooner than you think.'

She could feel the bile as it started to rise in the pit of her stomach at just the simple mention of his name.

'Oh Jill, we have had another bad morning with him, the aggression and violence. It's all getting too much. All I think about is Sophie, she has seen some terrible things. The guilt I feel is terrible. Why is he like this, Jill?'

Kate's thoughts drifted. Years ago, when Kate and Jill were at university, they were on a night out to the theatre in London's West End to see the play *Les Misérables*. It was during the interval that Kate bumped into a stranger and spilt her drink all down the front of his shirt as the thirsty stampede of theatregoers charged towards her to purchase their drinks from the bar. Kate cringed with embarrassment as she watched Jill launch herself at him. She started to rub a tissue across his torso in a seductive manner then proceeded to thrust her large chest into his face, as he gasped for air.

Jill's voice brought her back to the present.

'I told you from the start that bastard was no good the night you met him. There was something about him, I could see it in his face, Kate. I've met blokes like him before, but you didn't listen to me, though, did you?'

Kate eyed her friend, surprised that she had adopted a selective memory. She took a deep breath and raised her eyebrows, as she looked across at her.

'That's not quite how I remember it, Jill.'

'Well it was a long time ago, Kate, but he was still an arsehole in my book.'

Kate replayed the vivid comedy scene from her youth yet again. She remembered the shock on Alan's red, angry face as he struggled to force Jill's hands off him. Jill, rejected, was taken aback and told Kate not to entertain him and called him a loser as she walked away. Kate had caught his gaze and noticed his anger was short-lived as it dissolved from his face.

He was quite easy on the eye. His thick brown hair was clean cut and the subtle scent of his sweet-smelling aftershave filled her nostrils. He apologised and let out an awkward laugh as he offered to buy her another drink.

They talked and laughed through the whole

interval, as Jill watched them from the other end of the bar, perched on a bar stool with a face like a slapped arse. Kate decided to ignore her. It was when she had got up to leave for the second half of the show that he asked her out on a date.

A long week had passed by until he called her up and arranged to take her out. It was on that first date he told her that he couldn't stop thinking about her and after six dinner dates, he said one day he would marry her. Kate, embarrassed, brushed it off, as she turned a light shade of crimson.

It was almost four months later when he proposed, in front of his friends and family at a top-notch posh restaurant.

She had never seen such a place before, all crystal glasses, fine china and chandeliers. He had kept it such a surprise that none of Kate's friends or her dear Aunt Beth had been invited. But swept off her feet, in love and caught up in the moment, she had said yes, unable to believe she could feel so happy and content.

They had moved into the house his parents had bought for them after they were married, but it had been hard for Kate being left on her own as Alan continued to work abroad, sometimes six to ten months at a time, only to return for a week here and there, then off again to another secret location.

It was during one of Alan's return trips that by chance happened to fall on their three-year wedding anniversary that she became pregnant. She was ecstatic, hoping that the child would bring them closer and complete them as a family.

Having gone through a difficult pregnancy, it was during a scorching hot summer on the last day of June that she gave birth to a healthy baby girl at the local hospital and named her Sophie.

Jill had come to visit her and had brought Sophie some beautiful gifts. Kate was grateful but it didn't make up for Alan's absence. All she received from him was a drunk gibberish phone call telling her he would be home in a few months.

Devastated and alone, Kate balanced her job as a teacher in the local school and motherhood, which helped fill the void of Alan not being around.

She was eternally grateful and happy that Jill was nearby to lend a hand whenever she needed it.

They had been married nine years when Alan was offered a permanent position in London.

Kate was so happy he had accepted it, and although she had worried that they had never really lived together for long as man and wife, she was still pleased he would be home for good.

Once again, Jill interrupted her thoughts.

'You jumped in too bloody quick, let's face it, Kate. You didn't know him that well, or what he was all about, and not being there when Sophie was born, phoning you up drunk, that was unforgivable and selfish. That's when the alarm bells should've started ringing.'

She knew Jill was right, and the alarm bells should have been ringing like Bow Bells.

Kate's mind drifted back to the past again.

Alan had been home for almost a year and not much had changed as Kate started to wish he still worked abroad. He left the house before she got up in the mornings and came back most nights after she had gone to bed. Kate had started to notice how he would fly off the handle over the silliest of things and had a bit of a short fuse. He began to stay out most nights for a few drinks after work, which never bothered her much. She put it down to the stress of his job and didn't dwell on it for too long.

But on the rare nights out they had together,

he would end up paralytic and become vulgar and obscene as he tried to embarrass her. He'd play the big 'I am' as she tried, in vain, to get him home and when she did finally manage to, as soon as he was through the front door he would pick up where he had left off and drink the house dry. She often went to bed without him.

He became more and more distant and had no bond with his daughter. On weekends, he never played with or even acknowledged Sophie, which saddened Kate. She thought his job abroad was a lot to blame for how detached they had all become, and it left her with a heavy heart.

It was at his work's annual party that he began the abuse outside the marital home, in front of his colleagues. Alan had made jokes at her expense, hinting to them that his wife had put on a lot of lumber since he had worked away, and her arse just about got through the kitchen door most days. Kate was mortified and upset as to how cruel he had become as she walked out, flagged a cab and went home alone.

That night, she lay awake in bed trying to figure out where it had all gone wrong as she cried herself to sleep.

The next morning an almighty row erupted as he screamed at her about how she had embarrassed him in front of his work colleagues and who the fuck did she think she was?

Kate was gobsmacked by the way he had turned the previous night's scenario around in his favour. Scared, she watched in amazement as the hate manifested in his face and became physical, as Alan picked up his coffee cup and threw it hard towards her. Kate was petrified as it smashed against the kitchen tiles. Alan, without another word spoken, turned around and left the kitchen.

Alan had sulked for weeks afterwards and refused to speak to her. He spent more time in his study with a fresh batch of booze from the local shop, where he was on first name terms with the shopkeeper.

It was a good six months later when the shit really hit the fan. Alan told her he was going down the pub. Kate had asked him to forget the pub and suggested it would be nice if he spent the day with her and Sophie.

She knew it was a big mistake as soon as the words left her lips. His face turned red. He morphed into someone else as the veins in his neck stood out, and his eyes protruded from the sockets as they pierced into her. He exploded, punching her hard in the face. Her legs turned to jelly and she hit the floor hard.

Kate's body shook. Unable to speak, she tried to pick herself up. She wondered who this person standing over her was as he rained down blow after blow to her limp, fragile body. In that moment, she knew just how short his fuse had now become. She was terrified.

The next day he was like a sad puppy with its tail between its legs. She watched the tears flow from his big soppy blue eyes, all apologies and promises on how it would never happen again, and how ashamed of himself he was. She listened to him as he begged forgiveness. He blamed it on the stress and pressure he had been under at work. She looked at the slobbering mess before her, who promised he wouldn't go out as much if she were home more for him, and not teaching and running drama classes after school hours.

He convinced her she would be a better wife and mother if she stopped these things, and told her he earned enough to provide for all of them and that she didn't need to go to work anymore. She felt sorry for him and started to feel guilty. She thought maybe she could cut back the hours from her job a little bit and, going against her better judgement, she decided to forgive him.

She loved her job, but maybe he was right. Perhaps she should spend more time with her family now he had returned back home. He had made a sacrifice, why shouldn't she? So, both in agreement, she went ahead and handed in her resignation.

She felt a fresh start was on the horizon, and started to put extra effort into their home, being creative, decorating and cleaning more. She had Alan's dinner on the table every night when he walked through the door. This soon became a thankless task. Often, he stood with a perplexed look on his face at the dinner plate, refusing to eat most nights. He always asked what the fuck it was he was meant to be eating. Kate could hear his voice in her head as he protested;

'I should be rewarded a *Blue Peter* badge for attempting to eat that lot of shite!'

How she wished she had never succumbed and given up her job and her independence. She had little money of her own and never got to see her friends any more. Depressed and isolated, she was on a downward spiral and so was Alan's drinking, and then the dreaded phone call came.

Alan had been made redundant. Kate knew it was because of his alcohol consumption but was too frightened to mention it. He fell quickly back to his old ways. He preferred to spend most evenings with a bottle of cheap Scotch in his study as he tinkered with his computer gadgets.

He became more venomous with each mouthful of the golden nectar, and continued to mentally abuse her. Putting her down for one thing or another with every opportunity he got.

Jill's voice brought Kate back to the present again...

'Kate, I'm talking to you, are you listening to me, honey? Kate?'

Kate turned her head as she looked at Jill. 'Sorry, Jill, I was miles away. I was just thinking about years ago. Do you want another cuppa?'

The sound of whistling from the hallway panicked her as she stared hard at Jill.

'Well, to be honest, Kate, I need to get home and have a shower. I've been out all night. Are you going to be okay?'

Kate reeled back in shock as she heard his voice behind her. He staggered in the doorway as pissed as a pudding.

'Oh, look who it is! Jill, how are you, darlin'? Bloody hell, you look like Marilyn Monroe in that outfit. All you need is a windy draught between your legs, and I can sort that out for you, sweetheart.'

Kate cringed. Repulsed by him, she watched Jill as she laughed out loud at Alan's lame joke.

'Hello, Alan, how are you? I just popped in quick to see Kate. So sad about Aunt Beth passing away like that, you must be gutted.'

Kate kept her eyes on him as he stumbled towards the kitchen table.

'Yes, shame about the old bird but she did creep me out with that glass eye of hers. It was like one eye was going down the shop and the other was coming back with the change. To be honest, I couldn't look her in the face, she made me go cross-eyed.'

Kate sat bolt upright in her chair, as he laughed at his own joke, and looked across at Jill.

'Well, look on the bright side, Alan, as I said to Kate, she might have left you a few quid, so don't go knocking her just yet. Anyway, I've got to make tracks, my lovelies.'

Alan continued to make a fool out of himself. Embarrassed, Kate sensed her face was the colour of Jill's red lipstick.

'Going already, Jill? Don't you fancy a quick

one before you go? Drink that is,' he went on.

Kate rolled her eyes towards Jill. Standing up, she shook her head in amazement. 'Jill's busy today, Alan.' The cheesy grin that had accompanied his eyes as they fixated on Jill's large breasts made her feel sick to her stomach.

She shuddered at the image she had conjured up in her head, of him panting like a dog.

'Another time, Alan, got to dash I'm afraid. Kate, I will give you a call in the week. Oh, and if you need to call me, do it on my old pay-as-you-go mobile number. Take care and look after yourself, and don't forget to give my love to Sophie. Bye.'

Jill left the same way she arrived, in a whirlwind. Unnerved as her friend banged the front door, Kate was faced with a pissed-up Alan.

'So, what's going on?'

She didn't answer as he started his verbal assault. The cheesy grin that was plastered across his face had dispersed, replaced by a much more sinister one.

'So, what the fuck was she doing here today? And what's her fucking problem? Leaving in such a fucking hurry? I suppose you've been sitting here slagging me off no doubt, you pair of fucking whores.'

She knew he was three sheets to the wind and not wanting to argue with a drunk, she tried to stay calm.

'Don't be silly, Alan. Jill just popped in because she heard about Aunt Beth, that's all. Don't be so paranoid, for heaven's sake.'

She wished she had kept quiet and not opened her mouth at all, as he was at her once again.

'You're a lying cunt! You've been sitting here mugging me off. I can see it in your fucking face.'

Her hands trembled. He reached into his pocket and she watched nervously as he pulled out one of his prized Cuban cigars and lit it.

'We haven't even mentioned you, Alan. Not once.'

The stench of the cigar smoke made her throw up a little in her mouth, as the colour drained away from her face.

'I've told you before, Kate, the trouble with you is, to be a liar you need to have a good fucking memory.'

She watched Alan as he took a long drag on the cigar and blew it straight into her face. Kate coughed and waved her arms about frantically, as he continued to take deep drags on the rolled Havana concoction and blow it towards her.

'I'm not a liar, Alan, why do you keep saying...'

He lunged at her with the cigar before she had finished her sentence and as the pain seared through her arm, she screamed out.

'Why are you doing this to me, Alan? Why?'

She ran towards the sink, turned on the cold-water tap, and placed her arm under the running water. Alan's face it lit up like the hot embers that had just pierced her arm.

'You're a fucking parasite trying to put me down, and mug me off. You never told me she was coming here today. My house, my rules, and as soon as that sinks into your one fucking brain cell the better.'

She didn't answer him. The pain was insufferable and as the tears flowed from her eyes she looked at the burned crater in her arm.

'You think you're such a clever cunt, don't you? But you're going to have to get up a bit earlier to get one over on me, Kate. Do you hear me?'

Deciding safety was her better option, she gritted her teeth and complied with him.

'I will tell you next time if Jill turns up, Alan,

but she took me by surprise also. I swear I didn't know she was coming around here today. I promise you I'm not lying, I swear.'

She focused on her arm as the ice-cold water started to sooth the burn a little. She waited for another mouthful of abuse, but none came. She apologised once again.

'I'm sorry, Alan, I don't want to upset you.'

She turned around from the sink to face him but he was gone. The stench of cigar smoke still lingered strong in the air. Kate walked across the kitchen, reached out her arm, opened the window and took in a long, deep breath, as she let out a heavy sigh of relief.

CHAPTER 3

The rest of the day and evening had gone by peacefully, with no further sign of Alan. Relieved, but still on tenterhooks, she glanced across the kitchen and caught her daughter's gaze, as Sophie swung her legs back and forth at the kitchen table doing her homework.

'Mummy, where's Daddy? Do you think he's coming home tonight?'

Kate looked up at the kitchen clock. It was nine o'clock. Almost certainly he was slaughteredin a run-down back-street north London boozer somewhere. She didn't want to worry her daughter, so she lied.

'He had to go and see someone about a job, Sophie, so I'm not sure what time he'll be back.' She hated the fact she had to make excuses for him, so changed the subject as she felt her nerves start to resurface, she snapped at Sophie. 'Have you nearly finished that homework Sophie?'

'Yes mummy, all finished.'

Kate started to feel tired and anxious as she felt his arrival could be imminent.

'Come on, Sophie, it's time for bed now, chop, chop. I'm going to have an early night. It's been a busy day, to say the least, and you have school in the morning, my angel. Upstairs please and don't forget to brush those teeth tonight!'

It had been another horrendous day, but she always tried hard not to let her true feelings show in front of Sophie. In fact, she had become a master at hiding them.

'Okay, Mum. Do I have to? It's not that late.'

'Yes. I'll be right behind you, my angel. Just going to switch everything off down here and I'll come and tuck you in, okay?'

Kate glanced across at Alan's dinner as Sophie left the kitchen. Covered in cling film on the worktop, she knew it would be the first thing that greeted her the next morning.

'Come on, Mummy, hurry up, I want to show you something,' Sophie called from upstairs.

Kate locked the back door and made her way upstairs. As she met Sophie outside the bathroom in her pink pyjamas, she showed off her clean teeth.

'Look, Mummy, squeaky clean.'

She smiled at her daughter. She was a good

child and never once gave her a day's worry, not like some of the kids she had encountered. Some of them had been a total nightmare.

'Wow, I think I need to go and find my sunglasses, they are so bright.'

Sophie giggled. Her laugh was so infectious that Kate soon found herself laughing with her.

Sophie had always laughed. She had never cried much, not even when she was a baby, unlike the ones she had endured on the bus into town that made the journey a living hell and often brought on a migraine. She felt blessed.

'Come on then, angel, into bed before you blind me with those teeth.'

As Sophie had gotten older, she was always up in the mornings, dressed and ready for school, and never once complained. She was the only person Kate lived for these days, and she loved her child with every beat of her heavy heart.

'Okay, Mummy.'

Kate followed her into her room, reached out her arm, and pulled the covers back as Sophie bounced into her cosy, warm bed. Kate covered her up tight and kissed her on both cheeks. As she cuddled her, she heard Sophie's voice.

'Wow, Mummy, that was a big hug.'

She loved her daughter. Out of all the misery and pain there had never been something so pure and innocent in her life. How she wished Alan still worked away and had never come back home for good. She yearned for it to be just her and Sophie again.

'I love you, Mummy. I wish you were happy and Daddy was nicer to you. It's not fair.'

Kate's heart ached as the words left Sophie's lips. She tried to hide her emotions.

'I love you too, my angel.'

She felt the Catholic guilt that had been pushed upon her as a child, not from her own mother—a legal secretary she never saw, who sent out subpoenas or summonses to poor unsuspecting bastards—but from her dear Aunt Beth.

'Don't you worry about me Sophie, or Daddy, okay?'

She could hear Aunt Beth's voice as clear as day in her head. She had warned Kate to be careful and not to inflict any long-term damage on to her child but she had chosen to ignore her advice. Her words had come back to haunt her.

'What's the prayer we say, Sophie?'

Sophie looked at her with knowing eyes, and recited the prayer off pat. Sat perched on the end of her bed while Kate listened to her.

'Good night, God, I'm going to bed, school is over, prayers I've said. God bless my Mummy and my Auntie Jill, and please look after Aunt Beth in heaven.'

To Kate's horror, that's where it ended.

She frowned at Sophie. Aunt Beth's warning words hit her like a sledgehammer through her heart again.

'That's not right, Sophie, you've not mentioned Daddy.'

'I don't want to say a prayer for Daddy because he doesn't deserve one, Mummy. He is horrible to you.'

Kate was guilt-ridden at how her daughter's hatred for her father was so apparent. The irony of it was that she had just switched off the lights downstairs as one had switched on with such brightness it burned deep into her soul. She looked into Sophie's eyes. She tried to hide the sadness from her face and her tone softened as she spoke to her.

'You must say a prayer for Daddy, Sophie, he is your father. I know he is not happy at the moment, and he is sometimes angry with me but he still loves you, my angel, you must never forget that.' She knew the statement wasn't right, as the guilt once again invaded her mind. It washed over her like a giant tidal wave. 'You mustn't be silly, Sophie, and think those thoughts, okay?' Kate stood up. Bending over, she kissed Sophie twice on the forehead.

'I'm sorry, Mummy, I didn't mean to upset you.'

Kate looked at her sad face, as Sophie's eyes became tearful.

'It's okay, my angel, we can repeat it properly tomorrow night. Don't worry now, get some sleep. That alarm clock will be ringing out before you know it.'

She made her way towards the door and turned around as she blew her daughter a kiss and switched off her light. She heard Sophie's voice call out to her as she closed the door.

'Night, Mummy, God bless you.'

In her heart of hearts, as she entered her own miserable room, she knew the damage had been done. Her little girl was scarred by all the goings on within her doomed marriage. She ignored her own bruised body as she undressed. She climbed into the vast empty bed, thankful his fat carcass wasn't in it. The warm tears streamed down her tired face onto her pillow. Mentally and physically exhausted, she drifted off into another worrisome sleep.

Sophie, however, found it hard to sleep that night. Fearing her father's arrival, it gave her a sick feeling in the pit of her stomach. The palms of her tiny hands sweaty, like they were most nights when she awaited his return. She tried to put her father to the back of her mind as she started to think about seeing her best friend, Megan, at school the next day. She managed to drift off to sleep, only to be woken up by a loud thud on the stairs as she heard him swear at the top of his voice.

'Fucking stairs are a right fucking nuisance, who needs fucking stairs?'

Sophie could hear the anger in her father's voice and as she lay there still, she couldn't breathe properly. Her senses rose to another level, and she could hear the sound of her own heartbeat. Sophie strained her ears as she listened to the door handle to her parents' bedroom rattle. It creaked open, then slammed shut.

Her heart in her mouth, she lay awake, her body tense. She heard the loud snoring that echoed through the bedroom walls. Relieved her father was asleep, she relaxed and as her eyelids started to feel heavy, she closed them and fell asleep.

Sophie had been asleep for less than thirty minutes but the heaviness in her bladder made her stir. She knew she needed to go to the toilet and pee, but didn't want to get up from her warm, cosy bed. Then the smell hit her nostrils. It was an unfamiliar smell. She opened her eyes, stretched out her arm and pulled off her bed covers. Sophie jumped out of her bed. Scared, she switched on the light, opened her bedroom door and panicked as the smell of smoke intensified, filling her nostrils. Sophie ran towards her parents' bedroom, reached out her arm, flung open the bedroom door and switched on the light. Petrified, she ran towards the bed. Scared by what she saw, Sophie wet herself on the spot, the yellow urine trickling down her legs as she screamed at the top of her voice.

'Mummy! Please wake up! Mummy! Please wake up, please, Mummy, Mummy.'

Kate woke up with a start and as she looked at her daughter standing in front of her, she could see the fear in her eyes as the smoke thickened from Alan's side of the bed.

'Mummy, Mummy, what's wrong with Daddy? Why is he making that funny noise?'

She listened to the weird noise from the

creature next to her. Kate screamed at him to wake up as she got up out of bed, and ushered Sophie out of the bedroom.

'Alan, wake up. Alan, the room is on fire! Wake up will you, Alan!'

Kate could see by the look on his face as he opened his eyes that he had no idea what was going on and was still half pissed. As the proverbial penny finally dropped, he was up out of bed and on his feet.

Kate coughed hard as she got Sophie out of the bedroom. She guided her downstairs into the kitchen and grabbed the fire extinguisher from the cupboard. His voice boomed behind her as he entered the room.

'Where's the fucking fire extinguisher, woman? For fuck's sake, hurry up! The whole place will burn down.'

She almost threw it at him. Watching him fly back out of the kitchen and up the stairs, she turned her attention to her daughter.

'Are you okay, Sophie? Talk to me, is your throat sore?'

Sophie was traumatised. She coughed a few times as Kate, worried, stared at her daughter's face. Sophie started to cry.

'I'm okay now, Mummy. I was frightened you

were dead and I think I've wet my pyjamas.'

Kate remained calm as she reached out her arm to grab a glass from the cupboard by the sink. She filled it with cold water and handed it to Sophie.

'It's okay Sophie, I'm fine. We're all fine, thank God. It's going to be okay, my angel, don't you worry. Mummy will get you some clean pyjamas in a minute. You've had a terrible shock. Now sip this slowly.'

Sophie's hands trembled as she held the glass in her small hands. Kate hugged her tight. 'It's okay Sophie, Mummy's here.'

The anger rose from within her as she heard him pounding back down the stairs. Kate turned around to face him in the doorway as he stood with a supercilious look plastered across his face, holding the fire extinguisher in his hand.

'Panic over. Nothing to worry about. The carpet is a bit singed but no real damage. I've opened the windows, so we can all go back to bed in a bit. My cigar couldn't have gone out properly.'

Kate's blood boiled as he opened the cupboard door to put away the fire extinguisher. She stood there, livid. She wanted answers.

'Nothing to worry about? What the hell were

you thinking, smoking in bed? If Sophie hadn't woken up, God knows what would've happened to us all.'

The smirk appeared on his face again. As he banged shut the cupboard door, Kate jumped and thought it might come off its hinges. She wondered if he was still drunk or in some kind of delayed shock!

'Stop being so fucking melodramatic, and if I want to smoke in my bed, I fucking well will.'

She found it hard to register that he wasn't taking any responsibility for his actions as his slurred words left his lips.

'So, shut your mouth, and if you hadn't moved my ashtray, then this wouldn't have happened. Now I will have to buy a new fucking carpet because of you. More money you've cost me! You're such a fucktard, Kate, you do know that, don't you?'

Kate was gobsmacked as Alan ranted like a man possessed. She was angry but, as she glanced down at Sophie, she decided not to pursue it further, aware her daughter had been through enough for one night. Instead, she kept her mouth shut and ignored him.

'Come on, Sophie, let's go upstairs and get you back to bed, sweetie. You've been so brave tonight.'

She led Sophie from the kitchen back upstairs into her bedroom and removed the wet pyjamas. Kate cleaned her and dressed her in fresh pyjamas as she got her back into bed and sat down next to her.

'You can have a shower in the morning, Sophie, but you need to get some sleep now.'

Kate had started to feel the pinch. Angry and worn out, she was mentally exhausted.

'Mummy, how can Daddy blame you for what happened? It's all his fault. You weren't the one smoking.'

She knew her daughter was one hundred percent right, but didn't want to talk about him now, frightened she might say something she would regret. She tried instead to settle her down.

'Right, Sophie, enough now. We all need to get some rest, or we're all going to be walking around like zombies in the morning, okay?'

She didn't want to leave her alone after what she had been through, so decided she would spend the night with her. Kate was too upset to be in the same room as him, let alone in the same bed. It seemed like the best solution all around.

'Would you like Mummy to sleep here, in

your room with you tonight, Sophie?'

Sophie's smile widened. It lit up the whole of her face.

'Really? Yes, Mummy! You can have a sleepover in my room. That would be cool.'

Kate tried to push her angry thoughts to one side as she climbed into Sophie's bed and cuddled up next to her, happy that Sophie felt some kind of security. She stroked her daughter's face.

'Night, night, Sophie.'

After a while, Kate, unable to sleep and still furious with Alan, decided to get up and make herself a cup of tea. She crept downstairs and tiptoed towards the kitchen, and was taken aback as she opened the door and heard his voice.

'What do you want now?' Alan sat there, glass in hand. The half-empty bottle of Scotch sitting between the remnants of the slopped casserole on the kitchen table made her feel sick.

'I said what do you want now? Shouldn't you be upstairs asleep, with your precious fucking daughter?'

His face hardened as she made her way into the kitchen. She didn't recognise him anymore.

'Look, Alan, all I want is a cup of tea, then I'm going back to bed. I don't want any more rows tonight, it's been a stressful enough day as it is.'

Kate walked across the kitchen and grabbed the kettle off the worktop. She placed it onto the hob as she waited for what seemed like an eternity for it to boil.

'You get on my fucking nerves,' he spat. She turned her head as she heard his chair screech hard across the tiled floor. With her teeth on edge, she watched him as he stood up, unsteady on his feet, and manoeuvred towards her.

'You make me fucking sick, Kate! How did I ever end up with such a fucking cunt like you? Do you actually think you're better than me? Do you? Well I've got news for you, you're fucking not.'

In hindsight, she wished she had stayed in bed with Sophie. She had no feelings for this man that was standing in front of her.

'Okay, Alan.'

He had battered any love or respect she once had for him out of her. She couldn't even bear to look at him anymore. He had brought her down. Her nerves fraught, the stress had started to take its toll on her once attractive face.

'Alan, I'm getting a cup of tea, and I'm going

back to bed. I have no energy to argue with you. There is nothing you can say to me or do to me that can upset me any more than you have already, I'm so done!'

The kettle boiled at the same time as he lunged himself at her and grabbed her by the hair. She spun around like a rag doll as he pushed her face down onto the kitchen table into the pieces of the spilt casserole. She struggled as he held her down with one hand and hoisted up her nightie with the other. Kate felt his fingers inside her knickers as the damp between her legs made his limp dick harden and stand to attention, an occasion his military father would have been proud of.

She could hear the sound of his zip. As he released his belt, he pulled down his trousers and pants and he thrust hard into her wetness.

'You're not done yet, bitch. You're done when I say you're done.'

She pleaded with him to stop. Kate struggled hard to break free from him, but he applied more pressure.

'Please, Alan. Why are you doing this? Please. Please stop.'

Her cries fell on deaf ears as he continued to thrust himself deep into her. She could feel the hardness of him against her tense vagina. The pain now unbearable, she cried out.

'Please, Alan. Stop!'

Her eyes dead, her body limp, she switched off altogether, as she focused her eyes on the calendar that hung on the kitchen wall. She fixated on the pug puppy with a silly hat on that adorned the month of May. She couldn't speak any more. It seemed like the whole world had stopped. What felt like an eternity was over in a few minutes.

'You whore! Now I'm done.'

Her body was numb. She was frightened to move as he left the room. She heard the front door as it slammed and broke her from her trance. Kate fell to the floor. The sound of the kettle whistled on the hob as she cried like she had never cried before.

She could feel the coldness of the kitchen floor as it set in to her bones. 'Please, God, don't let that be Sophie.'

Her lips trembled as she shivered, and she forced her body up from the cold floor. Her legs were like jelly. Kate reached out her arm and gripped the back of the kitchen chair to steady herself. She removed the screeching kettle from the hob and as her mind raced, she tried to come to terms with what had just happened. The floorboards creaked above her head. Kate stood still and listened. She turned around and made her way across the kitchen towards the door, as she tried to find her voice. Then she called out.

'Is that you, Sophie?'

Kate stood and listened again, but heard nothing. She could feel the tears as they welled up inside her. She started to cry again as she went back in to the kitchen and closed the door behind her, unaware that upstairs Sophie, her head under her duvet, sobbed hard into her pillow as she tried to make sense of what her father had just done to her mother.

CHAPTER 4

Kate spent the rest of the night in the kitchen, with her head in utter turmoil. She tried desperately to make sense of everything that had happened as it played out, over and over in her mind.

'I have got to get away from him.'

She was unable to comprehend what she had done that was so bad that the man who had swept her off her feet years ago, that she had married and born a daughter to, could have sunk so low. Part of her had wondered if it had really happened at all. She doubted herself. Maybe it was her mind just playing cruel tricks, but as she broke from her reverie, she knew it was all too real.

The sun was breaking through the kitchen window as she heard Sophie's voice call out, 'Mum, I will be down in a minute, okay?'

She couldn't remember how she cleaned the kitchen, it had all become a blur, but she had managed to have Sophie's breakfast on the table and ready for her earlier than usual. 'Wow, I can't believe you're dressed and ready to go.'

She was thankful that Megan's mother was picking her up this morning and taking her to school early for netball practice, then collecting her after school and taking her home with her for a few nights. Kate was grateful to Penny and relieved Sophie was out of Alan's way.

'I'm so looking forward to tonight, Mummy.'

Kate looked at her and forced a smile.

'I bet you are, I'm sure you and Megan will have lots of fun.'

Kate, for the first time, was relieved when she heard Penny's car sound its horn. Sophie kissed her goodbye, grabbed her bag and bolted excitedly out of the house as she shouted back to her, 'I love you, Mummy. I'll see you tomorrow.'

She had noticed Sophie had been a little bit quieter than usual but put that down to the trauma of the fire and lack of sleep, so didn't dwell on it for too long as her number one priority was to get into a hot bath and wash the stench of him off her.

She made her way down the hallway. As the sound of the telephone rang out, it startled her and she paused for a moment, but before she could grab the receiver, they had hung up.

'I didn't want to speak to you either.'

She climbed up the staircase to the bathroom and placed the plug into the bottom of the tub, turning on the hot and cold taps simultaneously. Then she got annoyed as she heard the telephone ring again.

'Whoever you are, I'm not racing down those stairs.' Kate poured bubble bath into the water that turned it blue. She undressed and eased her abused body into the soapy water. Lying back, she rested her head. Her heavy eyelids closed down and then quickly opened again as she heard the ring of the telephone once more. 'For heaven's sake, not again.' She ignored it. As she reached for the soap and washed her body, she wondered who the persistent caller could be but, at that moment, she didn't care as the clean fresh scent of the bubble bath washed over her and removed all traces of him. She lay there silently, lost in her own thoughts as the telephone rang out again and broke her from her reverie. She shouted out.

'For crying out loud, someone's bloody impatient.' Leaning forward, she pulled out the plug. She got out and wrapped a fluffy white towel around her body, unlocked the door and raced down the stairs. With her arm outstretched, she answered the phone and spoke.

'Hello. Kate speaking, can I help you?'

Kate became intrigued, as the man's voice on the other end of the phone spoke to her.

'Hello, Mrs Saunders. My name is Henry King from Moore and King Solicitors. We wanted to inform you that we have been dealing with your late Aunt Elizabeth Goldsmith and her last will and testament, and wanted to ask you if you could come and see me tomorrow at our offices on the high street.'

She was gobsmacked and found it hard to speak. His words reeled around inside her head.

'Really, I don't know what to say, Mr King. I'm at a loss for words. She never, ever mentioned anything about her will to me.'

'Try not to worry, Mrs Saunders. I won't hold you up any longer, but I and my colleague James Moore look forward to seeing you tomorrow. Shall we say about eleven o'clock? We're just clearing the last of the paperwork. We have known your aunt for over forty years. She was an exceptional woman, and on behalf of us all, we offer our sincere condolences. It's all in hand and hopefully will be completed by the end of today.'

Kate stood still in the hallway, glued to the spot. She tried to take it all in but, unsure of what to say next, she just said, 'Well, thank you for being so persistent in calling me, Mr King, and I will definitely see you tomorrow morning at eleven o'clock.'

Kate pushed back the wet hair out of her face and listened to him.

'You're very welcome, Mrs Saunders. We look forward to meeting you.'

She almost dropped the receiver, unable to comprehend everything that had occurred in the last twenty-four hours of her life. Kate looked up and into the hallway mirror at her reflection.

'Bloody hell, Aunt Beth. Thank you.' She pinched her pale cheeks just to make sure she was awake and not hallucinating. Then she continued to stare at herself in the mirror until her body started to feel cold. She realised she was standing in the hallway naked with just a towel around her.

What am I doing, standing here? I'm bloody freezing, she thought to herself. Kate made her way back upstairs again and as she opened her bedroom door, the aftermath of the fire lingered in the air, like one of Alan's bad farts. She felt sick. Pausing by the bed, Kate bent down and opened the drawer next to it as she rummaged around inside for fresh underwear. She pulled out a pair of knickers and a bra, then, making her way across to the wardrobe, she took out her favourite blue denim jeans and a blouse. 'That'll do.'

Dressed, she grabbed the hairdryer off the dressing table, and dried her wet hair. She thought about her unexpected phone call and the possibilities it could hold for them. She tried her best to keep focused, as she felt it was probably only a couple of hundred quid, if that. Then as quick as a flash, her thoughts reversed. Excited, she imagined — what if it could be more than that?

She remembered what Jill had said to her. 'I must go and ring Jill, she's not going to bloody believe this.' She couldn't help but hope that maybe this could change their lives. Pumped, she made her way downstairs into the kitchen. Kate picked up her mobile phone and tapped in Jill's number. She never answered, so Kate left a message.

'Hi Jill, it's Kate. Give me a call when you get this message.' She re-dialled but still got no answer, and she wondered if maybe she had been out all night with her new squeeze. But then Kate remembered that Jill never mentioned she had any plans. She racked her brain as she stood perplexed as to where her friend could be?

She tried to put Jill to the back of her mind. Despondent, she looked across the kitchen and noticed the giant pile of ironing that had been sitting on top of the worktop was still there. The thought of getting through it all brought her back to reality once again. Undeterred, she walked across the kitchen and picked up and shook the half-empty kettle, then she placed it on the hob and switched it on, determined to get the ironing finished, but not until she had made herself a much-needed strong black coffee. Her body felt tired again. The latest events had now taken their toll, as they caught up with her.

She retrieved a cup from the cupboard above her head and placed it down on the worktop, added a large spoonful of coffee and two large spoonfuls of sugar, then, once boiled, she poured the hot water into the cup. Kate stirred the thick dark liquid as she thought about her friend again. She sipped the hot beverage, disappointed she couldn't contact her to share her exciting news. Undefeated, she decided she would try and call her back again after she had completed the mundane task that lay ahead.

An hour had passed by as she stowed away the ironing board, placing it back in the cupboard, amazed at how fast she had sailed through it. Relieved, she eyed the massive pile of pressed laundry that sat folded on the worktop. Turning her head, she glanced up at the kitchen clock, worried if he was going to put in an appearance and grace her with his pissed-up presence anytime soon. She pushed the churning thought to the back of her mind as she reached into her back pocket and pulled out her mobile phone to redial Jill's number. The call connected and Kate hoped and prayed that she would pick up this time, but as it diverted to Jill's voicemail, she spoke.

'Jill, where you? I've been ringing you all morning, please call me back when you get my messages.'

Kate felt low-spirited as she replaced her mobile into her back pocket. She picked up the pile of ironing, turned around and made her way towards the door. Caught off guard, her side tingled as she heard her ringtone vibrating down her leg. She dropped the large pile down on the kitchen table, reached into her pocket and pulled the phone out with Jill's illuminated name displayed on the front of the screen. She answered it.

'Hi, Jill, where the bloody hell you been? I've been trying to call you all day.' Her voice sounded desperate as she spoke.

'Hi, honey. What's the emergency? Is everything okay? Sorry it's taken till now to call you back but I've been a bit busy with my new man, if you know what I mean.'

Shocked, she ignored Jill's revelation, along with the image she had conjured up in her mind.

'Jill, you're never going to guess what happened today! I had a call from Aunt Beth's solicitors. King, or something like that. They have asked me if I would go to their office in town tomorrow morning.'

She felt relieved as she unburdened herself to her best friend.

'Bloody hell, Kate, what did I tell you? I said she might leave you something when I was around at your house the other day. I don't believe it. I might be a bit psychic, you know. My mum always said I was, but then again, she did spend the best part of her life round gypsies. Probably why we always went on holiday in caravans. Anyway, what did Alan say? I bet he was pleased?'

Taken aback by Jill's latest revelation, Kate was dumbfounded that her friend assumed she was going to share that information with him.

'Anyway, Jill, I just had to tell someone and I wanted it to be you. I don't know what she has left me. It could be money, or a painting. I will have to wait and see what tomorrow brings. As soon as I know, I will give you a call.'

Everything started to seem real as she spoke about it out loud.

'Mind you it would be great if it's a few quid though, like you said. Believe me, I could do with it. Then maybe Sophie could get away from here.'

She didn't mean to speak so fast, but she couldn't help it.

'Oh, Kate, that's marvellous news. Fingers crossed, girl. I couldn't be happier for you and Sophie. Give me a call tomorrow, I have my fingers well and truly crossed for you.'

Kate composed herself, as she took in a deep breath.

'Okay, Jill, I'll call you with any news when I get back from town tomorrow. So sorry for the persistent calls, but I have been dying to tell you.'

'No worries, Kate, I'm glad you finally did, as

it sounds like you're about to burst. Try and stay calm.' Kate listened as Jill let out a half laugh. 'I've got to go now, Kate, he's calling me and he can't keep his hands off me. I'll speak to you tomorrow, my honey. Good luck.'

She ended the call and as Kate threw her mobile phone onto the kitchen table, she felt a mixture of emotions wash over her. Overwhelmed and feeling fatigued, she sat down at the kitchen table with her head in her hands. She breathed a sigh of relief. The sound of keys jangling startled her as she lifted her head and turned it towards the direction of the hallway. Her heart raced as the front door opened and she watched him fall through it. He stumbled as he slammed it shut behind him. With one arm outstretched, he used the wall to steady himself as he guided himself towards her. Unable to move, she could feel the colour as it drained from her face as he approached, making eye contact with her.

'Well, I was expecting a better welcome then this, Kate. No sexy little nightdress? I am disappointed.'

She couldn't speak. The perverted look that had manifested across his face made her want to throw up in her mouth.

'Or maybe you want to come down later and surprise me again when you're in the mood?' he continued.

She was angry. He was so drunk, she could just about make out what he was saying. She wondered if he had taken some kind of hallucinogenic drug along with the alcohol that reeked from him.

'Alan, what you did to me last night was despicable! You should be ashamed and disgusted with yourself. I can't bear to look at you.'

He stood open-mouthed, with a puzzled look on his face as she sat bolt upright.

'What are you talking about, woman? I've got nothing to be ashamed about. You came down here last night, flaunting yourself in front of me... You know what you wanted, you wanted sex, and I gave it to you.'

She stared hard at him.

'What you did to me last night wasn't sex, Alan. How can you think it was? And no, I didn't want it, or you.'

His face reddened and she kept his gaze. Alan leant across, stretched out his arms and placed both hands onto the kitchen table as he came face to face with her.

'You're fucking lucky I touched you at all, and I hope you're still popping those little pills. You already trapped me once and I don't want any more fucking mouths to feed in this house, do you hear me?'

Scared, she couldn't move in her chair, overcome by the smell of alcohol on his breath. She could feel her body as it shook. The palms of her hands sweated profusely. He pushed himself back up from the table and turned around. Kate kept her eyes on him as he made his way towards the fridge. Reaching out his arm, he opened it.

'Where's all the food? There's fuck all to eat in here. What the hell do you do all day? You really are a lazy cunt, Kate. Would it hurt you to do a bit of shopping once in a while?'

He rummaged around inside the fridge as she sat glued to the chair, still frightened to move. He pulled out an empty packet of ham and threw it on the floor.

'When was the last time you cleaned this fucking fridge out, for fuck's sake? That's it! I suppose I'll have to go out again now because of you.'

He banged the fridge door shut and as he turned his head they made eye contact. He manoeuvred towards her. She looked away, scared. She could sense his presence as he stopped dead in his tracks. Her heart raced. He punched her hard in the back of her head and as she fell forward, she smashed her face onto the kitchen table.

'That's for being a lazy fucking bitch and not doing the shopping, and don't think I'm bringing any fucking takeaways back for you either!'

Her head throbbed with pain as she raised it, in bewilderment, off the kitchen table. She turned it towards the hallway as she caught sight of him disappearing through the front door. Kate was relieved as he slammed it shut behind him. She took several deep breaths and eased herself up out of the chair, then turned and made her way out of the kitchen along the hallway. She reached out and gripping the bannister, she forced herself up the stairs to her bedroom. Once inside, she walked at a snail's pace across the room. She lay down on top of the bed. She knew the punch was harder than the ones she had received from him before. Dizzy, the room spun as her head connected to the soft white fluffy pillow. Kate was unable to stop the flow of tears as they streamed down her face.

CHAPTER 5

Kate was washed and dressed ready for her appointment in town with the solicitors. She was pleased that Alan had gone out before she got up that morning. She felt blessed when those rare occasions took place and grateful she didn't have to deal with any of his nonsense. Kate was surprised at how calm she was, but intrigued about what lay ahead. Her mind wandered back to the telephone call she'd had with her aunt's solicitors the day before. Excited, she spoke to herself as she left the house and made her way down the path.

'Right I must not let myself get carried away today.'

Outside it was a cloudy north London day, like many others. The substantial grey brick house stood back from the long line of parked cars behind its wrought iron fence. The long strip of paved garden displayed a border of geraniums which contributed splashes of red and pink against the monochrome of the Victorian house. Kate continued down the long narrow road. She glanced across to the other side and made eye contact with her Jamaican neighbour standing on the doorstep. Kate smiled. As she nodded her head in her direction, she disappeared back inside her house and closed the door.

Kate looked up at the grey clouds that had formed in the sky, quickening her step as she felt the first droplets of light rain on her face. She arrived at the bus stop and stood under the shelter, catching sight of her bus as it approached the stop. Pleased that she had timed it just right before the torrential downpour started, she got on and sat by the window. Peering out as the rain pounded the pavements and people outside took shelter, she hoped it wouldn't last long. Kate's mind wandered again as she thought about her meeting with the solicitor. What were they going to tell her? What was so important that they couldn't give her any more information over the telephone? She pushed it to the back of her mind, distracted as the bus travelled through the town centre and the vast array of brightly coloured multicultural shops that brought life to the street.

It had changed so much since she had lived there. She remembered what it looked like before — it hadn't even been a town. All that had been there was a pub, a fish and chip shop and a mini market. Nowadays it was a place you could purchase almost anything you wanted. Kate was happy it was more or less on her doorstep so she didn't have to venture too far out of her way. The sound of the bell on the bus broke her from her memories as she realised it was her stop and got up from her seat. She pulled her coat up over her head as she disembarked, worried about her hair. She didn't want to look like a drowned rat. Along the high street, she looked out for the name of the solicitors on the signs above the shops. She noticed it in big gold letters: Moore & King Solicitors. She paused for a moment in the doorway as she removed the coat from over her head. She reached into her handbag, pulled out a small mirror and checked herself out. Content with her appearance, she replaced the mirror back inside her bag, opened the door and entered. The solicitor's office was a plush establishment that was adorned with large gold-framed pictures that hung on every wall. Mesmerised, Kate eyed the antique gold ornaments. She approached the dark-haired girl with thick black-rimmed glasses, sitting behind the oversized desk.

'Hello, my name is Mrs Kate Saunders. I have an appointment with Mr King.'

The girl looked up from the computer on the desk in front of her.

'Yes, hello, Mrs Saunders. I will let them know you're here. Please take a seat, they won't be too long.'

Kate admired the décor as she walked across the room and took a seat near the unlit open log fireplace. Uneasy as her eyes wandered around the lavish room, she started to feel out of her depth. She heard a man's voice as the deluxe swanky office enveloped her.

'Mrs Kate Saunders?'

The impeccably groomed gentleman surprised her. She noticed he was as austere as the city and smelled like money.

'Yes, I'm Mrs Saunders. Hello. You must be Mr King,' she answered as she shook his outstretched hand.

'No, I'm afraid not. I'm Mr Moore. Mr King is my partner, who I believe you spoke with on the telephone yesterday. He deals mainly with probate these day even though I help out. I tend to deal more with criminal law.'

She realised he had not been educated around this neck of the woods. Kate felt overwhelmed by his posh accent, that wouldn't have been out of place in Chelsea.

'Oh, I see.'

Kate noticed his smile softened his whole face as he spoke to her.

'Please come this way, Mrs Saunders.'

She followed him along a long narrow corridor, which seemed to go on forever. When she came to the end of it, he opened the door for her to enter. Kate smiled at him as she walked past him in to the swanky office. It took her breath away. Like the reception area, it was posh in here but it was more lavish. Crystal chandeliers hung from the ceilings while gold paintings adorned the walls and animal rugs covered the polished floor. Kate felt like her eyes had been given a treat today. Never before had she seen anything like this. Kate looked over towards the opulent desk that sat in the middle of the large room, as an older man with his arm outstretched made his way towards her.

'Hello, Mrs Saunders, I'm Henry King. Thank you for coming down to see us this morning.'

She shook his hand gently. She noticed he was older than Mr Moore, his receded hair a darker grey. He wore glasses that wouldn't have been out of place in the seventies era, but he still had that same smell of money about him. Kate tried to speak in her best posh voice.

'Hello, Mr King, that's quite alright. I must say, I'm overwhelmed to be here and somewhat intrigued by the sudden urgency.'

They were interrupted by a quick knock on the door that surprised her. It opened and in walked a tall dark-haired man in a dark navy-blue suit. Kate, perplexed, listened to Mr King as he spoke to the man.

'Oh, Charles, good timing. Mrs Saunders has just arrived, come and sit down.'

Kate, unsure who the man was, listened as Mr King continued to speak.

'Mrs Saunders, this is Charles Golding, head manager of Barclays Bank on the high street. We have asked him along today as we thought he might be of some assistance to you. But all will be revealed.'

Mr Moore seated himself next to Mr King and started up the conversation. Kate noticed how in sync they were with one another, like a well-rehearsed Morecombe and Wise double act.

'Firstly, once again, I would just like to say how sorry we all are at Moore and King solicitors, for your terrible loss, Mrs Saunders. Mr King relayed to you on the telephone yesterday that we have been dealing with your aunt's estate, and she has left you and your daughter rather wealthy.'

Kate remained silent as she digested the information.

'I'll get to the point, Mrs Saunders. Your aunt has left 2.8 million pounds to your daughter, Sophie Saunders. This has been placed in a trust fund for her. But you, of course, have immediate access to your share. You both obviously meant a great deal to her.'

Kate's jaw dropped open for a second. She reeled back in her chair as she tried to talk.

'How, how much did you just say, Mr Moore?'

Kate felt the colour drain from her face. In shock, she tried to concentrate.

'I said 2.8 million pounds. I can see this has come as a bit of a surprise to you. Henry, get Mrs Saunders a glass of water, will you? Or would you like a brandy, Mrs Saunders?'

She coughed nervously and tried to clear her throat.

'Water would be nice, thank you.'

Kate was transfixed on Mr King as he walked

across the room to the large drinks cabinet and poured the translucent liquid into a crystal glass. He made his way towards her and without a thought, she grabbed it out of his hand and took a big gulp as Mr King took control of the conversation.

'Well, another delicate matter we need to discuss is the money in cash, found with all your aunt's other belongings. That is also rightfully yours. The total sum amounts to one hundred and fifty thousand pounds. We have that here in the office. In fact, that's why we have invited Mr Golding here today, to give you some advice. Maybe you would like some information about investing it? Or maybe you would like it transferred to your bank account?'

Kate realised the only account she had was a joint one with Alan. Panicked, she refrained from answering his questions as she spoke and took it all in.

'I have never seen one hundred and fifty thousand pounds in cash before.'

She watched Mr King bend down and retrieve a black holdall by his feet. He put it on the desk and opened it.

'Well, Mrs Saunders, this is what one hundred and fifty thousand pounds in cash looks like.

Come and take a look.'

She rose from her chair, walked across to the desk, and looked inside the bag at the endless fifty-pound notes that were bound together. Kate was gobsmacked and unable to believe all this was real.

'So, this is also mine? I'm having trouble taking all this in.'

Kate heard the unfamiliar voice of Mr Golding. Startled, she looked across the room and stared at him.

'Well, Mrs Saunders, would you like to talk to me about investing it? Or maybe I can help you with something else. High-interest-rate accounts maybe, or ISAs?'

Kate made a decision fast.

'Well to be honest, Mr Golding, I think I would like to take it home with me today, then make a decision down the line once all this has sunk in, if that's okay with you. But thank you so much for your help on the matter.'

Kate's legs started to feel like jelly. She turned around and walked across the room, thinking her brain was going to explode. Sitting back down in the luxurious chair, she listened as Mr King spoke to her.

'Right, Mrs Saunders, let us finalise all the

details of the trust fund. Do you have a guardian for Sophie in case anything should happen to you? Hopefully, it won't, but it's good to have these things in place. Your husband, maybe?'

Kate's stomach churned at the mere mention of his name. She felt sick and began to stutter.

'No, no, Mr King, I don't. I know it's not the norm, but I would like my best friend Jill Reynolds to be named as my daughter's legal guardian, if you could draw up the paperwork please. She is not a blood relative but she is like an aunt to Sophie.'

'Very well, Mrs Saunders, we will sort all that out for you, so you don't have to worry about any of that.' She watched Mr King as he reached into his jacket pocket. Pulling out a shiny gold pen, he held it in his outstretched hand.

'Well, if you could just sign a few things, Mrs Saunders. First, the receipt for the money, then the trust fund and guardianship form. Then we can finish up there.'

Kate stood up again and walked towards him. She removed the luxurious pen from Mr King's hand and noticed the initials HK engraved deep into the side of it. She wondered for a moment if he indulged all his writing implements this way as she signed all the forms and handed the pen back to him.

'Well, Mrs Saunders, that's everything done and dusted. Don't look so worried. We're only too pleased it was only the one hundred and fifty thousand pounds in cash she wanted you to have today and not the 2.8 million. We would've needed a bloody lorry otherwise.'

She half smiled at him as he threw his head back and laughed at his own joke. Mr Moore joined in with his comedy partner.

'Well, thank you all so much for everything you have done for my Aunt Beth. I have really enjoyed meeting everybody today.'

The laughter stopped as Mr King and Mr Moore both spoke in unison.

'You're very welcome, Mrs Saunders.'

She turned to Mr Golding, who stood up and shook her hand. Kate smiled at him as she gripped it. 'Thank you, Mr Golding, and maybe I will contact you in the not so distant future.'

She leant across the desk, picked up the holdall and as she turned her head towards the door, she noticed Mr Moore had opened it for her. She walked out of the office as he showed her the way out back down the long corridor into the reception area. She stopped in her tracks as she felt his arm on her shoulder and turned to face him.

'Would you like us to ring you a taxi, Mrs Saunders? The weather is dreadful, and you are carrying a rather large sum of money.'

She didn't want a fuss. She tried to get out of there as fast as she could.

'That's okay, Mr Moore, I don't want to put you to any trouble. Plus, I have a few things to do in town.'

They shook hands again and she walked outside on to the wet street. Once outside, she walked away from the solicitor's. The black holdall clutched tight by her side, she paused by the edge of the pavement as she looked out along the road for a taxi. Excited, she could feel the palpitations in her chest. Kate spotted a taxi approaching and lifted up her arm and waved to flag it down. It halted by the side of the kerb and without hesitation, she opened the door, and let out a sigh as she informed the driver of her destination. Her heart still pulsated fast, panicked about Alan. She thought about what she would tell him as to where she'd been. What would she say was in the holdall? She prayed he would still be out when she got home.

When the taxi pulled up outside her house, she noticed the gate was still closed as she paid the driver and got out, and he pulled away. Kate knew it was a good sign. She noticed the Jamaican neighbour with her curtain pulled back, staring out from her window. As Kate made eye contact with her, the woman reeled back inside. Unconcerned, she turned around, opened the gate and made her way up the path. Reaching inside her coat pocket, Kate pulled out her keys and opened her street door. The house was silent, but as she entered, she called out his name to make sure he wasn't home.

'Alan, are you home?'

She pulled her keys out of the lock on the front door, stood still and waited for an answer, but never got one. Relieved, she closed the door and rested against the back of it, as she dropped the holdall on the floor for a moment. Once she had caught her breath, she removed her coat and bag and hung them on the coat rail. She composed herself as she looked down and stared at the black holdall by her feet. With both hands outstretched, she bent down and lifted the holdall off the floor, holding it tight against her rib cage and closing her eyes for a second. She smiled to herself as she sprang into action. Taking the stairs two at a time, she reached the bedroom and dropped the holdall to the floor again. She stood still as she surveyed her depressed domain. It looked tired. Despite her creative input, he had overruled her as usual. Instead, he had decided to paint it creamy beige, the *neutral look* as he called it! She knew if walls could talk, this room had been anything but neutral. If she'd waved a Swiss flag, it wouldn't have stopped him as he kicked the crap out of her. Deep down inside, she knew the only real reason he had painted it one colour was not due to his lack of creative flair or DIY skills, but his thriftiness.

She put him out of her mind as she closed the door. She bent down one last time as she gripped the holdall and threw it onto the large double bed that dominated the whole room. Kate sat down and pulled the holdall across onto her lap as she thought about the solicitors.

If Mr Moore smelled like wealth, the real thing felt like hope. Her head spun as she tried to take stock. Her life had become like an out of control roller coaster, twisting up and down, turning in different directions. But, this was one ride she didn't want to get off.

She unzipped the bag carefully as she gasped in amazement at the sight of the neatly bound bills, fearful as she touched them in case they disappeared. The clouds outside dispersed behind the crisp white net curtains and as the strong sun shone through, it illuminated the colours of the fifty-pound notes. The Queen's enigmatic smile was conspiratorial. Kate zipped up the holdall, straining her ears and listening for a moment to the silence of the empty house. All she heard was the sound of her own racing heartbeat. Excited, she re-opened the bag, once more entranced by the possibilities it held. She reached inside, pulled out a stack of fifty-pound notes and fanned the money. She stared at it like she'd never handled cash before. She thought maybe she should've tipped it all out onto the bed and rolled in it. She giggled to herself. As the bathroom pipes creaked it brought her back to reality and she stuffed the money back inside the holdall and closed it up. Kate looked around the bedroom for somewhere to hide it. Fixated on the chunky wooden wardrobe in the corner of the room, she picked up the holdall and stowed it behind it. Despite it being hidden, she could sense its presence and vulnerability. Spurred on by this, she left the bedroom and made her way back downstairs, pausing for a moment by the coat rail. She opened her handbag, reached inside and took out her mobile phone, then closed the bag. Kate continued down the hallway into the kitchen. She tapped in Jill's number as quick as her fingers would let her, anxiously counting the rings before Jill answered.

'Hi, Jill… Yes, it's Kate. I said I would call you once I got back from the solicitor's.'

Kate could hear the excitement in her own voice.

'Flaming hell, Kate, you been there already this morning? How did you get on?'

She couldn't get the words out quick enough.

'Well, you're not going to bloody believe this. She had money, and it's a lot more than I thought it would be.'

Kate was excited as she started to put her plan into place.

'Fucking hell, Kate I can't believe it. I'm in shock! Oh my god, I'm speechless. That's amazing. I'm gobsmacked, I don't know what else to say, that's fucking fantastic.'

Kate tried to keep a straight head on her and listened as Jill lost hers.

'I know, I can't believe it's been so quick either. I need you to do a big favour for me. Can you get over here and bring a big black holdall and don't say anything if Alan is here. If he asks, you're coming from the gym, okay? Is 1.30 pm alright, Jill?'

Kate started to feel the first beads of sweat on her forehead.

'Yes, Kate, I'll be there by 1.30 pm. Try and calm down. I know it's a shock but stay calm in case Alan comes back before I get there. I'm excited myself.'

Kate took in a deep breath, then, as she let it out slow, she said, 'Okay, Jill, I will see you soon, and thank you.'

She placed her mobile phone into her back pocket, then walked across and reached behind the back of the kitchen door for a set of keys.

'Please, God, don't let him catch me now,' she prayed.

Kate left the kitchen and approached Alan's study. Her hands shook while her fingers fumbled through the vast collection of keys. She hesitated, unsure what most of them were for, but managed to find the right one on the keyring. Kate unlocked the door to his domain and as she entered, closed the door behind her!

CHAPTER 6

Kate watched the kitchen clock as she counted the minutes, waiting for Jill's arrival. She felt sick, unable to eat since she had got up that morning. Her emotions were high as she tried to settle her nerves with another cup of coffee. Kate nibbled on a chocolate biscuit and wondered if Jill would put in an appearance anytime soon as she spoke out loud to herself.

'Bloody hell, Jill, hurry up. I can't stand this.'

The front door hadn't alerted her as Alan snuck into the house and stood behind her. She almost dropped the coffee cup as she heard his voice.

'Can't stand what? You waste of fucking space.'

She struggled to find an answer as she turned around to face him.

'Err, this countertop. I can't stand cleaning the thing; it always looks tired and dirty.'

While she hoped her answer was a believable

one, she stood glued to the spot.

'Funny you should say that, that's what I see when I look at you.'

She watched him as he roared at his own joke. Alan's eyes narrowed.

'Why are you still here anyway? Are you not going out today? I thought you might have had places to go and people to see down King's Cross with all the other washed-up old tarts seeing if they can pick up some pin money?'

His contempt, even his cruel words, couldn't hurt her today. She knew she had bigger fish to fry.

'I'm not going anywhere, just cleaning, so no need to go on, Alan!'

Her voice was soft but tense. Alan relentlessly continued to goad her.

'Cleaning, my arse. You say you're cleaning...'

She watched his arm as he waved his hand over the cup of coffee that sat on the kitchen table.

'But it looks like you're just sitting on your arse, getting fatter, stuffing yourself silly with chocolate biscuits.'

The muscles in her body tightened. Kate ground her teeth hard and tried to be diplomatic. 'Did you want a cup of tea or coffee? I can make you one if you want one.'

She noticed the disgusted look as it surfaced. It spread across his face like she'd just offered him a pile of shit with sugar on top.

'You tried to give me hard boiled salmonella the other day, so do you think I'm going to risk a cup of tea or coffee if you've touched it? Think on, woman…'

She picked up her cup of coffee and ignored him, distracted, as she glanced up at the kitchen clock.

'You need to get me some of those ready meals next time you go shopping. I am a lot safer eating those.'

She gulped the sweet syrupy liquid as Alan's eyes burned into her. Unprepared as the doorbell rang, she almost choked on it.

'What the fuck's the matter with you today? Talk about jumpy. You're like a rabbit caught in the headlights.'

Kate nervously sat upright and tried to pull herself together.

'There's nothing wrong with me, Alan. It just startled me, that's all.'

Alan continued the abuse.

'Well, that's more exercise than you've had in

a while. Why don't you sit down and take the weight off your feet, my dear? Let me get the door, you must be fucking exhausted.'

He chuckled to himself as he marched out of the kitchen towards the front door. Jill was through the front door before Alan reached it. Her flaming red hair was ruffled as she barged past him. Her cleavage preceded her down the hallway to the kitchen. As she got closer, Kate could see her plastered-on make-up had cracked at the creases of her eyes.

'Hi, honey, sorry I'm a bit late. Are you ready?'

With a blank expression, Kate stared at her friend as Jill rolled her eyes towards her and winked.

'By the look on your face, Kate, I'd say you've forgotten about our little shopping trip today.'

She played along as they continued to improvise.

'Oh, my god! I'm so sorry, Jill, it totally went out of my head. What am I like? I've been so busy, it slipped my mind.'

She eyed Alan as he walked past Jill and centred himself between the two women like some sort of referee.

'She always forgets things lately, Jill. I keep

telling her to go and get some pills from the doctor. But I don't think they can cure stupid, ha!'

Kate listened as Jill tried to stick up for her.

'It's easy to forget something like shopping. Kate has Sophie to worry about. My brain is like a sieve most days.'

Kate was disgusted by him as his eyes focused on Jill's large breasts.

'I must say, Jill, you're looking rather sporty today. Is that a new tracksuit?'

Kate smiled as she looked at the garish outfit and day-glow trainers she thought wouldn't have been out of place at a nineties rave.

'This old thing? I've had it ages, Alan. No, I've just been to the gym, the new one that's just opened on the high street. In fact, I signed up for a year.'

Amused, Kate listened to her fabrication. She knew even if Peter Andre was giving free personal training and it was full of fit blokes, you wouldn't get Jill's arse inside a gym. She hated them.

'If only every woman took care of herself like you do, Jill. You look great.' He repulsed Kate as he gushed. She was unsure if he was about to start foaming at the mouth. 'I keep telling Kate she should make an effort and join a gym or some kind of class. A bit of exercise might help her memory also.'

Unruffled, she listened to his cruel insults, like she wasn't even in the room.

'Well, you don't get this figure eating junk food, and I need to stay in shape, don't I?' she said, wiggling her shoulders. As her breasts jiggled up and down, Kate looked across at Alan, who was fixating on them like he was in his own porn film.

'Oh, I can see that, Jill. Not really sure it would benefit Kate though. At this point, she's probably ninety-nine percent pizza and chocolate.'

Embarrassed, she screeched her chair across the tiled floor as she stood up, walked across the kitchen and poured the rest of her coffee down the sink.

'Well, if it's okay with you, Alan, I'm going to go shopping in town with Jill for the rest of the afternoon.'

His eyes were still focused on Jill's large breasts as he continued to talk like she didn't exist.

'You don't need my permission, Kate. She uses my joint account, Jill, so I don't know why she feels the need to ask my permission. Anyway, I'll be working in the back garden today.'

Kate raised her eyebrows and stared at him. As he tried to impress Jill, she swallowed a sarcastic laugh.

'The garden, Alan? What's in the garden that would take you away from your study?'

She recalled it was about five years since he last set foot in the garden. She knew all Alan's talk was for her friend's benefit. Kate was amused by Jill as she played along and started to flirt with him.

'Anyone would still think you were working for the government, Alan, hid away in that study of yours with your high-tech stuff. You're like a younger, sexier Q from *James Bond*. All smarts and gadgets,' Jill simpered.

She made allowances for the banter between her husband and her best friend because she knew that Jill took the piss out of him, which tickled her when he beamed like a lighthouse.

'Oh, get away with you, Jill. What are you bloody like?'

She noticed his erection pushing through his trousers as he laughed for no reason, apart from his hormones.

'Flattery will get you everywhere, Jill. You know that you're a naughty girl.'

Her eyes followed him. As he walked across to the back door that led to the garden, he called out as he exited.

'You are a big bloody tease, Jill Reynolds. That's what you are, you little minx.'

Kate rolled her eyes towards Jill, walked across the room and stared out of the window into the garden, which she noticed was in need of some urgent attention. The grass had become overgrown, replaced by weeds that bordered the edges of the lawn.

'Has he fucked off, Kate?'

He walked along the path and disappeared into the old shed that stood at the back of the jungle-like garden.

'Yeah, he's bloody gone at long last, the bastard. I was beginning to think he wasn't going to leave. I've been a bloody nervous wreck all morning. I couldn't stop looking at the sodding clock.'

Jill placed the holdall at her feet, and as she leant back against the worktop, she stared at it.

'God he's such a sleaze, Kate. Of course, I was coming! How long have we known each other, honey? We've been best friends for over twenty-five years, through thick and thin, like them off the TV. Hmm … what's their names? Hmm. Oh yeah, Ant and Dec. I'm always here for you, Kate, you know that.'

On another day, she might have found Jill's double act comparison to Ant and Dec quite funny, but not today. Kate glanced back out of the window into the garden and let out a big sigh.

'I'm sorry, Jill, it's just been one of those mornings.'

'You don't deserve this grief, Kate. There's nothing I want more than for you and Sophie to get as far away as you can from that evil bastard.'

Kate felt Jill's arms around her waist and as she hugged her back, she looked out over the garden, watching his fat arse trailing behind the old petrol lawn mower.

'I know I play nice with him, Kate, but it's just for show, honey. You know I have your best interests at heart.'

Kate's eyes welled up as she tried to get a grip on her emotions.

'Tell me he hasn't been knocking you about again?'

She didn't want to divulge too much, so tried

to shrug it off.

'Pulling hair and some verbal but you know what he's like. Every little thing sets him off lately. And I know you have my best interests at heart, Jill. I'm so glad I have you to talk and offload too'.

Her eyes glazed and blurred, she looked at Jill.

'Oh, don't you start crying, Kate ... you'll set me off and have my mascara running down my cheeks if you're not careful.'

After one last glance into the garden at her nemesis, she noticed Jill rub at dry eyes as she tried not to smudge her spidery false eyelashes.

'To think how Alan has treated you and Sophie all this time ... I don't know how you put up with it every day, Kate.'

Kate shook off the emotional moment as she got practical. She concentrated on the present as she thought about the money.

'Can you imagine what would happen or what he would do if he ever found out about all this, Kate?'

Kate shuddered at the thought.

'It doesn't bear thinking about. It makes my blood run cold. Brrr.' She rejected the thought straight out of her mind. 'I can't think like that,

Jill. It would paralyse me. So, pass me that holdall and I'll get the one with the money in it.'

Jill walked across the kitchen and picked the holdall up off the floor, handing it to Kate.

'Jill, you stay here by the window and keep an eye on him. If he comes in you will have to alert me somehow.' She turned around, made her way towards the kitchen door and raced out down the hallway, up the stairs to the bedroom. She ducked into Sophie's bedroom and glanced out of the window that overlooked the garden and was relieved that she couldn't see him.

'Oh fuck, please stay inside your bloody shed, Alan.'

Her heart raced as she spotted him. She ran straight out of Sophie's bedroom into her own, reached behind the chunky wardrobe and swapped the holdalls over. She listened out for the sound of his voice as she headed out of the bedroom, down the stairs, through the hallway and back into the kitchen. She noticed Jill standing by the window, smiling as she waved out at Alan in the garden.

'Jill, come on. What are you doing?'

Kate surprised Jill and she jumped as the smile plastered across her face morphed into a look of disgust.

'Oh, bloody hell, Kate. You nearly scared the crap out of me.'

Confused for a moment, Kate placed the holdall on top of the kitchen table as Jill joined her. Jill reached out and picked up the holdall with both hands. She lifted the bag up and down before she placed it back on the table.

'It's not that heavy, Kate. How much is in here?'

Kate didn't want to discuss figures so changed the subject.

'I will tell you all about it later. Let's get it out of here first. Do you have your car outside, Jill?'

Jill laughed excitedly as she bounced up and down on her toes in her day-glow trainers.

'Don't be silly Kate, I don't need a car. I go to the gym and I jog everywhere. I'm super fit, don't you know?'

Kate smiled at her. She thought to herself that her large chest might do her some severe damage if she didn't stop soon.

'Right, come on, Jill, let's get a move on. Where's the bloody car?' She felt hot as tiny beads of sweat appeared on her forehead.

'Yes, Kate, it's outside. Don't panic, Mr Mainwaring! Don't panic!'

Unimpressed with her *Dad's Army*

impression, Kate ignored it.

'Well, thank God for that. I'm out of breath just going up and down those stairs ... but maybe that's because I'm finally on the verge of escaping him and I'm terrified of having all this within his reach.'

Kate sensed Jill had picked up on her nervousness. She put on her sensible head, lifted the bag up off the kitchen table and held it tight against her ribcage.

'Come on, Kate, we can take it straight round and drop it off at mine. It'll be safe there. You don't need to torture yourself anymore.'

She looked at Jill's outstretched arms. As she gripped the handles, Kate hugged it tighter as she spoke.

'It's finally here, Jill. I can touch it, it's real. It feels like I've been waiting a lifetime and maybe I have, for something good to happen. He can't ever find out about this. Promise me you'll never mention it.'

She released her grip as Jill removed it from her arms.

'Don't be so stupid, of course not. I would never say anything, especially to him. Right, let's go. Time to put dreams into action. Okay, let's do this.'

The pressure lifted, Kate was relieved it would be out of the house so he couldn't find it.

'You know how he pokes into everything, Jill. Nothing gets past him.'

Still panicked, she listened to Jill.

'You need to relax, love. We'll go and have some lunch after we drop this off at mine. I found a new place, and it is really nice. That'll take your mind off things and we can treat ourselves.'

Kate forced a smile at Jill as she tried to ease the tension.

'That sounds lovely, Jill, but can we please just go? We have to get out of this house now before he comes back inside and sees us still here. Thanks for doing this for me.'

Jill carried the holdall out of the kitchen. Kate followed behind and paused by the front door as she watched Jill make her way out down the path. Kate grabbed her coat and handbag off the coat stand and caught up with her.

'Kate, there is no need to thank me, I'm your friend, always remember that. I'm happy I can help you out when I think about all the favours you have done for me over the years.'

Kate's bond with Jill was a solid one. Forever grateful, Kate watched her as she made her way down the road. Jill paused, turned around and shouted out to her.

'Come on, Kate, hurry up will you, before that pig comes out and makes himself busy.'

Kate looked round for Jill's old Volkswagen Beetle, not that it wasn't easy to spot—bright green with several knocks. It was Jill all over.

Jill opened the car door. Unable to resist, Kate glanced back towards the house, sure he would be standing there on the doorstep, but there was no sign of him.

'Come on, Jill. Let me in, will you?'

She breathed cold fresh air hard into her lungs as she watched Jill place the holdall on the back seat. Jill leant across and opened her door.

'Sorry, Kate, this bloody door keeps sticking.'

Inside, overwhelmed at the mess, Kate wondered if Jill had set up her own car boot sale.

'I'm so sorry about the mess, Kate. I haven't had time to give this car a good clean this week.' Empty cola cans and sweet wrappers littered the floor. There was even a half-eaten kebab in a box that had been slung under the front seat. The traffic light air freshener that hung off the inside mirror next to the pink furry dice couldn't even mask the stench of sweaty onions that emulated from it.

'Wow, Jill, this week? You sure you don't mean this decade? When was the last time you actually cleaned this bloody car? It flaming well stinks!'

She rolled down the window to get a reprieve, overcome by the body odour smell. It filled her nostrils.

'Well, funny you should say that, Kate. I was going to get it valeted the other day, but as I went past, I thought I saw Alan in there, so I changed my mind. Has he still got the same car?'

Kate tried to answer her, frightened she might gag or even throw up because of the foul stench.

'Yes, he still has the same car he's had for the last four years.' Kate looked across the road. As she spotted his car, she pointed her finger towards it. 'It's the one over there, Jill. Look, can you see it?'

She watched Jill as she opened her handbag and retrieved a pair of gold-rimmed glasses, put them on and looked in the direction she had pointed to.

'Oh yes, I can see it now. Yes, it's the same number plate: POB 6NOB1. So it was him.'

Taken aback, she jumped as Jill burst into uncontrollable fits of laughter. She stared at her.

'Oh, Kate, take a good look at Alan's number

plate, can you see what it spells out? It has NOB1 in it.'

Kate had never noticed it before. Amused by Jill as she started the car and revved the engine, she laughed at Jill's acute revelation as they drove off towards Jill's flat. Never in her life had Kate seen a number plate that suited someone so well. It was better than if she had chosen it herself.

CHAPTER 7

Jill lived above the local pizza takeaway that filled her small flat with the smell of oregano and tomatoes. Kate hadn't had a slice in years. She decided to wait in the car and watched as Jill grabbed the holdall off the back seat. 'I won't be long Kate, don't worry!' Silently, she looked out of her passenger window as Jill walked towards her front door. Opening it, she disappeared inside. Kate started to daydream about her future free of Alan and maybe London altogether. Kate thought about how she and Sophie would get the life they deserved. A fresh start somewhere far away from him. She started to feel like there could be light at the end of the tunnel. Startled as the car door opened, Kate came back to reality as Jill got in. She sat behind the wheel as she tried to catch her breath.

'Well, that's now been taken care of, Kate, so you can stop bloody worrying now, okay?'

Kate smiled at Jill as she breathed a sigh of

relief. She noticed Jill had transformed out of the cocoon of the garish tracksuit and sprung into a gold lamé butterfly. All thighs and dangly earrings.

'My god, Kate. Don't think I've ever changed that fast in my entire life. That tracksuit was bloody ugly, but we're celebrating now.'

Jill straightened her tight dress as Kate compared their clothes, unhappy in her sensible, mum-of-the-year outfit. She felt underdressed compared to Jill's gold creation. Calling all moths — here's something shiny. As she turned to her she moaned, 'Jill, have a good look at me. I don't feel very dressed up today to be going somewhere fancy.'

She watched Jill as she reached behind her seat and hoisted up a carrier bag. She put it on to her knees and stared at it.

'Don't worry, Kate, I have thought ahead. There are a few tops and skirts that I borrowed from you in that bag, and some you had left here ages ago. I'm sure there is something in there for this occasion. Pop back into mine quick and change.'

Kate looked at her thoughtful friend and smiled as Jill reached out her hand and relinquished her flat door key into her hand.

Getting out of the car, Kate walked across, opened the door and let herself inside, making her way up the stairs into Jill's living room. She was shocked by the mess. Her stomach churned with the smell of the pizza parlour below combined with the stale smell of cigarettes. She ignored her surroundings as she threw the keys down. Kate opened the carrier bag, sorted through the clothes, changed and went back downstairs. Once outside, she closed the front door and walked across to the car. She got in and let out a sigh.

'That's better, Kate.'

She had emerged with a glimmer of a new glow. Not from lamé, her black V-neck blouse only hinted at cleavage and her skirt, slit at the back, was long enough to be subtle.

'Do you think so, Jill?' Unlike Jill's flame of red hair, which fed off the oxygen in the car, her burnished blonde illuminated the darkness around her as she smiled. Jill punched her lightly on the arm as she spoke.

'I don't know about you, Kate, but all this cloak and dagger stuff has made me hungry. I could eat a scabby cat. Let's go and get some lunch at that new place I told you about.'

Kate could feel the rumbles in her stomach as

she watched Jill turn the key and start up the noisy engine.

'Okay, Jill, but it's my treat and no arguments. It's the least I can do for all your help today.'

She relaxed as the car pulled away from outside Jill's flat. She felt like a weight had been lifted from her shoulders. With the money safe and out of Alan's way, they chatted as Jill drove them to the restaurant.

'You're going to love this place. It's called the Corkscrew. It has a great menu, and it's not far, only around the corner.'

Relieved the journey wasn't long, Kate heard her stomach as it growled.

'Maybe I'll start going to restaurants in the future, Jill — try new things. All Alan ever wants is chips with everything. If I have to cook one more batch of them I might deep fry his head.'

She laughed out loud as Jill joined in.

'I doubt anyone would put that on a menu Kate! I remember when I went to my very first restaurant. We never ate out when I grew up. Mum would bring leftover food back home with her from school. Being a dinner lady all those years, she had first dibs on what was left, plus it saved her cooking so she could have more time down the pub. I remember it was fish and chips at Southend-on-Sea and I didn't care how it tasted. I was just relieved it wasn't second-hand goods.'

Kate recalled the time when she first went to a restaurant. A smile spread across her face as she told Jill.

'My dad, Jill, was too cheap to go to restaurants. He had a great job in the bank but couldn't walk past a menu without making some comment like the food was better and cheaper at home when my mum cooked it.' She continued as Jill laughed. 'In fact, it was Aunt Beth who took us all out one year to a Chinese restaurant. We even brought my gran, who put her false teeth in a finger bowl! I remember the raspberry jam rising off of them and floating to the top. Dad was so embarrassed he walked out.'

The laughter continued as Jill pulled the car up outside the restaurant. The place looked familiar to her.

'Didn't this place use to be a charity shop, Jill? I'm sure I have been here before and bought a few second-hand blouses.'

She reached out and flipped down the sun visor in front of her and looked in the mirror. She tidied her hair behind her ears and put on some lip gloss.

'Nothing second hand here now, and definitely not for you from now on, eh Kate? Onwards and bloody upwards, that's what I say.'

They both got out of the car and Kate walked along the pavement and stopped outside the restaurant to look at the menu by the door. Jill locked the car and caught up with her.

'This looks fantastic, Jill. Might take a bit of getting used to but I'm up for it. And maybe a bottle of wine too! What do you think?'

She didn't get a reply. Jill slipped through the door like a whippet and Kate followed behind her. 'It's busy, Jill.' She noticed there were several diners already seated. They wove through the tables, checking out what they were eating.

'I know, Kate, it's meant to be very good in here.'

Kate admired the Impressionist prints on the walls, as she followed Jill past the highly polished maple tables to a table near the bar. They sat down.

'This place looks really classy and expensive, Jill.' She smiled as she looked around and surveyed her surroundings.

'Just something I found on my travels, Kate.

You know me, always looking for adventure. Come on, let's enjoy ourselves. Anyway, how long's it been since you let your hair down?'

Kate tried hard to recollect, as Jill looked at her.

'Do you know what, Jill, I honestly can't remember. I know it was before Sophie was born. Alan was a stone lighter and even smiled now and again.'

Her face dropped as she remembered the good times they once had, a long time ago.

'Come on, Kate, cheer up. Just think, you'll be leaving that bastard soon. All the more reason to celebrate. Come on, live a little.'

Kate knew full well that Jill was right and she pulled herself together.

'Well, as long as we don't stay here for too long or else he'll start on me as soon as I get home and I'm not in the mood for him today.'

She picked up the exciting menu off the table and studied it, as Jill waved out to the waitress.

'Forget about him. You're a new woman now, Kate.'

She listened as Jill gave the waitress their drinks order. She was back within minutes. Kate smiled as she placed the champagne on the table with a plate of appetisers, her mouth-watering.

'This is the bloody life, Kate. Cheers!'

She raised her glass towards Jill's as they clinked together. She took a sip of the champagne. They nibbled on the plate of cured meats, olives and baguette slices as both of them studied the menu.

'Oh, look at the price of mussels, Jill! I can't believe they're so expensive. When I used to go on holiday with Mum and Dad, we could buy them for pennies.'

It had been years since she had been anywhere decent, she couldn't believe the price of things. Jill laughed.

'Listen to you! Are you serious right now? Worried about the price of bloody mussels, when you've just come into a few quid?'

Jill drained her glass in one mouthful. Kate leant across and refilled it.

'Shush, Jill. Keep it down. Don't shout it out. I don't want to jinx anything.'

Kate picked up her glass and took another sip of the fizzy drink. She savoured the bubbles as they slipped down the back of her throat.

'It's still not real, Aunt Beth leaving me that money. I can't seem to get my head around it. I mean, the one hundred and fifty thousand was a shock, but then the 2.8 million she left Sophie...'

Kate jumped as Jill slammed both hands down on to the table. Her mouth fell open, displaying most of her poor dental work.

'Oh my god, Kate! You kept that quiet until now. 2.8 million pounds! I can't believe it. That's unbelievable.'

The colour had drained from Jill's face. Kate was amused as Jill turned fifty shades of pale.

'Well, I guess I was waiting for the right time. I wanted to tell you I have put your name down as Sophie's guardian. I hope that's okay with you, Jill? It all happened so quickly, and I had to think on my feet.'

Jill's face still in shock, Kate waited for her to answer.

'I can't imagine how you must be feeling, Kate. Think what you can do with it. You and Sophie can go anywhere you like and never have to worry about Alan again.'

The waitress approached the table and Jill stuttered through the order. Kate's attention was drawn to a man standing at the bar. She ignored him as he waved across at her. She turned her attention back towards Jill.

'Right, Kate. We're going to have mussels, to hell with the expense.You can afford them dipped in gold now, and we will have another bottle of champagne.'

Embarrassed, Kate remained silent, as Jill continued.

'Kate, I can't imagine what it must be like to have that kind of money. My poor old dad was a bin man who never saw a fifty-pound note, let alone handle one.'

Sometimes Kate felt sorry for Jill. She refilled her glass again and topped up her own. Her mind wandered back to the past as she played around with the baguette slice on her plate.

'Alan went through everything I inherited when my parents were killed in that car accident. It only took the bastard eight years. He sold it all. Everything from jewellery to paintings.'

Kate picked up the bread, angry, and crushed it in her fist. The bread crumbs fell like memories onto the plate. She could feel her eyes well up but composed herself.

'He left me with nothing, Jill. He thinks he's taken everything from me, but now I have a chance. I just have to keep reminding myself this is real.'

The waitress approached with more champagne and a bowl of steaming mussels and placed them down on the polished table in front of her. Kate's nostrils were filled with the aromas of garlic and white wine. The restaurant seemed busier as she looked around. She saw the same man at the bar. He smiled at her. Ignoring him, she looked away as Jill interrupted her thoughts.

'It's as bloody real as we are. Like this bottle of champagne is, Kate.'

Jill swirled the golden liquid around in her glass and as she gulped another big mouthful, Kate hoped she wouldn't have to carry her home.

'It's no dream, Kate, so you'd better work out what you're going to do, and soon. You need an escape plan.'

She eyed Jill as she licked a drop of champagne off her fingertip and started to realise the world was her oyster.

'Where would I go, Jill? How do you choose when you can go anywhere?'

'Kate, I know where Brad and Angelina would go. You have a wider choice now they're single again, and Johnny Depp's out and about also. You could stalk the rich and fuckable.'

Kate giggled as she looked across the table at Jill.

'Oh, you can always make me bloody laugh,

but I think you're talking about your dreams, not mine.' She smiled as she listened to her ideas.

'What about France, Spain or even America? You can travel first class anywhere. Why not the United States of Disney?'

Jill dabbed at the garlic butter on her chin with a serviette. While Kate watched her, she thought about her daughter.

'Actually, that's not a bloody bad idea, Sophie has always wanted to go and see Mickey Mouse. She loves him. I think that would be my first stop.'

She thought about how happy Sophie would be if she knew she was going to see Mickey Mouse.

'I'm sure she would love it. Not that it would be my first choice though. With all those theme parks and oversized fuzzy characters, they would freak me right out.'

Kate giggled at the thought, confident it would be Jill's worst nightmare.

'I don't think you've ever been a child, Jill. But, as for Sophie, she still believes in magic and would be over the bloody moon.'

Kate noticed the man from the bar was now standing behind Jill, who was oblivious to him.

Nervous as he approached their table, Kate listened as Jill continued to talk.

'I believe in magic, Kate. The magic moments between a man and a woman and all his money.'

Jill's face was a picture as he stood in front of them. Kate watched Jill's face as she looked the newcomer up and down. Then he spoke to them.

'Hello, ladies, I hope you don't mind, but I couldn't help notice you both enjoying yourselves. What're you celebrating then?'

Kate looked at him, up close. He was about their age but with that youthful appearance that covered up manly sins.

'What the bloody hell has it got to do with you what we're celebrating?'

Shocked by her friend's quick retort, Kate stared at her.

'I'm just back in town, and to be honest, I'm not having a good time of it today, but I could hear you girls laughing and having fun and wondered if I could possibly join you for a drink.'

Kate stayed silent but, amused, fixated on her friend's face. She smirked as she appraised him.

'There is a spare seat but only if you're buying the next bottle of champagne.'

The stranger picked up the bottle of

champagne from the table and called out to the waitress. 'Could you send another bottle over here please?'

Kate felt uncomfortable as he pulled out the chair and introduced himself. He sat down next to her.

'My name is Jonathan Jacobs, but you can call me John. I'm delighted to meet you both.'

She watched as the waitress approached with the champagne. He told her to keep the change as he handed her a fifty-pound note. His jet-black hair was slicked back and shaped neatly around his ears, and he was clean shaven with noticeable cheekbones. Kate wondered if he could've been a model a couple of decades ago. She started to feel an unfamiliar warmth inside her belly as she caught his gaze.

'So, what's the special occasion? Is someone getting married? In which case, I would like the chance to stop the wedding right now.'

He planted his elbows on the table, rested his chin on top of his hands and as he winked at her she noticed his soft deep brown eyes. As Jill spoke, Kate felt herself blush.

'Just the opposite. My friend Kate here is finally going to get shot of her pig of a husband. She's leaving him for good, and not before bloody time.'

Kate was mortified Jill had just blurted this out in front of a complete stranger. Annoyed, as she gulped back another glass of champagne, she heard herself saying, 'Jill, bloody hell, do you mind! Please stop. I'm sure John doesn't want to hear my bloody life story.'

Her mood changed as the sound of Michael Bublé rang out around the table and she was amused as he pulled out a mobile phone from the inside of his jacket pocket. 'Bloody hell, I haven't heard him in years? Is he still alive?'

Both were taken aback as he shot up out of his chair. 'I'm so sorry, ladies, excuse me, but it's imperative I take this call.' Kate turned to face Jill as he walked away from the table towards the bar.

'This is bloody ridiculous, Jill. We really need to leave soon.' She started to feel uneasy and out of her depth.

'Don't be daft, Kate. What's the matter with you? He likes you. I clocked him at the bar looking at you as soon as we walked in the bloody place.' Kate could feel the intense burn on her cheeks. 'This is what happens when a man wants a woman, Kate. I know you have been living in a cave for years, but out here in my world, these things happen. Sometimes you really worry me, you really do. Can you honestly say you can't see how he is looking at you? Being married to Alan has made you short-sighted. I've got some vouchers for Specsavers in my bag, you should go.'

Kate laughed and Jill joined in. The other diners, unamused, looked over in their direction. John returned to their table. Kate noticed Jill purse her lips in a kissing action as he sat down. Moving in closer as she spoke to him.

'So, what line of business are you in then, John? Must be good if you keep having to tear yourself away and answer phone calls all the time.'

Kate noticed his eyes narrow for a moment as he gave out a half laugh. He backed away from Jill and positioned his chair closer to her.

'Well, right now I'm in the business of getting to know your friend Kate better, if you don't mind, Jill. The quiet one, but probably the brave one. Tell me about yourself, Kate.'

Mortified, Kate looked across the table at Jill's face, sensing Jill wasn't happy. Kate noticed there was an edge to John's voice as she re-joined the conversation.

'There's not much to tell really, John. I'm not

that interesting.'

Kate stopped talking as Jill got up out of her chair and turned her head in his direction. She stared at him hard, as she said, 'Well, I can see that I'm surplus to requirements, so I'm off to the ladies to powder my nose. I'll be back in a bit.' Jill grabbed her handbag off the back of her chair, flounced off in the direction of the toilets and disappeared inside.

'I think you have really upset my friend.'

She noticed that as he laughed, the humour didn't seem to hit his eyes. Mesmerised, she stared hard at him as she tried to figure him out.

'I'm sure she's had worse things said to her than that and survived. I didn't mean to upset her. Don't worry. I'll apologise when she gets back, I promise.'

Not one bit sure he meant it but intrigued by him, Kate decided to let it go as she tried to find out more about him.

'What is your line of work, John? I'm guessing something to do with computers.'

She studied him as she imagined him in an office somewhere, behind a desk.

'No, I'm a stockbroker. I work for a large firm in the City of London, been there a few years now.'

Impressed by his line of work, she said, 'That must be a fantastic job, getting to play around with other people's money all day.' She grabbed a mussel off the plate and sucked it from its shell.

'Oh, believe me, it has its moments. Anyway, I don't mean to pry, but it sounds like you're going through a bit of a rough patch at the moment.'

She sighed, retrieved the serviette from the side of her plate, and wiped her lips.

'It's okay. My husband is having a bit of a hard time at the moment. He recently got laid off. He worked for the government. Surveillance, all that sort of thing.' She laughed. 'Jill calls him Q from *James Bond*. Without the fashion sense, and a few other things, but I won't repeat those.' She laughed again, lifted her hand to her mouth and muffled a half burp.

'Don't tell me, you're Miss Moneypenny, or maybe even Pussy Galore!'

She snorted.

'Well, I wouldn't go that far. More like the bloody maid that cleans up after James Bond trashes another hotel room.'

Kate fidgeted in her chair and glanced down at her watch. She felt uneasy as Jill returned.

'Bloody hell, Jill, I wondered where you had got to. I was beginning to think you had got lost. Anyway, we've been having a nice chat.' She noticed Jill staring across to the other side of the bar.

'Well, Kate, I have been talking to a very nice man over there at the bar.'

Kate turned her head and eyed the dapper old dinosaur that was propped up at the bar. Jill blew him a kiss as she listened to John. He apologised to her.

'I'm so sorry, Jill, about earlier. I really didn't mean to be rude, and it wasn't my intention to upset you.'

She stared at Jill's unreadable expression.

'It's fine, John. I'll forgive you but only because you have put a smile on my friend's face.'

Kate looked at Jill. A decision made, she summoned the waitress and paid the bill.

'Oh, don't tell me both you lovely ladies are going to leave me already? Who's going to drink the rest of this champagne?'

The glow of the champagne kicked in, as she doubted his sincerity.

'I need to get home I'm afraid, otherwise there will be a search party out for me with torches and pitchforks.'

He grabbed her elbow to pull her closer to him. He whispered into her happy ear.

'Maybe we could do this again some time, Kate. Preferably without your friend Jill. Maybe dinner or drinks somewhere nice?'

She fought her baser self as she pulled away from him.

'I'm not sure that's going to happen, but it's been lovely meeting you.'

She panicked as he reached into his jacket pocket. He pulled out a business card and forced it in to her hand. Not sure how to react, she blushed as she popped it into her coat pocket.

'Come on, Jill, let's go.'

Kate thought Jill might want to hold on to those Specsaver vouchers as Jill kept stopping and turning to blow kisses at the little old man she had spoken to at the bar while Kate tried to steer her through the tables and out the door into the bright light of day.

'I'm thinking taxi, coffee and shower, Kate, before you go home and face that arsehole.'

Kate had to be practical. She had been out too long and knew Alan would have a full head of steam but, convinced her punishment would be far worse if she turned up drunk and messy, she agreed.

'Okay, Jill, I need to get my clothes out of the car. Give me the keys.'

Jill leaned up against a convenient No Parking sign as she opened her handbag. She rummaged around inside it and pulled out the set of car keys. Kate reached out and grabbed them out of her hand.

'You get your clothes, Kate, and I'll see if I can seduce a taxi.'

Kate wobbled over to Jill's car as she targeted the door and homed in on the keyhole. She opened the door, reached over the seat, rescued her dowdy duds, got out and locked the car.

'Come on, Kate. Hurry up, will you, I have a taxi.'

Amused, Kate noticed Jill had her head through the passenger window of a taxi. Her arse stuck out like a sore thumb in her tight, short dress, like it was in need of someone to park its bike there. 'Alright, Jill, I can hear you. I'm not bloody deaf.' She wrestled her out of the window and into the taxi, away from the charming bistro. As she reached into her pocket and pulled out the card John had given her she smiled to herself as she looked at it for a second. Kate contemplated throwing it out of the window, but instead she opened her handbag, placed it inside and closed it.

CHAPTER 8

Once back inside Jill's flat, Kate made several cups of strong black coffee to sober them up. She showered and changed back in to her average day-to-day attire. Nervous and increasingly anxious, she retrieved her mobile from her handbag and called Alan's number. Kate was surprised when he answered on the first ring.

'Where the fucking hell are you, Kate?'

She stuttered. 'I told you I'm shopping with Jill, I shall be home soon.' Kate's hands shook and her heart pulsated, as he hung up on her. 'I need to get home right now, Jill.'

Worried, she called herself a minicab to take her home.

'Kate, I have had such a great day today. We really need to do this again soon. It's been too long.'

Jill was sprawled out on the sofa with one arm above her head and her other hand covering her bloodshot eyes.

'Me too, Jill. It was good fun and a good laugh, and it's been a while since a man has done that.'

Jill stood up from the sofa.

'What you talking about? Done what, Kate?'

Kate removed her hairbrush from her handbag and laughed as she brushed out her almost dry hair.

'Given me their phone number.'

She was amazed as Jill jumped up off the sofa and stood in front of her with her mouth open.

'No way! Not that John. No, he never did. Are you kidding me? Where is it? Let's have a look.'

Kate opened her handbag and took out the business card, giggling as she waved it playfully at Jill.

'Come on, Kate, let's see it. Don't mess about.'

Amused, Kate toyed with Jill's outstretched hand, as Jill tried to grab the card from her. Kate laughed then relinquished it, as Jill, eyes wide open, studied it.

'What! He's a stockbroker in the bloody city! Christ, Kate! He must be flaming loaded.'

Kate pondered.

'That must be such a stressful job, Jill. Not sure that I could ever do a job like that.'

Jill laughed.

'Never mind a stressful job, Kate. Wake up and read the noughts, will you!'

Kate looked down and checked her watch as she stood up. Annoyed, she reached out her arm and snatched the card back out of Jill's hand.

'Bloody hell, Jill. Why has everything got to be about bloody money with you?'

Kate felt annoyed but sad that money was Jill's God, aware that Jill only ever met men for what she could get off them and then moved on to the next poor unsuspecting bastard.

'Money is power, Kate. Imagine what you could've done if you'd had the money before it got this bad with Alan, eh?'

Kate reeled back in shock at Jill's short memory.

'I did have money, Jill! Remember, I told you, when my parents were killed in a car accident by a drunk driver? I got money and it didn't make a lot of difference to my life.'

Jill took a deep breath.

'Well, you have a lot more now. I know you're angry with Alan and everything he's done to you, and that's good, but it's also good to feel alive and know you can still pull the blokes, and a good-looking one at that. That John is fucking fit. Are you going to call him?'

Kate stared hard into Jill's face.

'He seemed like a really nice man but I'm married, Jill, and still living with Alan. But I was flattered that he was sort of interested.'

'Listen, Kate! I'm used to pulling blokes and I know when they're interested and if he had set his sights on me instead of you, I would definitely be calling him. Wild horses couldn't stop me.'

'I do not really want to meet anyone at the moment. My bloody life is a bloody mess and complicated enough with Alan. I feel like I need time out to concentrate on me for a change.'

A decision reached, Kate had made up her mind.

'No one said you have to marry him. Just give him a call. The worst that could happen is that you don't like him.'

Like it arrived on cue, Kate heard the car in the street below beep its horn twice. She ran across to the window and looked down into the street. She could see the minicab sign in neon lights across the roof of the car.

'That's my cab. I've really got to go. Thanks again for today and everything you've done for me. I don't know what I would do without you.'

Kate, arms open wide, moved towards her

friend and hugged her tight. She checked her minty fresh breath against her shoulder, as Jill lifted her head and looked at her.

'Don't be silly, Kate. You know it's here when you need it. You're my best friend for fuck's sake! Now go on, get going, and I hope that miserable bastard doesn't give you a hard time when you get home!'

As Kate turned and made her way out the door and down the steep steps, she heard Jill's voice call down after her.

'Don't forget, Kate. Give that John a call. Never say never. New beginnings and all that.'

Jill always had to have the last word, but this time, Kate decided not to let her have it. As she slammed the front door she called out,'Bye, Jill!'

Kate made her way across the road to the minicab, opened the door and got in. She closed the door, her heart racing as she wondered what waited for her when she got home.

It was like Blackpool illuminations when the minicab pulled up outside Kate's house and disgorged her onto the pavement. The curtains were wide open, and all the lights were on. Kate's heart was heavy as she opened the wrought-iron gate and made her way up the steps to the front door. She reached into her pocket, pulled out the door keys and put the key in to the lock. She almost fell through it and stumbled as it opened from within. She saw him standing there. His face flushed, he was at her again.

'Where the fucking hell do you think you've been?'

She noticed the glass in his hand. The stench from his breath turned her stomach as he exhaled cheap whisky into her face.

'You've been gone all fucking day.'

She didn't answer him and, as she regained her composure, Kate brushed past him down the hallway, her heart racing. The street door banged shut behind her and she heard his heavy footsteps as they followed her into the kitchen.

'Well then. The happy fucking wanderer returns, and no word for her fucking loving husband? What the hell have you been doing all day, woman?'

Kate realised he was more pissed then she thought he was. Her nerves surfaced and she started to feel sick again.

'You know where I've been, Alan, please don't start as soon as I'm through the door.'

She had sobered up fast from her afternoon out with Jill.

'Start? I haven't even scratched the surface yet. And where's your precious daughter? Is she off swanning about and whoring too? She's not even home from school and it's just about to get dark outside, like your mean soul.'

She turned away from him as she walked across the room, reached for the kettle and put it on the hob. Kate hoped she could coax him into a strong black coffee or three.

'I know she's not home from school, Alan. I'm making coffee, do you want one?'

'What, is she taking after you, not coming home early, not calling? And no, I don't want a fucking cup of coffee.'

He gripped the glass of whisky tight in his hand as Kate watched him slide along the counter. He halted by the sink and raised the glass to his mouth, gulping his favourite drink.

'I did call you, Alan. And I told you yesterday—Sophie is having two sleepovers at Meghan Wheeler's house this week. Don't you remember?'

Perplexed, she watched him look down on the floor near her feet. Then, as he wandered across to the kitchen table, he bent down and looked underneath it.

'What are you doing, Alan?'

He lost his footing and wobbled. She wondered what the hell was up with him.

'So, come on, tell me what you have been spending my money on? Where are all the bloody shopping bags then, Kate?'

Her hands started to shake as she looked up at him. He lunged at her with his arm outstretched and slapped at the empty air as he missed her and stumbled back onto the kitchen table.

'Mrs bloody Moneybags, I'm talking to you. What did you buy?'

She backed away from him as he raised his glass, gulping the potent brown concoction again.

'I didn't buy anything, Alan. I couldn't find anything I liked and when I did find something, they didn't have it in my size.'

Kate's stomach flipped. She could taste the mussels she had earlier in the back of her throat and pictured them in her mind all regurgitated over the kitchen floor.

'Are you fucking telling me you've been gone all this time and never bought one bloody thing? I don't believe you. You're fucking lying to me again.'

The colour started to drain from her face as he

moved closer and closer towards her.

'That's right, Alan. I didn't buy one thing, fucking or otherwise.'

His face turned red, complementing his bloodshot eyes. She thought his head was about to explode as his veins protruded and pulsated around his neck.

'I bet curvy Jill bought loads of things, tits and arse, she has a good sense of style that woman.'

Kate felt repulsed by him as he stood in front of her. He lunged at her again. This time he didn't miss and grabbed hold of her hair tight, pulling her back to the kitchen sink.

'You should've asked her to pick a few things out for you, but then I forgot, you're like one of those really ugly dogs they put ballet dresses on... Ha! A bulldog in a frock, you would come last in Crufts.'

She watched his fist come towards her face. Kate wriggled and twisted and broke free as his fist connected to her hip. She fell back. Her agony stoked the fire of her anger. As she held her sensitive side with one hand, she moved towards the kitchen door.

'I think I'm more than capable of choosing my own clothes, thank you very much.'

Alan lifted his arm and pointed his finger

towards her, as he winced.

'You're one fucking wriggly bitch and this isn't over yet, you fucking whore.'

She regarded him icily as he lost his balance and slid down the side of the kitchen cupboard like a sack of shit. She looked at him, flabbergasted, as he reached out his arm up onto the worktop to retrieve the glass of cheap booze. Kate was amazed as he took another swig and missed his mouth altogether, pouring it down the front of his chest.

'I've had enough of this. Look at the state of you. I'm going to wash the stink of you off me and go to bed. Don't bother trying to get up again. Goodnight.'

Angry, she looked at the man on the floor, unrecognisable, as though he wouldn't be out of place sitting on a park bench somewhere with a bottle of cider attached to his hand.

'You fucking whore.'

She walked out of the kitchen, turned around in the doorway and looked him up and down.

'You're a bloody hateful bastard. I might be ugly, but you will still be a bloody drunk tomorrow, and the day after that.'

She closed the kitchen door behind her, and made her way down the hallway and upstairs into the bathroom. She locked the door as she removed her clothes. Kate grabbed a towel off the rail. As she stood in front of the full-length mirror to gauge her body, she spoke out loud to herself.

'I fucking hate you. I don't know who you are any more, Alan.'

The bruises covered her body and her head throbbed as she checked out her scalp, still sore from the last lot of abuse. Her fire became her fury. She could still smell the acid of his breath in her nostrils. She quickly turned on the taps, picked up the soap and scrubbed her face clean. Kate grabbed her clothes from the rail, unlocked the bathroom door and walked along the landing and into the bedroom.

She paused for a moment and looked across at the whole empty bed as she anticipated the space she could stretch into unencumbered by her vile lump of a husband. She opened the drawer of the night table, removed a pair of cotton pyjamas and put them on. Ready for bed, she bent down and picked up her jeans. As the card fell out of the back pocket, it fluttered on to the floor.

'Oh my god, shit.'

Kate bent down again and picked it up,

holding it tight in the palm of her hand. Silent, she listened out for any sign of Alan and as she opened her hand to look down at the business card, she heard Jill's words in her head.

'I don't think I can go through with this.'

Kate opened the door of the wardrobe and focused her attention on an open handbag in the corner. Bending down, she concealed the card inside the torn lining. Standing up, she walked across and perched herself on top of the bed and stared hard at the closet, aware of what it contained inside.

'Oh, Jill's right. What the heck have I got to lose? He's probably already forgotten about me.'

She jumped up and grabbed her mobile phone off the bedside table as she raced over towards the wardrobe and opened the door. She retrieved the handbag, opened it and pulled out the business card. She tapped the number into her mobile phone.

'Hello, John, it's Kate.'

CHAPTER 9

Summer started to wind down into autumn and the breeze brought the scent of the changing leaves. She had agreed to meet John for a picnic. It was still warm in the sunlight as she watched him lay down a blanket for them to sit on under a big tree. She unpacked the overstocked picnic basket.

'This is lovely, John, but I'm not sure we're going to eat all of this.'

She stared at him as she removed the last of the food. She felt anxious, hoping he hadn't invited anyone else along to their secret rendezvous.

'A lovely picnic for a lovely lady. Thank you for coming today. How did you manage to get away from Alan?'

The mention of Alan's name sent shivers up her spine and made her stomach turn.

'Alan's at an electronics warehouse. He'll be there all day but I'd rather not think about him now if that's okay with you?'

She looked at him as he held a glass of wine towards her. Kate took the drink from him and started to relax. Leaning back against the tree, she watched a dog chase a Frisbee.

'That's more than okay. In fact, that's perfect. You don't have to think or talk about him.'

She stretched out her legs and felt the sun on her shins as she tried to draw in the last of the summer. She wondered why this attractive man had gone to all this trouble for her.

'John, can I ask you something?'

Kate sat upright and looked into his face.

'You can ask me anything you want, Kate, as long as it's not religion or anything to do with Brexit.'

She smiled as she placed her glass down on the floor next to her.

'Why me? I mean out of all the women you could have, why choose me? I'm just an ordinary mum from north London and nothing special.'

Her body tingled as he reached across and grabbed her hand. Kate felt his soft skin.

'Why, it's simple. You're so different. I mean, some women come across like high-speed trains and play games but you're straightforward and understated, and you don't put yourself out there as a shop window, like your friend Jill.'

Kate was taken aback as John raised her hand to his mouth and kissed her middle finger. Working his way up, he stopped at her wrist and spoke.

'I'm sure Jill has her good points, but you're classy and real, and very attractive.'

She breathed through her nose and licked her lips and as she started to feel the full heat of the sun, she undid the top button on her blouse. He manoeuvred across towards her face.

'You are a wonderful woman, Kate. Where have you been all my life?'

She froze as he leant in and kissed her, gossamer soft, on the cheek. He whispered in her ear.

'I really want to get to know you, on all levels, if you know what I mean.'

The blush started in her chest and bloomed over her cleavage, throat and face as she moved her hips against the ground. She coughed and pushed him away.

'Oh, John, you're getting me flustered. Can we just have the picnic? It looks delicious.'

She looked at his disappointed face, frustrated as he backed away and composed himself. Kate felt awkward and apologised.

'I'm sorry, I'm just not used to this kind of attention. Plus, you do realise I'm still married?'

He sat crossed legged on the blanket, as she watched him pour himself a drink. He took a big sip.

'I'm sorry, you're right and I'm wrong. I got carried away. It must be the wine, or I'm drunk on you. If I go too far I want you to tell me. I just want everything to be perfect.'

She looked at him, smiled and giggled.

'You say the daftest and nicest things, thank you, and I'm flattered, but I'm coming out of this bad marriage and I have so much to deal with at the moment.'

She considered him carefully as she picked up her wine glass and sipped it. He was an attractive man and her pulse raced whenever she saw him, more than she liked to let on.

'And that is another reason I want to be with you. You've got courage. You're on your way out of this bad marriage and becoming the new Kate. I'd like to be with the new Kate. Whoever she is. Okay?'

They were the sweetest words Kate had heard in a long time. Unable to hold back any longer she leant into him, closed her eyes and kissed him on the lips as he pulled her tight towards him. She opened her mouth a little to his and could feel his tongue slide along hers.

She opened her eyes at the exact moment the orange Frisbee came out of nowhere and cracked him on the side of the head. She reeled back, as he jumped up and shouted out at the top of his voice.

'Hey, what the fuck!'

Shocked, she watched as a young boy approached, alongside a panting golden retriever. Unapologetic, he asked for his Frisbee back, as John scolded him.

'You should watch what you're fucking doing. I mean, be careful in the future.'

She looked at him askance as he returned the Frisbee to the small child then turned around and stretched out his hand towards her. She grabbed it and he pulled her up onto her feet from the blanket.

'Are you okay, John? Do you want me to take a look at your head? I didn't see that coming until it was too late.'

His face still angry, she noticed his nostrils flare as she dusted herself down and straightened her dress.

'Those bloody things pack a punch. Bloody Frisbee took me by surprise, that's all. I'm sorry if I upset you.'

She thought he had overreacted, as she started to pack away the untouched picnic.

'I'm going to have to make a move after we tidy this away, but I have had the best day out I've had in a very long while.'

He reached out and gripped both her hands and held them tight.

'I really hope this will be the first of many times together, and I promise we will have much more fun the next time. Please say you will see me again.'

She couldn't remember the last time she felt so good. Lost in his dark brown eyes, she threw caution to the wind.

'I shouldn't really, but I will.'

Alan hated most things that were associated with fun and despised the park. Never once had he taken his daughter there. Kate used this to her advantage when Sophie wanted to go. She adored the playground, and while she played with the other children, Kate had the freedom to talk and text John. Kate always deleted her traces afterwards and never left her phone unattended. She sat on the park bench and watched all the children, enough to keep Sophie busy as she led the little ones in an adventure story around the play equipment. Kate had started to feel more content of late. She was happy she had met up with John, having had many coffee and sandwich dates with him over the last couple of weeks, but tonight was the perfect time to take things to the next level. With Alan away at some sort of gadget fair that was being held somewhere in the middle of the country, and Sophie off for the weekend on a school field trip, Kate was period free and frisky! She had even bought herself a new dress for their romantic dinner date at the exclusive Alejandro's Restaurant.

The sound of the Michael Bublé ringtone she had uploaded to her phone startled her. She could just about hear his voice as she answered it and the very loud PA announcement in the background nearly drowned him out.

'Hello, babe, I just had to hear your voice. You are still okay for tonight, honey?'

She heard 'Foolish Fancy, 10-1, is this year's winner'. She assumed he must be at some kind of dog track or race meeting but didn't ask.

'Yes, I'm really looking forward to it. The house will be empty so come over.'

Kate looked down at her phone and frowned.

Unable to hear what he said, she told him she would see him later. Annoyed, she hung up on him.

'What the bloody hell?'

She shook her head, tapping Jill's number into her mobile phone. Jill answered for a change.

'Hey, Kate, what's up, buttercup?'

Paranoid, Kate spoke to her.

'Maybe nothing but I had a strange call from John; sounded like he was at a race track or in a betting office when he should be at work. Do you think that's a bit strange? I hope he's not got some sort of problem I don't know about.'

She worried that this man that was so nice to her was just too perfect.

'Kate, it sounds like you've got cold feet. From what you've told me, he's mister wonderful. If he's treating you right, you shouldn't get your knickers in a twist just because he's skived off to have a flutter.'

She listened as Jill continued but she started to wish she hadn't called her.

'Now don't start second guessing people like you did at university. Start believing in yourself. You were always putting yourself down even though you thought you were better than the rest of us. I grew up with nothing, and you always had everything handed to you on a plate and complained about the big house you lived in with your posh parents.'

Gobsmacked, Kate started to get defensive as she wondered what had rattled Jill's cage today.

'I never meant to do that, Jill. That's how my life was. I had nothing else to compare it to.'

Kate grew worried. She had never heard Jill speak to her like that before in her life.

'Listen, you have found a good-looking man, you have money and you have the world at your feet. Some of us are just scraping by with nothing to look forward to. So, stop complaining and give yourself a day off, girlfriend.'

She digested her advice in silence.

'Are you still there, Kate? Look, I'm sorry, maybe I'm just a bit jealous, and who wouldn't be? He's a fit bloke. Now, if I had my hands on him...'

Kate laughed as she broke free from her uncertainty.

'You're right, Jill, I'm the one who should be sorry. Maybe I need to try and relax a bit more and start enjoying it.'

She started to feel stupid at how pathetic she sounded.

'Listen, Kate, look on the bright side. He

might win big and take you out on the town tonight. Anyway, I have to go now, honey, I have a job interview at John Lewis and it could mean a decent wage for once.'

Surprised at her revelation, Kate couldn't remember the last time Jill had a job interview. 'Really, Jill? Well, I'll have my fingers crossed for you.' She was happy for her and pleased that she had started to make good changes in her life.

'Thanks, I know you will. Speak soon and stop bloody worrying.'

Kate ended the call and placed her phone into her back pocket. She shrugged off her insecurities and wandered across the playground to speak to Sophie.

'Come on, Sophie, time to go home and pack for your trip.'

Sophie punched the air, excited. She watched her daughter's happy face as they both made their way back home.

The house felt eerie and quiet as early evening approached. With both Alan and Sophie away, she had started to tidy up Sophie's bedroom. She stripped down the bed and noticed a white piece of paper folded in half with the word Mummy scrawled across it. Kate picked it up, and as she sat down on the edge of the bed, she read it out loud to herself.

"Dear Mum, I love you very
much and you deserve a better
life. One day I will get a job, and
we can get a new house along
the way for me and you to live
in. I have noticed that you smile
a lot more lately, which makes
me happy. See you when I get
back from my trip.'

Lots and lots of love

Sophie xxx"

She held the note tight to her chest and smiled. Happy, she lay back on the bed as she started to daydream and take stock of her life, convinced she was on the right track for once. She noticed that the room had darkened. Panicked, she turned her head towards the clock that sat on the bedside table and, shocked at the time it displayed, Kate bolted upright.

'Shit! Shit! Look at the bloody time. He'll be here in a minute.'

In less than thirty minutes she had managed

to shower and change into her new dress. Standing in the kitchen, she decided to open a bottle of wine. She poured herself a generous glass to steady her nerves. She was all fingers and thumbs as she raised the glass to her lips. The sound of the doorbell echoed through the empty house. She placed the glass down on the kitchen table and raced down the hallway to open the front door.

'Hello Kate. Wow! You look a million dollars.'

Her nerves had all but disappeared. She felt like a teenager all over again.

'Come on in, John. Can I get you a drink?'

She stood aside as he entered. The smell of his expensive aftershave wafted past her as she closed the front door. She turned around to face him.

'I would like a drink but there is something I need much more than that.'

Kate was taken by surprise as he reached out his arms and pushed her back up against the front door, his mouth on hers as her body pressed itself against John's length. Her brain was on holiday as she felt his erection grow. It jingled the change in his pocket as he pulled away from her.

'I don't know where that came from. I'm so

sorry, am I going too fast again? I wanted tonight to be special.'

After years of drought she unfolded like a flower, but a hungry one. She wanted him and needed to be entirely connected to him. She reached out her hand, fumbling for his zipper to free him from his prison. Kate knelt down and took him in her mouth. His penis swelled in her hand as she licked around the tip of his hot straining cock. He caressed her head with gentle fingers. She sucked lightly as she felt him shudder. He pushed her away.

'Not like this, Kate.'

She looked at him, confused, as he grabbed her hands and pulled her up onto her feet. She led him up the stairs towards the bedroom. Once inside, he pushed her tenderly down onto the large bed and mounted her. She could feel his erection once again as it rubbed up against her mound, her insides screaming out as they groped each other's clothes off. She reached down and caressed him slowly. As she steered his penis between her inner lips and towards her damp moisture, she rubbed him around her clitoris and labia, as he nuzzled at the opening.

'Oh, Kate, I have been waiting for this moment for a long time.'

Kate gasped as he pressed forward and eased the tip of his cock past her tight entrance a little at a time. She opened her legs wider, hooking her heels firmly behind his knees as he slipped deep inside and filled her. She rotated her hips against him. She could feel every inch of him. She stopped him as he tried to withdraw, raised her legs and locked them tight around his waist, as he said to her, 'Oh, it's like that is it?'

She laughed as she felt him push hard into her as his rhythm accelerated. She could feel the tide was rising and had no idea how high it would climb as she let go. Bound to him, she rode his passion and the waves of her own pleasure, as he plunged into her again. The earthquake inside her shook her from her fingertips to her toes as he accelerated faster. She felt him shudder. As he groaned above her, she watched the rush of bliss as it appeared across his face. He collapsed on top of her as she tried to catch her breath. Her body still tingled from the aftershock. She had never felt so good. She was in heaven, pleased that they never made the restaurant that night.

CHAPTER 10

After Alan and Sophie both arrived home, Kate was adamant she wasn't going to let him upset her. With a spring in her step, she decided to take Sophie into town. Kate stood in the hallway, buttoned her coat, and shouted out to him.

'Alan, Sophie and I are off out into town now, okay? We will be back later.'

She spotted him in the kitchen as she stood by the front door with Sophie. He shouted back at her.

'Okay, good, maybe I'll get some fucking peace and quiet around here now.'

She ignored him as she rolled her eyes at Sophie, who giggled as they left the house and headed for the bus stop.

'Come on, Sophie, let's leave misery guts to his peace and quiet.'

The short bus ride into town was packed. Relieved as they got off, Kate and Sophie wove through the parked cars which had constricted the traffic.

'Can I look for a DVD, Mummy?'

Kate looked down at Sophie's excited face. 'Of course, you can.' She grabbed Sophie's hand as they entered the store and she led her over to the DVDs, watching her as she looked through hundreds of them. Happy that she had decided on the one she wanted, Kate paid for it at the cash desk.

'Thanks, Mum, for buying me that DVD. I have wanted that for ages.'

Kate watched Sophie as she skipped along next to her out of the shop onto the street. They continued their shopping spree for the next two hours. Kate, weighed down with bags, noticed Sophie had started to look tired.

'How about we go and get a burger and a milkshake, Sophie? My feet are starting to ache.'

Sophie never answered her as Kate paused and placed the bags down on the floor. Kate opened and reached into her handbag. Rummaging around inside, she retrieved her purse and closed her handbag. Intrigued as Sophie stood on her tiptoes, Kate noticed the serious look on her face, as she stared out across the road.

'Sophie, what are you doing?'

Sophie, still engrossed, frowned, as Kate wondered what was wrong with her.

'Mum, that looks like Auntie Jill over there, getting into a taxi with that man. She has the same colour hair.'

Kate turned her head and looked across the road as two people, one with a flash of red hair, got into the back seat of a taxi. She smiled, as she looked down at Sophie.

'No, Sophie, it's not Auntie Jill. A lot of people have that colour hair. You can buy it in a packet from the supermarket.'

Kate glanced across the road again, unable to make out the two people. She watched as the taxi drove off along the high street.

'It could've been her, sweetie, but it's probably someone that just looks like her. They say everybody has a double in the world.'

Sophie turned around fast and made eye contact with her.

'Really, Mum? So, there's another one of me in the world then?'

Kate laughed.

'Oh, there can't be another one of you, you're definitely a one-off. Now come on, let's go and get that burger and then get this lot home.'

On the bus, Kate eyed Sophie, as she ripped

the cellophane off her DVD with her teeth and read all the cover notes.

'Wait till I tell Megan I've got this DVD, Mummy.' Glad they had both had a nice day, she knew it would only last until she stepped through the front door and saw her pig of a husband again.

'Next time you have a sleepover, you can take it round to her house.' She pushed Alan to the back of her mind as they got off the bus and walked the short distance home. She reached into her pocket for her keys as she made her way up the front steps. She opened the door and called out, 'Alan, are you home? Were back.'

Thrilled she hadn't got a response, she made her way down the hallway into the kitchen. As she bent down and placed her shopping bags on the floor, she spoke to Sophie.

'Why don't you go and put the TV on, Sophie, and Mummy will make you a nice milkshake?'

Kate watched as Sophie's eyes widened.

'Can I have strawberry one please, Mummy? That's my favourite.'

Kate smiled at her, as she watched her excited daughter jump up and down.

'You can have whatever one you want, my angel, now go and set the DVD up.'

She started to think about Jill as she unpacked the shopping. She wondered if it was her Sophie had seen in town. Intrigued, she reached for her handbag, pulled out her mobile phone and tapped in Jill's digits. She was just about to end the call, as Jill answered.

'Hi, Jill, it's only me. Just thought I'd give you a quick call. I didn't have a chance earlier as I've been out all day in town with Sophie. How did your job interview go the other day?'

She waited a while for Jill to reply.

'That's nice, Kate, I hope you both had a nice time. Not been much good on the job front. I will just have to keep on looking. But never mind.'

She thought Jill sounded bored and pissed off.

'I'm sorry to hear that. You will find a better one I'm sure. Anyway, we had a great time. Sophie enjoyed herself and funnily enough, she thought she saw you in town today.'

The pause at the end of the phone crackled.

'Did she, bless her? No, it wasn't me! She must have been seeing things, or my double. I haven't been out all day.'

Kate laughed, not bothered any more. She changed the subject and started to talk about John.

'I had a great weekend with John. It's getting

quite serious. He wants me to leave Alan.'

Jill's sigh was just a hiss.

'Well that's good, isn't it? You'd be leaving Homer Simpson for Ryan Gosling. What's the fucking hold up?'

Kate laughed at her comparison.

'I don't know if the time is right yet. I will have to have it out with Alan, probably over dinner one day next week, when Sophie is out the way.'

Sophie's voice distracted her, as she called out from the living room.

'Mum, can you stop talking to Auntie Jill and bring me my milkshake and watch this film with me? This one's even better than the other one.'

Kate acknowledged her, then spoke to Jill.

'I'm coming, Sophie. Sorry, I'm going to have to go. I promised Sophie I'd watch a film with her this evening, I'll give you a call soon. Bye.'

She replayed the conversation she had just had with Jill in her head, perplexed as to why she had paused so much. She brushed it off, putting it down to one of her friend's idiosyncrasies, as she heard Sophie's voice.

'Mum, what are you doing? Come on, I'm waiting for you.'

She thought no more about it as she spent the

rest of the evening snuggled up with Sophie on the sofa. They watched the film and went to bed before Alan showed his face.

The next day, after she had waved goodbye to Sophie from her bedroom window and made her way down the stairs, she was startled as she heard Alan. His voice boomed through the whole house, followed by a tremendous bang.

'Fucking bollox! Fucking stupid thing!'

In a trance, without any thought, she stopped and straightened a picture that featured Alan's father, the bully of all bullies, then flicked her finger into his face. She noticed the morning post still on the mat and bent down and picked it up.

'What the fuck is wrong with this bloody thing?'

She walked towards his study, turned her head, paused, and looked into his secret hideaway. She noticed the computer screens, all blank and lifeless. Alan was on his knees, his arse in the air like he was at prayer, surrounded by cables.

'Fucking stupid cables.'

Kate was amused when he rammed a plug into a socket and shocked himself.

'You fucking bastard!'

She rolled her eyes as she made her way into the kitchen and turned her attention to a letter addressed to her. Puzzled, she opened it to find it was for an urgent meeting that day at Sophie's school. Worried, she removed her mobile phone from her pocket. She called the school and confirmed the appointment. Then she heard Alan.

'Who the fuck you talking to, at this time in the morning? You look worse than usual, what's up with you?'

Kate was in no mood for him today.

'There is nothing the matter with me, Alan. You're the one making all the racket. I bet half the street can hear you banging and crashing about.'

She knew she had to get out of there fast before he started his antics again.

'I will make as much fucking noise as I see fit, so don't you dare fucking dictate to me.'

She eyed him as he moved towards her. Panicked, she turned around and darted out of the kitchen and down the hallway as she heard his voice.

'Where the fucking hell are you going?'

Kate didn't answer him. She grabbed her coat and bag, opened the front door and slammed it shut behind her.

Kate had taught drama for years at Sophie's school. Miss Jenny Slater sat down in a position of power. Kate was forced to sit in a small child's chair, worried she would lose the feeling in her legs under the foreshortened table. Sophie's teacher spoke to her.

'Hello, Kate. I'm so glad you could come in and see me at such short notice.'

She looked at her old colleague, a veteran teacher with no kids. Her pupils were her substitute family.

'What's wrong, Jenny? What's the urgency? Has something happened?'

Jenny got up, walked across the small classroom and picked up a sizeable green folder. Then she walked back across the room and placed it on the table in front of her.

'It's Sophie's drawings, Kate, they're very worrying. Let me show you.'

Kate watched Jenny as she opened the folder. Surprised, Kate reeled back and looked down at the images of her house on fire. The vivid shades of red and orange and deadest black surrounded all of them. Kate sat dumbfounded.

'How long has this been going on for, Jenny?'

Kate looked up at her and noticed she held

another drawing in her hand. Without thinking, she grabbed it from her.

'I'm really sorry, Kate, but this has been going on for about three months now.'

She turned over the picture. With a blood red beard and eyes to match, the jagged black outline of Alan's body was surrounded by a sea of crimson red. The sound of Jenny's voice pulled her out of the disturbing picture.

'I know I don't have to tell you, but they're quite disturbing.'

Alarmed, Kate couldn't take her eyes off the pictures.

'Yes, I can see that, Jenny, but why didn't you contact me sooner, for heaven's sake?'

She placed the picture down onto the table and pushed it aside.

'Well, to be totally honest with you, Kate, most children draw odd things from time to time, and I didn't want to worry you at first.'

Kate's eyes welled up as she watched Jenny gathering the pictures up from the table and placing them back inside the green folder.

'I'm still having trouble believing she did all those pictures.'

Kate reached out and accepted a tissue from Jenny, then dabbed her wet eyes.

'Look, Kate, far be it for me to pry, but is everything alright at home? I mean, Sophie is not seeing, or around, any violence, is she? Because if she is, you know, I'll have to report it to social services.'

Kate dead-eyed her.

'Don't be daft, Jenny. Alan and I are having a bit of a rough patch because he lost his job, but things will be back to normal when he gets another one.'

Jenny was a busybody. Even if she was an old work colleague, Kate didn't trust her. Most of the teachers that worked at the school knew she had her own hotline to social services.

'I'm sorry to hear that, Kate, but you know why I had to ask you to come in so urgently today.'

Kate fought her way out of the quirky undersized chair, stood up and faced Jenny.

'It's fine, Jenny. Don't worry. I will be having a good talk to Sophie, I'm sure it's just a phase or some cartoon she's been watching on the TV.'

With a heavy heart, she had lied through her teeth.

'Well, Kate, it's been lovely seeing you again, but I'm going to have to run, as I have a year two meeting. Is it okay if you make your own way out?'

Kate was thankful Jenny had something else to do with her time. 'That's fine, I think I can manage to find the exit. I worked here long enough.'

With Jenny gone, she walked across the classroom and inspected the projects and galleries of pictures that hung on the wall. She noticed not one of them featured fire or exploding dismembered dads. Upset, she turned and left the classroom.

Outside the school she waited at the bus stop. With no one around, she reached inside her handbag and retrieved a picture of Sophie. She traced her fingertip across her daughter's face, overcome by guilt as her emotions got the better of her.

'I'm so sorry, Sophie, it's all my fault. I've really let you down.'

She realised things had to change, and tonight she was going to sit down with Alan and try her best to get through to him one last time.

That evening she had gone beyond the call of duty. She placed the wine glasses down on the table next to the cutlery. Alan had ignored her activities. Sitting in a chair across the table, he read the newspaper. Nervously she started a conversation with him.

'Sophie is eating over at Megan's house tonight, so I thought we could have a special dinner.'

She removed the foil lids from the stack of hot food containers that sat on the kitchen worktop.

'I never know where that girl is any more. She's never here. It's like having a fucking cat around.'

Kate ignored him as she transferred the hot food onto the table, opened a bottle of wine and poured them both a glass.

'I have got us a nice Chinese and a very nice bottle of wine.'

She noticed his head as it popped up occasionally over the newspaper.

'This is all very thoughtful of you, Kate, but anyone would think you had a guilty conscience or something.'

He folded the newspaper and threw it down on to the floor, as she persevered.

'Don't be silly. I know how you love Chinese food, I've even got your favourite — beef in black bean sauce.'

Sitting down at the kitchen table, she picked up a serving spoon and transferred the food onto the plates, as Alan started to take more of an interest.

'I can see you have got my favourite, and the noodles I like. It's all very nice, very nice indeed.'

Pleased he was in a better mood, she tried to recollect the last time they'd had a Chinese meal together.

'Are you sure you haven't got a guilty conscience, and there's nothing you might want to tell me?'

She stared at him as his mood changed. His face paled. His eyes were like pinheads as he suddenly jumped up out of his chair, grabbed the edge of the table, and tipped it and its contents all over her.

'Don't think I don't know what you've been up to, you lying fucking bitch.'

The hot food cartons seared her skin and blistered her arms and chest as the wine left a sticky film that intensified the burns. Petrified, she couldn't move.

'You've been in my study again. Don't think I don't know about it. What have I told you about interfering with things in my study? But you never listen to me.'

She watched him as he kept his distance from

the mess of food and broken crockery. She found her voice, as she forced herself up from the floor.

'I don't know what you're talking about. Honestly, I would never interfere, you know that. I haven't been anywhere near your study.'

Her scalded arms outstretched as proof, she screamed at him, 'Why in God's name do you do this to me? What is wrong with you? Why?'

From that moment onwards, she knew it would be her last-ditch attempt. Standing there, she watched Alan's twisted face as it turned to delight. He laughed from his oversized gut.

'Look at you, you have to be the most pathetic fucking creature on the planet. If you can't take the heat, stay out of the kitchen, bitch!'

Caught up with her inner fury she didn't register the noise as he stormed out of the house and banged the front door. Instead, she looked around at the mess he had created as her eyes smouldered.

CHAPTER 11

She focused her eyes on the paracetamol bottle and the empty glass that sat on the bedside table. Unable to break out of her usual routine, she had cleaned the kitchen before she had gone to bed the night before. In pain, she prised herself out of her bed as she called out.

'Sophie!'

Standing up, she made her way out of the bedroom and down the corridor. As she entered Sophie's bedroom, she called out again.

'Sophie! Time to get up, my little pumpkin.'

Kate walked across the room, sat down on her daughter's bed and shook her gently.

'Okay, Mummy, you don't have to shake me, I'm awake.'

Sophie wriggled away from her touch and sent shards of pain up her blistered arms.

'Sophie, I want to talk to you about something.'

Kate gripped Sophie by the shoulders as she

encouraged her to sit up. The bright sunlight snuck through a gap in the curtains and sparkled around Sophie's profile.

'What do you want to talk to me about, Mum?'

Sophie's eyes widened. As she stretched out her hand and touched Kate's bandaged arm, Kate flinched.

'Oh, Mum, what happened to your arms?'

Sophie's concerned face as she waited for a response worried Kate.

'Oh, that's nothing. I had another accident last night, love. Don't worry, it looks worse than it is.'

Sophie's angry face reminded her of her own expression the night before.

'Did Daddy do this to you?'

She dismissed the statement and changed the subject.

'No, just me being clumsy with the oven again. Anyway, let's talk about you, please.'

She looked at her daughter's worried face.

'What have I done? Did I do something wrong, Mummy?'

Kate reassured Sophie while her eyes still focused on the bandages on her arms.

'Don't be silly, when do you ever do anything

wrong? I love you, you know that, don't you? I wanted to talk to you about school.'

She watched Sophie as she cocked her head to one side like a little poodle puppy and pouted.

'What about school?'

She resisted the cuteness and got serious.

'I had to go and see your teacher yesterday about the pictures you've been drawing in your art class. They're very violent, Sophie.'

A look of horror appeared on her daughter's face as she reeled backwards.

'I just draw what I see, Mummy, and I see Daddy always being mean to you and doing nasty things. And he never talks to me, just gives me funny looks all the time. He is a big fat mean pig, and I don't like him.'

It was a statement of fact. Sophie's lack of emotion scared her.

'You mustn't say awful things like that, Sophie.'

Sophie started to sob as Kate reached out both arms to cuddle her tight.

'It's alright, Sophie, please don't cry. You know I'm always here for you and you can talk to me about anything. It will be okay. I promise you, Sophie.'

She regarded Sophie with determination as

she held her in her arms. She rocked her back and forth.

'It just upsets me, Mummy. Why can't we go and live somewhere else, or better still, why can't he?'

Kate cupped Sophie's face in her hands and looked hard into her face.

'I know you're upset, Sophie, but things will change for the better soon. You must promise me no more scary pictures at school though, okay? Let's start drawing nice ones again.'

Still worried as she cuddled her daughter, she knew it was time to escape Alan once and for all.

She no longer referred to the menu at the Corkscrew restaurant, it had become her local for her affair with John. She thought of it as her romantic destination. Kate spotted him as she entered and he quickly caught her gaze.

'Kate, over here.'

He stood up from a reserved table at the back of the restaurant to greet her as she approached him.

'Wow, Kate, it's so good to see you. You look absolutely amazing. Sit down. I have got us a nice bottle of Chablis.'

She leaned in to him and kissed him on the

cheek, then sat down at the table and watched as he poured them both a glass of wine.

'I'm so glad you called me, Kate. I have been so worried about you, especially after you told me about what happened at the school and Sophie's drawings. How is she?'

Kate looked sad.

'I didn't realise what all this was doing to her. Alan's temper has definitely had an impact, and I feel awful, so guilty.'

She noticed his eyes divert towards the attractive waitress as she passed their table. But he kept it to a sidelong glance as he said, 'The good thing about kids, Kate, is they're very resilient. She'll bounce back, you'll see. She's a survivor, just like her mum.'

She relaxed and as the tension left her brow, it made her look younger. Startled, she felt John's hand on her arm.

'What the bloody hell has happened here? Did Alan do this to you?'

Embarrassed, she watched him as the anger hit his face. She pulled her hand away from him.

'Oh no, that's nothing, I just tipped some hot food on myself, being bloody clumsy as usual.'

She looked at him, concerned as he steered his eyes away from her. His hand toyed with the base of his wine glass as he spoke.

'I don't want to sound pushy, but have you given any more thought to leaving him?'

She had thought about nothing else for weeks.

'Yes, I'm going to leave him. I'm done trying, my marriage is as good as dead.'

He looked into her eyes and grasped both her hands as she smiled at him.

'I'm going to make you so bloody happy, Kate. The thought of you living in that house with him and what he is doing to you and Sophie... Well, it makes me so upset. You don't have to do this alone, we will tell him together.'

She listened to the bravest, but the stupidest thing she had ever heard.

'First, I need to get Sophie out of the way — she can't be there. And it's not going to be easy.'

Her mind raced as she watched him raise his hand to his chin and massage it as though he had a beard.

'Didn't you say that Sophie was having a sleepover next weekend?'

She took a sip of the chilled white wine.

'Yes, she's having dinner and staying with her friend Megan.'

He paused for a moment.

'Right, that's it then. Next Saturday, I'll meet

you outside your house—shall we say eight o'clock?—and we will tell him together. Let's get this over and done with, then we can concentrate on us.'

Kate's mouth felt dry. She began to feel sick at the thought of what Alan might do to him.

'I'm apprehensive. I don't want him to hurt you. He is a violent drunk and so unpredictable.'

The wine almost reached her face as it sprayed out of his mouth. She reeled backwards, as he laughed.

'Listen, he is not going to hurt me. He is a control freak and a pickled bully. Men like Alan only prey on women, so stop worrying, okay?' Still unsure, as she looked at him she forced a smile. 'Now promise me you'll stop the worrying. Let me get the bill and I'll get you a taxi home in time to pick Sophie up from school. I will call you in the week, okay?'

Kate's emotions were all over the place as she watched him but she felt comforted as he reached across and stroked her cheek. She couldn't wait for Saturday to be over and done with.

After breakfast the next day Alan had disappeared. Kate was happy at the lack of his high-pressured presence. It had taken the stress off the laundry as she stood in the garden pegging out the washing. Interrupted by her mobile phone, she answered it and heard Jill's voice.

'Hi, honey, it's Jill. How they dangling?'

Kate laughed as she held the phone under her chin and pegged Sophie's blouse on to the washing line.

'Downwards, Jill. I was going to call you for a chat after I'd finished the daily mundane chores.'

She retrieved a pair of Alan's pants from the washing basket, held them at arm's length, and then tossed them across the garden into the compost heap.

'Oh, you can talk? I take it happy bollox is out then? So, don't keep me in suspense, how did it go with John? Did you have another conversation about leaving Alan?'

She could hear the excitement in Jill's voice.

'I don't know or care where Alan is any more, to be honest with you, but I told John I'm going to leave him. You should've seen his face, he looked so happy, and he wants to be there with me when I tell him.'

She had come so far. She knew this was as

real as it could get.

'Sounds like you've got a good one there. You're not going to back out, are you? After everything that bastard has done to you, I'm surprised it's taken you this long.'

She thought Jill's tone sounded like a challenge.

'No, not at all. John said there will never be a right time to tell him. He has told me to stop worrying, and said he is going to meet me at the house next Saturday night at eight o'clock.'

She listened for a reply as she shook out one of Sophie's tops.

'He's right, Kate, you must stop worrying. You'll feel so much better once this is all out in the open. Stay strong, and you know where I am if you need me. Call me any time if you need a chat.'

Jill ended the call with Kate, pulled her open shirt across her chest then tossed her mobile phone on to her bedroom nightstand. She surveyed the clothes strewn across her bedroom floor as she heard the sound of his heavy footsteps approach. Her eyes re-routed towards the bedroom door.

'I can't believe it. Kate's actually going

through with it. I didn't think she'd have the bottle to be honest with you.'

Jill watched him as he made his way towards her. She smiled as he sat down on the bed and curled his body around her back, kissing her shoulders.

'Bloody hell, Jill, miracles do happen then. So, when is this all meant to be taking place? Soon, I fucking hope?'

She noticed his hairy hand as it appeared on her chest and fondled her breasts. She reached out and gripped it.

'In a couple of weeks maybe, I'm not one-hundred percent sure yet.'

He removed Jill's hand then flipped her on to her back, laughing as he climbed on top of her.

'Stupid fucking cow thinks she's leaving me! We're the ones doing the leaving. To think how much time I've wasted with her when I could've been with you. Now get that shirt off, Jill, I haven't finished with you yet, you sexy bitch.'

Jill giggled. 'I was hoping you would say that, Alan, round two is well overdue.'

The week had been a long one. It had crawled by. Kate was relieved as Saturday finally arrived. She sat beside Sophie on her bed and helped her pack for her sleepover with her best friend, Megan. Kate watched Sophie as she packed most of her stuffed animals into her small case.

'How many things have you got in there, Sophie? You're only going for the night.'

'I know, Mum, but I can't sleep without them and Megan won't share her teddies with me.'

Sophie tucked her head under her armpit as she snuggled up close to her.

'Okay, Sophie, but you can only take a couple of them, and you have to be good for Megan's Mummy. I don't want her phoning me up telling me you're not listening or dropping broccoli under the table for her cat.'

Sophie's sheepish look amused her.

'I won't feed the cat again, I promise. I will be a good girl, don't worry about me. Will you be okay, Mummy?'

Sophie, who could be both mother and daughter at the same time, took Kate's breath away.

'Don't you go worrying about me. You just have a great time and remember your pleases and thank yous when you speak to Megan's parents, okay?'

She stood up as she heard the sound of a car's

horn drifting up the street.

'That must be them. Now, have you got everything? Remember, I'm only around the corner if you want to come home for a cuddle.'

Kate gripped the handle of Sophie's pink rolling suitcase as she made her way out of the bedroom and down the stairs, passing the dead-eyed uniform portraits. She opened the front door and spoke to Megan's mum.

'Thanks for having Sophie again, Penny. She is so happy to be having yet another sleepover.'

She liked Penny. She was a good mother and she was pleased Sophie had such a good friend in Megan to play with.

'That's fine. Kate, I know you have a lot on. It's no trouble, honestly, we're happy to have her anytime.'

She placed Sophie's pink case into the boot of the car and wondered whether Sophie had enough happy childhood memories to balance out the bad ones. Standing alone on the pavement, she chided herself as she waved them goodbye. Back inside the house, she entered the kitchen and noticed Alan standing there suited and booted. He checked himself out in the microwave door as he spoke to her.

'I'm off down the pub. Got to see a man about

a dog. I might be home later.'

Mortified he had somewhere to go today of all days, she tried to think fast.

'What about dinner? I'm going to town to get shopping, and something nice for dinner.'

He squinted his eyes at her as she tried to remain unruffled.

'Well, Kate, if you're going to go to the bother, I may be home about seven thirty, but on second thoughts, scrap that, I'd rather eat at the pub.'

She didn't react as he marched out of the kitchen. She was immune to the sound as he banged the street door and she was annoyed that he might not be home that night. She waited a few minutes for the coast to be clear before she walked down the hallway, grabbed her coat and bag, and left the house talking to herself to herself as she did so. 'Shit! Shit. No. You must be home tonight.'

It was a spectacular day as she wandered amongst the many window shoppers and stopped for a quick coffee break. Before she braved the travel agents she called John, who answered her call straight away.

'Hello, Kate, is everything okay?'

The sound of his voice calmed her.

'Yes, I'm fine. Are you still okay for tonight? I

just wanted to double check that you're going to be there. Alan's gone to the pub. I just hope he comes back early.'

Kate could hear the nervousness in her own voice as she spoke to him.

'Stop worrying, Kate, everything is fine, and I'll be there. Give me a call later, okay. And don't forget, I love you.'

Reassured, she ended the call. Her stomach growled to let her know how hungry she was. Kate dined at a sushi restaurant for the first time, thankful she was on a solo adventure when it made her gag. She vowed never to eat it again. Caught up in her own thoughts, she lost track. Worried, she called John but got no reply, so left a message.

'Hello, John, it's Kate. I'm in town but now on my way home. Please be patient, I won't be late, I promise.'

The spectacular day had taken a complete turn for the worse, and so had the traffic that had backed up along the busy road. Greasy rain was illuminated by the oncoming car headlights. Frantic and disappointed, she tried to call him again, only for the call to go to his voicemail.

'Hello, John, it's me, Kate. I'm so sorry, I lost track of time, but I'm on my way home. I should be there soon, but the traffic is horrendous. Please call me back.'

Pleased when the bus approached, she got on and snuck into a front seat. Her heart throbbed hard in her chest. Kate wondered if the people on the bus could hear it too. Relieved as she listened to the dulcet tones of Michael Bublé from her handbag, she took out her phone and answered it.

'Kate, I have got your messages, I have told you I'll be there. Now stop worrying. I know all this is a big deal for you—well, for us, really. I'm on my way, sweetheart, you know I wouldn't let you down.'

There wasn't enough moonlight to make out the dark shadow that crept through the garden that night and entered the back door to the kitchen, making its way upstairs to the master bedroom. They opened the second drawer in the bedside cabinet, and after they had removed the oil-stained cloth, they made their way back down the stairs. The TV was louder than usual and as the light pulsated from the living room, it illuminated the barrel of the gun. Alan sat in his armchair, half cut, watching his favourite game show. Sensing movement he turned his head around. Shocked, he stood up.

'What the bloody hell?'

Andrew from Wetherby had just won the jackpot as the gun exploded.

CHAPTER 12

Once off the bus, Kate raced along her road feeling panicked after she heard a loud bang, which sounded like a car backfiring. Stopping dead in her tracks, Kate turned her head and looked up and down the dark street, but it was empty. She quickened her step and as she approached her house, noticed it was in darkness. Just the glow from the TV warmed the curtains. Kate pulled out her mobile phone and pressed the redial button.

'Hello, John, it's Kate, I'm at the house, but I'm not sure if Alan's home yet.'

Her hands trembled as she reached into her pocket to pull out her keys.

'Just go inside, Kate, I will be with you soon. Just leave the door on the latch for me, okay? I'm not far behind you.'

She opened the front door, surprised as she stood on something soft in the hallway. She picked up one of Sophie's gloves and tossed it on the hallway table.

'Alan, Alan, are you in?' she called out nervously.

Kate got no answer but as she made her way along the hallway, she noticed the door to Alan's study was open and the monitors were alive.

'Alan, are you home?'

Curious, she entered his study and took a closer look, puzzled as to why the monitors all flickered. She noticed the tape had finished so she pressed the rewind button.

John drove along the high street in his black Jaguar, pulling off a black glove with his teeth. He steered with his left hand, as he spoke out loud. 'Now that was the best rush I've had in a long time.' He indicated a right turn and pulled over to the side of the kerb as he tapped on the interior light and checked himself out in the rear-view mirror. John reached into his inside pocket, took out his mobile phone and pressed the same digit three times.

'Yes, police please.'

Kate left the study and walked along the hallway to the lounge. The sound of the TV escalated as she nudged the door open. Taken aback, she noticed Alan on the floor. His arms were stretched out above his head, and without a thought, she threw herself into the room and over his body.

'Oh, Alan, what's happened to you?'

She saw the blood. Kate quickly became overwhelmed by the stench of shit, piss and copper assaulting her nostrils. She saw the gun. Terrified and in a trance, she picked it up and stared at it. Kate was oblivious to the sound of the police sirens that echoed along the street and quickly broke from her reverie as she heard the male voice in the doorway.

'Mrs Kate Saunders, is it? I'm Detective Inspector Sebastián Roberts. Please put the gun down on the floor and put your hands in the air.'

Confused, she lifted her head as she noticed the strange people in uniforms in her house. She listened as he projected his authority.

'Mrs Saunders, look at me please. I'll tell you again, please put the gun down slowly on the floor and put your hands in the air. We need to know you're not a threat.'

She bolted into the present as she made eye contact with him and dropped it to the floor. Two uniformed officers pushed her face down onto the carpet and handcuffed her. She turned her head and watched the authoritative figure as he knelt down by Alan's body speaking to the young black man who stood next to him.

'I don't see any signs of life here. He's gone.'

She watched him as he shook his head and spoke to the young black man again.

'Looks like he took one bullet to the chest and one to the shoulder. Webb, help get her and caution her, then let's get her down the nick.'

She didn't react when the police cautioned her. Fixated on Alan's perforated body, she watched as the blood pooled and seeped into her best rug.

He left his car. John was on a mission as he took a detour to the canal and hurried along the unlit path. Hesitant, John searched for the right barge. Then, as the scent of marijuana hit his nostrils, he jumped on board and called out, 'Mickey, it's John. Are you here, mate?'

John opened the small door and wished he'd taken in more fresh air as he entered the cramped quarters and heard Mickey Hannagan's voice.

'I'm here, John, if you've got that money you owe me.'

The smell of diesel, damp and crack pipes,

with the underlying tones of Mickey's sweat, took John back to the time they spent inside together.

'Alright, Mickey boy.' Skinny as a whippet, Mickey looked like his skin had been painted onto him as he held the burning joint between his stained yellow fingers. 'I could give you that monkey, or you could wait and turn it into a grand.'

John looked around for somewhere to sit but thought better of it, distracted by Mickey as he offered him the joint. John imagined Mickey probably hosted several different infections at once and so declined.

'I remember you said you had plans when you got out, but I'd rather have the certainty of that monkey now, thanks.'

John sighed.

'Look, I'm a bit short now, but I do have the cash for coke if you can get your hands on any.'

John reached into his pocket and pulled out a wad of cash.

'Still breaking promises. Mind you, John, if it wasn't for you stepping in and saving my bacon with that bent screw inside I wouldn't be so generous, so I'll wait this time, and I better get the full grand. Now, how much Charlie do you want?'

John handed over a wad of cash. He knew Mickey was twice as greedy as he was smart, and bore the scars of a life lived cheaply.

'Whatever that will buy. I'll trust you.'

John watched him and as he looked him straight in the eyes, Mickey laughed.

'Ha! You like to be the funny man? Okay, let me see what I've got.'

John eyed Mickey as he entered the small galley and opened the oven door. Mickey removed a brown paper bag, reached inside and pulled out two wraps, replaced it back inside the oven, then closed the door.

'So, you still using that alias then, what is it again? Oh yeah, Jonathan Jacobs.'

Shocked, John eyed the scar on Mickey's face that stretched from his lip to his hairline. He'd got it for grassing up a couple of armed robbers from south London, back in the day.

'Bloody hell, you remembered that! Now that's a surprise.'

He reached out as Mickey relinquished the two wraps into his hand and smiled.

'Yeah, I'm full of surprises. I remember your big plan, so you best watch out. I can keep my eye on you, now I'm a free man, and I will.'

John's eyes bulged as he put the wraps of cocaine inside his jacket pocket.

'No need to be paranoid, Mickey. You can trust me. It's you I should be worried about with your fucking track record as a grass.'

The wood burner in the corner created waves of warm stink. John started to feel nauseous as he regarded Mickey coolly. He watched him as he rummaged in the chaos of the floor. Mickey picked up a pen and scribbled on a piece of torn paper.

'Anyway, here's my current number. If you need any more Charlie, or herbs, give me a buzz.'

He didn't answer but grabbed the piece of paper out of Mickey's hand. He turned and made his way out of the foul cesspit, along the canal path and back to his car. Angry as he got in, he raised his clenched fists and slammed them hard against the steering wheel as he spoke to himself.

'Mickey fucking Hannigan, you out and out fucking shitbag. If you think you've got me over a barrel, you can think again, you little mug.'

The White Manor was a well-established hotel, distinguished by well-tended lawns and a clientele to match. It was far from John's usual habitat. Inside the car park he handed over his keys to the valet, got out and entered the hotel through a side entrance. John took the lift to the fourth floor and made his way along the corridor until he found the right suite. He took the hotel key card and popped it into the slot.

'Bingo'

Elated as he entered the immaculate suite, he smiled to himself.

The stink of urine and nicotine had battled the fog of detergent in the hot interview room that multiple scrubbing sessions and repaints had failed to remove. Kate, dressed in weird overalls, sat next to the middle-aged, hunched duty solicitor. Tired from the arduous photos, DNA, gunshot and fingerprint tests, she spoke to him.

'Where is my daughter? I need to know she is okay. She is going to be worried about me.'

She looked across the table at DI Sebastián Roberts' expression. She was amazed at how quickly she had gone from wife and mother to just another criminal, as she raised her tone.

'Where is my daughter? Could somebody please tell me?'

She noticed from the angle of his shoulders to his vein-free nose, he was a self-disciplined copper that knew his fair share of low-life scum and was probably respected for it.

'Please be quiet, Mrs Saunders, you will get your chance to talk.'

Taken aback, her eyes diverted towards the younger detective. Dressed in baggy pants, he pressed the recording device that shrieked for far too long and pierced her ears. DI Roberts spoke.

'Mrs Saunders, would you like to tell Detective Webb and me what happened tonight?'

She watched as he leaned in closer and Detective Webb flashed her a fake smile.

'I don't know what happened. I'd been out all day.'

She eyed the young apprentice, the master of two buttons, as he stretched back in his seat.

'Mrs Saunders, we had a call tonight saying gunshots were coming from your home, and the sound of somebody screaming. Do you not know anything about that?'

She sensed he was all about business as he looked down his nose at her.

'I went into town, did some shopping,

stopped and had something to eat, then did some more shopping, and then stopped for coffee.'

She thought hard as she pieced together her movements that day.

'So what time did you get home from this so-called shopping trip?'

Her mind confused, she didn't want to answer any questions, as once again her thoughts turned to her daughter.

'I don't know what time it was. About eight o'clock, I think. I'm not sure. Now can anyone please tell me if my daughter is okay? Because as I told somebody else, she is staying with her friend and is going to be very worried.'

She stared hard at Roberts as he turned his head and looked at his detective sidekick.

'Don't worry about your daughter, we have sent a WPC to the address you gave us earlier to inform her and to check on her.'

She had never felt so relieved.

'Oh good, she is going to be so scared and upset. I need to be with her.'

Focused on his intense eyes, she tried to calm herself. Roberts interrupted her.

'Mrs Saunders. Mrs Saunders, please listen.'

Stopped in her tracks, she stared at him again.

'The sooner you're honest with us, the sooner this interview will be over. Did you and your husband have a volatile relationship? Your neighbours have told us they hear shouting and screaming coming from your house on a regular basis.'

Kate was unsure what to say about her bully of a husband.

'Well, sometimes, but he did most of the arguing. I do the standing there and taking it. We have had our ups and downs, and he had a run of bad luck and lost his job, which he was devastated about.'

He sat as still as a gargoyle as she watched the thoughtful expression hit his face.

'So, what did you argue about?'

She looked down at the faded scars on her wrists.

'Lots of things, I suppose. It got more intense after he lost his job. Alan started drinking a lot more. He'd smash plates and furniture.'

Ashamed, she linked her hands and squeezed hard.

'Well, we have checked with the hospital, and it seems like you've been there on several occasions over the years, having x-rays for breaks and sprains, as well as treatment for burns.'

Embarrassed as she watched him, he looked deep into her frightened eyes.

'Don't bother lying, he can't hurt you anymore. Just tell us the truth.'

Unnerved, she jumped as Detective Webb intervened and yelled at her.

'Is that why you shot him? Did you have enough of him knocking you about?'

Desperate, she turned her head and looked at the duty solicitor for guidance, but got none. Annoyed, she turned her head back towards him.

'No! I didn't shoot my husband, why would I?'

Detective Webb was relentless.

'Well, maybe you just flipped. It couldn't have been easy for you dealing with all that abuse over the years, with him punching and kicking you about. Did he go for your daughter one day? Is that what tipped you over the edge?'

Her head was all over the place as she tried to focus.

'Why are you saying all this? Are you nuts? Why would I leave her with nobody? Half the time he didn't even know she existed, said it was like having a bloody cat. She's the only person worth anything in my life. I wouldn't risk that for him. No way.'

She noticed Detective Webb stopped talking as DI Robert's raised his arm, gripped his shoulder hard and let go.

'Would you like a glass of water, Mrs Saunders?'

Glad of the intervention, she nodded. He glanced across at Webb, who got up out of his chair and left the room after stating his exit for the benefit of the tape.

'I'm sorry about that. Let's try and keep things calm, shall we? Did you know if your husband had any enemies? Anyone he may have fallen out with? Neighbours? You said he lost his job, how about at work?'

Reassured, she thought hard.

'No, not that I recall. We never really mixed with our neighbours and as for work, he did use to mention a few names to me over the years but that stopped when he started spending more time down the pub. He didn't speak too much about work after that.'

Her eyes diverted towards the door as it opened. Detective Webb re-entered and placed two polystyrene cups down on the table as DI Roberts mentioned his return for the benefit of the tape.

'What was your husband's line of work?'

Kate fixated on Webb as he sat back down in his chair, next to his master.

'Alan worked in surveillance for the government. He maintained, fixed and installed electrical equipment. Well, so he told me.'

DI Roberts picked up one of the polystyrene cups and handed it to her.

'Was his work classified?'

Thirsty, she drank greedily.

'I'm not sure. I already told you, he never spoke to me much about his work, and to be honest, I never asked. I suppose some of it could've been.'

Roberts leaned in and whispered in Detective Webb's ear. Without another word spoken, DC Webb stood up and left the room again as DI Roberts noted it for the tape. He continued with the questions.

'Well, Mrs Saunders, from our perspective, it's not looking promising at the moment is it?'

She watched him as he picked up the polystyrene cup and gulped it back.

'Look, DI Roberts, I walked in after everything had happened. I found him—my husband, Alan—just lying there, covered in blood on the floor, not moving. It was me that found him like that.'

Her eyes diverted to the door again as Detective Webb re-entered the room holding a piece of paper in his outstretched hand and passed it to DI Roberts. He studied it.

'Is there anything else you can remember?'

Kate closed her eyes for a second as she tried to think, then opened them.

'Yes, I remember the TV being on. In fact, it was quite loud. Also, all the lights in the house were switched off.'

She watched him as he looked up and made eye contact with her.

'Well, we have had the forensics report back on the weapon that killed your husband, and the only fingerprints they found on it were yours. Also, the blood on your clothes matched your husband's, Mr Alan Saunders.'

He sat back in his chair then raised his hands, like it was a done deal. Kate was scared.

'I'm telling you, I didn't kill my husband.'

Her eyes burned into him.

'Well, we're still waiting for the gunshot residue test to come back so let's wait and see what that tells us.'

'Look, I hated Alan most of the time. In fact,

he was a bastard to me but I have survived him this long, so why would I want to kill him now? Especially since my daughter and I have come in to money.'

Pleased she had got his attention again, he sat upright in his chair.

'Really, well this is news. Why don't you tell me about that, Mrs Saunders?'

She sighed.

'My aunt passed away and left us everything—me and my daughter that is. We were going to start again, a new life together, as far away from him as possible.'

Overcome with emotion, she started to sob with her head buried in her hands.

'Did Mr Saunders know about the money? Was he upset you were leaving?'

She looked up at him.

'No, no, no, no! You're not listening to me, it wasn't like that. I have put up with him for years, and had plenty of reasons to hurt him, but I never did. I wouldn't kill him and take Sophie's dad away from her. I'm not that sort of person—just ask my friend, Jill Reynolds. She knew what Alan was like.'

She noticed his eyes were cold, and Kate wondered whether he believed her.

'Don't worry, we'll be talking to everyone. So, let's just concentrate on your story for now, even if it takes all night.'

The minutes turned into hours as she repeated herself over and over again. The questions continued all night. Kate had never felt so isolated and alone.

CHAPTER 13

Clothes and empty champagne bottles littered the hotel suite. The remnants of the devoured crab and lobster platter that had sat on the table next to the bed made John feel nauseous as he placed it down on the floor outside his room for some lucky housekeeper to find.

'How can something that tastes so good, smell so bad the next day?' he wondered.

The ear-to-ear grin cracked his debonair expression, as he eyed the strewn money and boasted to himself.

'Well, that couldn't have gone any better if I had planned it.'

Jill clutched a handful of fifty-pound notes, raised her arms and threw them above her head. John watched them fall across her naked breasts, as she spoke.

'I knew you could do it. You cracked it! Balls the size of the London Eye, you have.'

Mesmerised by the money and nipples, he

jumped on to the bed next to her.

'You should've seen Alan's face. He didn't know what hit him.'

She ignored him, as she reached down between his legs and giggled. His eyes widened.

'Someone's awake early this morning. How about a spot of morning delight?'

He grinned and licked his lips as she lay on her back. He watched as she ground the bank notes between her breasts.

'Not like that I don't. I want you to feel just how powerful it was.'

He got up, reached out his arms and pulled Jill's legs down to the edge of the bed. He flipped her onto her stomach and positioned her feet on the floor as he stood behind her.

'You are a naughty boy this morning.'

He parted her buttocks, spread her open and as he reached down, he took his erect cock in his right hand and manoeuvred it against her moisture. He thrust into her hard, without foreplay.

'Oh, John, I can just imagine how powerful you felt.'

Arms outstretched, she clawed at the bedsheets. Excited, he pulled back then slammed into her hard again. 'Can you feel it, baby?' He could feel her as she clenched him inside. He ground against her in a circular motion, paused, and then withdrew his penis.

'Slow down, Jill, take it easy, not so fast.'

He flipped her onto her back, grabbed her ankles and placed them on his shoulders as he thrust into her again. He watched her outstretched arms as they clutched a handful of fifty-pound notes.

'You're making me so hard Jill, really hard.'

He listened to her pleasurable moans and as he climaxed, he fell on top of her and came face to face with more cash, as well the image of our monarch, the Queen.

'God save her.'

DI Roberts watched the bulb as it flickered in the corridor, creating a spooky ambience for interrogations. He noticed Detective Webb as he approached him holding two polystyrene cups.

'Why do you have to walk like you're out on the street, Webb? Time to smarten up, my lad, if you want to be an officer in this man's police force.'

Webb stared at Roberts as he offered him the weak acidic drink.

'Sorry, sir. I was just enjoying the great

moment of an open and shut case.'

He took the cup reluctantly and sipped it, then turned his head around and looked for a plant he could kill with it.

'Really, Webb, and what open and shut case would that be?'

The look on Roberts' face wasn't very celebratory.

'The Saunders case, boss. We have a motive — he was beating her up. Also, a convenient gun, and an opportunity. She was there at the exact time. Not to forget the fingerprints on the weapon and his blood all over her.'

Unhappy with his calm approach to police work, Roberts stared at him hard.

'Well, Mr Smart Arse, I have just got the gunshot residue report back and there was none on her. In other words, DC Webb, she didn't bloody fire that weapon.'

Roberts wondered what Webb was going to say next, as he looked at the perplexed expression on his face.

'Well, maybe she wore gloves, boss, and dumped them before we arrived.'

Amazed, Roberts looked him up and down and wondered if he was premature in all things, or just police work.

'The gun was a souvenir given to Mr Saunders by his late father and had been in the house for years. The only prints on it belonged Alan Saunders.' Annoyed, Roberts thrust the polystyrene cup towards him. 'Dispose of that somewhere, Webb. Also, she had years to plan her revenge. Why would she mess it up so badly to be caught red-handed? She's not a stupid woman. Something's not right here.'

DI Roberts raised his hand to his forehead and rubbed it hard.

'Well, what would you like us to do, boss?'

Deep in thought, Roberts paused for a moment as he tried to think.

'Right. I want a proper full search on the house. I also want you to contact the best friend she mentioned earlier, Miss Jill Reynolds, and see what she has to say. Maybe she can shed some light on the happy couple.'

He turned his head as the young constable PC Peters interrupted him, tapping him on the shoulder from behind.

'Just to let you know, Mrs Saunders' solicitor is here and is in the waiting room.'

Roberts looked at him.

'Thank you, Peters. I want to have a word with him before we start with her again this morning. Tell him I'll be with him shortly.'

He heard Webb's voice as he turned his attention back to him again.

'Okay, boss, don't worry. I'm on it as we speak.'

Roberts had a change of heart, not sure Webb was ready to be let loose on his own.

'Hold on, Webb. When DS Jones shows her face, take her with you, her instincts are good. Until then, I want you back in the interview room.'

His decision was not up for debate as Webb's jaw dropped open.

'Ah, come on, boss, I don't need her! She may have been an all-star at Hendon but what's an outsider from Wales going to know about our manor?'

Roberts started to lose his patience.

'Firstly, Webb, why do you think she's a DS and you're not? If you're smart, you could learn a thing or two from her. Show me you're serious about being a DC and not just a street cop with more ambition than sense.'

'Yes, guv.'

Roberts noted the dejected look on Webb's face as wandered off.

Roberts spotted Kate's solicitor almost

immediately, sitting on a bench, squashed between two bikers. He thought Mr Moore looked as comfortable as a rat surrounded by boa constrictors as he approached him and called out his name.

'Mr Moore, I'm DI Roberts. If you could come this way please —'

He was surprised as Mr Moore rudely interrupted him.

'Could I see my client now please? You have kept her here all night and had her represented by a duty solicitor, who was probably as useful as a knife in a gun fight, I expect.'

Roberts ignored him until he led him into an empty interview room.

'I really wanted to have a quick word with you, before we restart the interview, Mr Moore, if that's alright with you?'

The stern look plastered across Mr Moore's face didn't bother him.

'If you're quick and to the point, Detective Inspector.'

Roberts gestured for him to take a seat and took the chair opposite him.

'Could I get you a cup of coffee, Mr Moore?'

Mr Moore smiled at him and laughed.

'Are you trying to kill me? I know my way

around your vending machines and I would rather have a colonoscopy, thank you very much.'

Roberts, not surprised by his answer, thought that would probably be the only thing they would agree on for the rest of the day.

'Mrs Saunders told us about an aunt leaving her some money? I wonder if you could divulge some more information on this.'

Mr Moore nodded his head at him.

'Yes, that's correct. My partner, Mr King, dealt with her late aunt's estate but I was present while her final wishes were carried out.'

Roberts smirked at his discomfort and studied him.

'How long ago was this, Mr Moore?'

The two men were both around the same age with years of experience, but Roberts saw Mr Moore as the enemy, a defender of the guilty.

'Not long ago. She came in to our office about a month or two ago. She left with one hundred and fifty thousand pounds in cash and signed some legal documents regarding the rest of the estate that was left to herself and her daughter.'

Roberts reached into his inside jacket pocket, took out his notebook and pen, and started to write.

'So, she left with one hundred and fifty thousand pounds that day. So, the estate? How much was that worth?'

His curiosity was piqued as he looked across the table at Mr Moore.

'Mrs Saunders is a very wealthy woman. The estate is worth 2.8 million pounds and is held in trust until her daughter reaches eighteen, but Mrs Saunders has full access to it now. See, Detective, there was no reason for her to shoot her husband. There is no motive.'

Puzzled, Roberts sat back in his seat.

'That's a fine defence Mr Moore and now I'm really intrigued.'

Mr Moore pointed towards the door and stood up.

'Then it's time we wrapped this up, Inspector. Shall we?'

The daylight had illuminated the hotel suite with a weak sun as John and Jill finished the last round of their sex and drug marathon. He noticed the soft light was kinder to her performance as he sat perched on the edge of the bed to light a cigarette.

'You know, we're going to have to keep apart until the dust settles.' He took a drag on the cigarette and handed it to her.

'What do you mean keep apart? How long for?'

John was taken aback as she snatched the cigarette out of his hand and sucked on it sulkily.

'Well the police are going to want to question you, what with you being her best friend.'

He bent down, picked up his shirt, put it on and started to button it up.

'Best friend! Ha! Don't make me laugh, I hope she gets put inside for life. And to think Alan thought I was going to run off with him! The silly bastard.'

John smiled as he caught sight of himself in the long mirror opposite the bed.

'She was so fucking gullible. She fell hard for Jonathan Jacobs, but then who could blame her? She honestly believed I loved her. Talk about a desperate housewife.'

With the sheets bunched across her breasts, Jill sat up watching him as he grabbed his trousers off the chair and put them on.

'She doesn't love you. She's bloody obsessed. I had to listen to her banging on about you all the time. The stupid pathetic cow.'

He smiled at her and laughed.

'Well, she's going to be bleating in someone else's ear from now on.'

Amused, he pulled on his socks, found his shoes and polished them on the edge of the bed cover.

'Come on, Jill, you're a lazy cow. Get dressed will you, I've got things to do.'

The sullen look as it appeared on her face made him laugh again as she flounced off the bed and left a trail of crumpled fifty-pound notes behind her. 'Bloody hell, do you want to get rid of me already?'

His tone changed.

'For fuck's sake, Jill, you need to get back home for when the old bill turns up. This is serious shit and you need to keep the story simple, and whatever you do, don't mention me.'

Unsure about her, he retrieved his comb from his pocket and combed his hair in the mirror, eying her naked body as he did so.

'What about all the money?'

Aroused again, he watched her as she found her bra and pants and put them on.

'Jill, I have the room booked out for a month and the money stays here. If they find this lot at your flat it will be game over. Listen, once the heat is off, we can kiss this country goodbye for good.'

Dressed in red bra and panties and red high heel shoes, she sidled towards him as she held her dress in her hand.

'Make sure you book those tickets. I want to see two first class and no returns in your hand.'

The shivers up his spine caused him to pull back as she moulded herself to him. She ran her index finger down the side of his cheek as she breathed lightly on his neck.

'Yes, yes, I've already fucking told you, my first stop will be the travel agents. We'll be on a beach in Thailand very soon.'

His emotions were confused as he became angry and aroused at the same time. Jill carried on talking.

'Or Bora Bora. I can't wait for us to be together. How long have we waited for this moment?'

The urge overtook him and he couldn't hold back any longer.

'You still fucking talk too much. Still the same mouthy bitch since I got out of nick that time. Your first year at university, that's how bloody long.'

He grabbed Jill roughly by the hair as he

pushed her down on to her knees. He undid the zipper on his trousers.

'What the bloody hell are you doing, John?'

He didn't answer her as he forced his erect penis towards her face. John forced it in to her mouth as he listened to her gasp for air.

DI Robert's was followed in to the interview room by DC Webb and James Moore. Kate, relieved to see him, listened as DI Roberts restarted the interview and noted who was present for the benefit of the tape.

'Mrs Saunders, I would like to ask you some more questions about last night's events.'

She wasn't sure how much more of this she could take.

'Mrs Saunders, where is the money your aunt left you?'

She looked at Mr Moore who was seated next to her, as he nodded his head, and encouraged her to answer.

'It's with my best friend, Jill Reynolds. I gave it to her to look after as I didn't want Alan to know about it. I have known her for over twenty-five years and trust her with my life.'

Roberts, fascinated by the story, scribbled in his notebook. Kate didn't need any more proof to know he was the one in charge, the old-school copper.

'Why didn't you want your husband knowing about the money your aunt had left you?'

She shifted in her chair as James Moore leaned into her and listened as he whispered in her ear.

'You don't have to answer that question if you don't want to.'

Happy he was there to fight her corner, she forced a smile at him.

'It's okay, Mr Moore, I want to be honest. I was planning on leaving Alan and I was waiting for the right time to go. He was in such a bad way, I didn't want to leave him like that.'

Her eyes diverted towards DC Webb, as he interrupted.

'So, you're saying you felt sorry for him — a man that likes to get physical with you?'

Anxious, she dead-eyed him as she persisted.

'I know more than anybody what Alan was like but I just thought maybe it might send him over the edge. There was a time when he was a nice man.'

Her body started to feel drained as he carried on mocking her.

'So, you didn't have other plans? You just

made a diagnosis that your husband was on the verge of a nervous breakdown?'

Exhausted she raised both her hands in the air and let them fall into her lap.

'I was just waiting for him to get another job and get back on his feet, then we were both going to tell him.'

DI Roberts interrupted her. As he looked up from his notebook, she made eye contact with him.

'Who's we, Mrs Saunders? You said "we were both going to tell him".'

Panicked, she wasn't sure whether she should've mentioned him.

'John. I met him over a month ago in a restaurant, while I was having lunch with my friend Jill. It's all pretty recent.'

Embarrassed, she worried it didn't sound right as she said it out loud.

'So, you were having an affair?'

She demurred, as she explained herself.

'Not an affair. It was much more than that. John is my soul mate. We would sit and talk for hours. He was a good listener, and he knew how badly Alan treated me.'

She watched Roberts as he turned his head and raised his eyebrows at DC Webb.

'This John, what's his last name and address?'

Deep in thought, she paused before she answered him.

'His name is Jonathan Jacobs. He is a stockbroker and works in the City. I know he has a flat near there somewhere, but I have never visited his home.'

DC Webb amused, laughed out loud.

'I'm fascinated you were planning on running off with some guy whose address you didn't even know. Sounds like a love story.'

She looked across at DI Roberts as his mobile phone beeped. He turned and spoke to DC Webb.

'That was DS Jones. She's waiting for you outside. Go and follow up on what we spoke about earlier please.'

Thankful he was needed elsewhere, Kate watched him as he placed both hands on the table and leaned across towards her face.

'Don't you worry, we will find out if you're lying, Mrs Saunders, and I promise you I will be back very soon.'

Intimidated, the tears welled in her eyes and she started to sob.

CHAPTER 14

John had got what he wanted from Jill and impatiently he pushed her in the direction of the door, causing her to stumble as she scooped up her red dress from the floor.

'Hey! What's your fucking problem all of a sudden?'

Furious, he pulled the zipper up on his pants. Jill wiped her mouth with her hand, then struggled to put on her dress.

'You're the fucking problem. Now listen, and listen well, do you hear me?' He grabbed the mobile phone that sat on top of the dresser as he turned to face Jill and forced it into her hand. 'If the sky is falling in, or you're on your death bed and need to contact me, use this, okay? Jill, for fuck's sake, don't use a landline. I have already pre-set the number into it.'

He placed his hands on her shoulders and shook her.

'Do you understand me, Jill? I don't want to

have to chase you down and remind you. And did you get rid of that phone you used to call Kate on?'

He could feel her tensed, rigid body as he watched her. She tried to break free of him.

'Yes I did, okay? Keep your bloody hair on for fuck's sake. I get it, and let go of me.'

He marched her towards the door again, opened it and thrust her outside into the hotel corridor.

'Now, get a fucking move on and don't forget — if the old bill asks, you don't know me.'

The door slammed hard into her face. Amused, he turned around, smiled and rescued the crumpled fifty-pound notes off the bed and put them back into the holdall. He then stowed it in the wardrobe as he said to himself, 'Jill, you really are the biggest fucking idiot I have ever met.'

He poured himself a Scotch as he retrieved his mobile phone and the screwed-up piece of paper that contained Mickey Hannagan's number from his back pocket.

I can't fucking believe that was so easy, like taking candy from a baby, he thought as he tapped in Mickey's digits.

John switched on the TV. As he plonked

himself down in a chair, Mickey answered.

'Hey, Mickey! It's me, John. How's business?' he said, delighted as the lesbian fest played out in front of him on the porn channel.

'Same old, same old, mate. Do you have my money yet?'

John ran his finger over the coke-dusted mirror that sat on the side and rubbed it around inside his gums.

'That's why I'm calling you. I've got your money and I want some more Charlie if you're still holding?'

He took a hearty swig of the peaty drink.

'So, I take it you got the job sorted then, mate? Is that how you're paying for that ritzy hotel?'

His lips tightened as the blood drained from around his mouth.

'What the fuck you chatting about, Mickey?' Angry, he could feel the pulse in his neck as it throbbed.

'I know where you are, mate. I told you I'd be watching, didn't I? Well, the debt has just gone up to five bags of sand. Come by the barge with the money and I'll get you your sniff. Now don't let me down.'

John's knuckles turned white as he gripped the phone. He growled as Mickey Hannagan ended the call.

'Mickey Hannagan, you dirty fucking little toad. Don't even think about fucking me over.'

Jill's journey back home was beyond illegal. Still high from the cocaine, she had removed her make-up and changed into her dressing gown. She had let the doorbell chime twice, just for effect, before she raced downstairs and opened it.

'Hello, can I help you?'

She immediately recognised the pair that stood on the doorstep as Old Bill. She could smell them a mile off.

'Hello, my name is DC Webb and this is DS Jones. Do you mind if we come in?'

She stared at the contrasted couple. Him with a heavy and muscular build, her slight, blonde, and seeming almost see-through. Still feeling horny from her drug binge, she could picture them in bed together but fought it off and remained focused.

'No, I don't mind at all. What's this about?'

She stepped back as they made their way up the stairs into the living room. She closed the front door and followed them.

'Can I get you a coffee or something? I was

just going to have one myself.'

With the corner of her dressing gown, she wiped at the moisturising cream on her face.

'No thank you. We don't want to take up too much of your time. We just need to ask you a few questions about a friend of yours. Mrs Kate Saunders.'

Jill placed her hand over her mouth for a moment, as she acted like she was shocked by the news.

'Oh really? Why? What's happened? Is she okay? She's not been in an accident or anything has she?'

In full character, she stared at them both. DS Jones took the lead.

'No, Miss Reynolds, nothing like that. She's not been in an accident.'

Jill focused on DS Jones. She had a Welsh musical lilt about her.

'Oh, thank God for that. You had me worried there for a minute.'

'I'm sorry to have to tell you, Miss Reynolds, there was an incident last night at your friend's house which resulted in her husband, Alan Saunders, being shot dead and Mrs Saunders being arrested.'

Her jaw dropped open as she let out a wail.

'Oh, bloody hell! That's terrible.'

DS Jones continued as Jill lifted her hands to her face and sobbed, her shoulders shaking, 'I'm sorry, Miss Reynolds, it must be a terrible shock. Can I get you a glass of water or anything?'

She looked up, turned her head and pointed to the sideboard in the corner of the room.

'I think I need a large vodka.'

Carried away, Jill watched as DS Jones turned her head and looked at her sidekick.

'Are you sure? It's a little early in the day for the hard stuff.'

Jill started to feel proud of her Oscar-winning performance.

'Can't you see I'm in shock? Don't matter what time of the day it is. Anyway, I'll get it myself.'

She stood up.

'No, no, please you stay where you are, Miss Reynolds. I'll fetch it for you.'

Jill faked a smile as DS Jones walked across the room and retrieved the bottle. Jill grabbed it out of her hand as she approached.

'I can't believe I'm sitting here listening to this. Why would anyone want to hurt Alan?'

Thirsty for the hair of the dog, she unscrewed the vodka and gulped from the bottle, as DC

Webb spoke.

'Well, that's what we're trying to find out, Miss Reynolds.'

Jill gulped more of the vodka.

'Poor Kate, she must be in a right old state. What about Sophie? Who's looking after Kate's daughter?'

Jill was impressed with herself as she displayed the false look of concern on her face. DS Jones tried to reassure her.

'Don't worry, Miss Reynolds, she is staying with friends and is perfectly fine.'

DS Jones kept the tone friendly and continued with more questions.

'Have you known Mr and Mrs Saunders long, Miss Reynolds?'

Jill paused and thought for a moment before she answered her.

'Well, I've known Kate and Alan years, but not seen them for a couple of months, if not longer.'

Jill felt calm.

'Would you say they had a good relationship?'

She looked at DS Jones and spoke as if she was revealing a big secret.

'Well, I remember the last time I saw Kate, she

wasn't happy at all.' She leaned forward and picked up the packet of cigarettes and lighter that sat next to the overflowing ashtray, removing one and lighting it.

'Why was that, Miss Reynolds?'

Unfazed, she took a long drag on the cigarette as she replied.

'Well, from what I could gather, their relationship was rocky, to say the least. She actually told me she wished he was dead. I also witnessed him putting her down a few times and there were the bruises and burns. It was obvious he was knocking her about.'

Her eyes switched to DC Webb as she crossed her legs. She noticed it caught his attention as he changed the subject.

'What do you know about the money Mrs Saunders was left by her aunt, and her planning on leaving her husband? Did she mention anything about this to you?'

Jill leaned forward as she found a space in the ashtray and stubbed out the cigarette.

'What money? She never spoke to me about any money, and she sure never mentioned she was leaving Alan.'

She dead-eyed them.

'So, you're one-hundred percent sure? She

never asked you at some point to look after any money for her?'

She thought DC Webb had a better future as a poker player than her, his face was unreadable.

'I have already told you, no! You can ask me anything else, but I'm sorry I can't help you with that.'

DS Jones interrupted and stood up as Jill looked at her.

'Thank you for your time, Miss Reynolds. I understand that this has been very traumatic for you but we may need to speak to you again, if that's okay? Don't worry, we'll show ourselves out.'

Relieved, Jill prised herself off the stool onto her feet and wobbled.

'Of course. Anything I can do to help. You know where I am if you need me.'

They made their way out of the room and as DS Jones paused, Jill was taken aback as she turned around quickly.

'Oh, before we go, Miss Reynolds, I don't suppose you happen to know a Mr Jonathan Jacobs, by any chance?'

Gobsmacked as DS Jones mentioned his name, Jill answered her straight away.

'I'm afraid I don't. Never heard of him, sorry.'

Jill eyed DS Jones as she held a card in her outstretched hand. Jill reached out and took it.

'Well if you think of anything else that might be useful to our investigation, please don't hesitate to give us a call.'

Jill peered through a gap in the curtain as she watched them get in to their car and drive off. She reached into her dressing gown pocket, retrieved the mobile John had given her and called him.

'Hello, baby, it's me. The Old Bill paid me a visit and have not long left. It's all fine, I think they believed me!'

She picked up the vodka bottle, took another mouthful and sat down on the sofa. The vodka dribbled down her chin and she wiped her mouth with the sleeve of her dressing gown as she heard his voice. 'Good, well hopefully they won't be back.'

She thought he sounded tense.

'Is everything okay?'

Relaxed, she undid her dressing gown and revealed a massive pair of comfortable knickers.

'What are you doing, Jill? Please tell me you're not still fucking drinking.'

She laughed and gestured two fingers down the mobile phone receiver.

'Fuck off, John. Don't you tell me what to do. You're not the one who has just been interrogated by the Old Bill. Even if DC Webb was a bit of a sort.'

She'd never bedded a black guy before and she wondered if it might be worth a shot if all the rumours were true about how well hung they were.

'But I'll be fucking nicked if you don't keep it together. This is serious. You have to stay focused. Were you drinking while the Old Bill was there?'

Broken from her fantasy, she adopted a babyish tone.

'Maybe a vodka or two, just for show, and the terrible shock I got from the news when they told me Alan was dead.'

Surprised as the guttural noise erupted from the other end of the line, she held the phone at arm's length as he ranted at her.

'You dumb fucking bitch! What are you playing at? You can't take chances now. We're so close.'

She placed the phone back to her ear and said, 'You worry too much, baby. I'm not going to do anything to spoil what we have together, am I?' She waited for a reply but didn't get one. 'John, are you there? John? Have you put me on mute?'

Annoyed, Jill realised he had hung up on her and tossed the mobile phone across the room.

The canal looked shoddier as the day brightened. Noxious odours rose from the water as John noticed the multicoloured slicks of petrol that floated on the surface. He picked his way past the occasional dog turd as he spotted Mickey on the deck of the old barge.

'Mickey Boy.'

John watched Mickey as he turned around and spoke.

'Morning, mate! Those are nice threads you're wearing today. You're obviously doing very well for yourself, Johnny boy.'

Mickey clasped a cracked mug in his grimy hands. John noticed it contained something brown and steaming. He forced a smile at him.

'Well you're looking better then you did yesterday, mate.'

John noticed Mickey had changed his attire. The clothes looked new, even if they were a bit baggy for his undersized frame.

'Just some second-hand clobber I bought recently for special occasions. Come aboard. I've got what you asked for, that's if you've got what you owe me, matey.'

There was an edge to Mickey's voice John didn't like as he jumped onto the barge and followed him inside. It smelled a lot less funky than the previous day. John handed him the envelope.

'Here you are. It's all there plus a little extra.'

John watched Mickey's scrawny fingers as he opened the envelope and looked inside. Mickey raised an eyebrow and smiled.

'Well, well. I didn't expect you to come through with it, but fair play to you.'

Mickey reached into his pocket and pulled out three wraps of cocaine and pushed them into John's hand.

'I figure this should square us now. Mind you, if you want any more, you've got my number.'

Angry, John fought the urge to punch Mickey senseless and grab the giant bag of coke out of his grubby little hands.

'So, I don't have to worry about you singing to the Old Bill then?'

Focused on Mickey's face, John placed the wraps inside his jacket pocket.

'Fuck me, John! You know I'd never do that! I was just messing with you, mate. But you had to know I was serious about the money. Can't have you letting an old friend down now, can I?'

Every part of John's body screamed out for him to punch Mickey in the face.

'You should've trusted me, Mickey. No need to have me followed.'

John looked around and wondered if Mickey was hiding something or someone. There was enough rubbish in the barge to camouflage a witness or two.

'You know it's hard to trust once you've been inside, Mr Jacobs. Anyway, you worry too much. Now we're even. You're sweet with me.'

The muscles around John's face relaxed as he forced a smile at Mickey.

'Good. I'm glad to hear it, but I have to go. Things to do and all that.'

Before John exited he turned around and dead-eyed Mickey.

'Don't get any ideas about following me again, okay? You really don't want to piss me off now and make me come back here for something other than a bit of sniff, do you?'

Mickey never answered him as John disembarked the rusty shit tip. Mickey eyed him through the porthole as he clutched his money in his greedy hands and counted it.

DI Roberts entered the incident room and stared at the blown-up pictures on the whiteboard of Alan's bloodstained body. Then she turned to DC Webb and DS Jones.

'So, Jill Reynolds has denied all knowledge of the money and she doesn't know anyone called Jonathan Jacobs?'

Roberts pulled out his old notebook as he watched DC Webb on the new modern tablet.

'Well, that's what she told us, boss.'

Roberts turned and studied the pictures again on the whiteboard.

'Seems very strange your best friend wouldn't know about a new romance, don't you think?'

Unimpressed DC Webb interrupted him.

'Maybe she kept it a secret and didn't trust Jill Reynolds as much as she's been letting on.'

Frustrated, Roberts felt the urge to slap him across the back of the head, but restrained himself.

'Jill Reynolds was her friend. She even knew Mr Saunders was knocking her about, and we know Kate Saunders left the solicitors with the money. So, someone's bloody lying, Webb.'

Roberts sighed as Webb interrupted once again.

'Maybe Mrs Saunders is a bit confused and

gave the money to another friend to look after.'

Perplexed, Roberts' eyes narrowed.

'Don't be so bloody stupid, Webb. Would you forget where you left one hundred and fifty thousand pounds? In fact, don't answer that, lad.'

Roberts started to question how Webb managed to get into the police force, confused by what could only be classed as a big mistake as it churned over in his head.

'Have you been over to the Saunders' house yet?'

Fed up with Webb, Roberts directed the question at DS Jones.

'We're off over there now, guv'nor.'

Roberts replaced his notepad back into his jacket pocket and shouted at them both as he made his way out of the incident room.

'We need to gather more facts. Keep me in the loop, you two, and if you find anything, I want to know straight away. In the meantime, I'm going to speak to Mrs Saunders again.'

Kate was sitting alone with Mr Moore in the interview room. The door opened and DI Roberts entered. Kate watched him as he sat down and started the tape machine once again.

'Mrs Saunders, we have just spoken to your friend, Jill Reynolds.'

Composed, she smiled tautly at her interrogator. 'I take it she has confirmed everything I have told you?'

Her glimmer of hope was short-lived.

'Quite the contrary I'm afraid. She told my officers she hasn't seen you in over two months.'

Unconvinced, Kate shook her head.

'You can't be serious? That's not true. There has to be some kind of mistake.' Open mouthed, she stared at him.

'She also told my officers that she knows nothing about any money, and has never heard of anyone called Jonathan Jacobs.' Kate's head spun as she gripped the table for support.

'Why would she say that? That's not true. I gave her the money. Why is she lying?' She looked at Mr Moore's supportive hand as he placed it on top of hers. Roberts continued to bombard her with facts.

'She also said she had no idea you were planning on leaving your husband. We have even checked both mobile phones and I'm afraid they're untraceable. Probably pay as you go ones.'

Kate shook her head again in disbelief.

'So, in a nutshell, she has pretty much denied everything you have told us.'

Kate's thoughts turned to John as she sat bolt upright in her chair.

'John will straighten this all out. Jill was with me the first time I met him at the restaurant. It's called the Corkscrew, it's on the high street. He'll back me up. Have you found him yet? Talk to him, he will tell you the truth.'

Kate raked her hands through her messy hair, as she answered Roberts' questions.

'Did anyone else, apart from Jill Reynolds, see you at this restaurant?'

'No, only Jill, but John and I went there a lot, and they always had the same waitresses, so they might remember us as he sometimes did a bit of harmless flirting with them.'

She started to feel positive, hopeful that somebody would remember her dining there with either of them.

'Do you have a photo of him, or maybe he gave you a card or something?'

She remembered the card.

'Yes, yes, I do. He told me he was a stockbroker in the City and gave me his business card. It's in my handbag I think.'

Her mind raced as Roberts shouted out to the

uniformed officer stationed outside the interview room.

'PC Peters, get in here please!'

The young uniformed rookie appeared from behind the door.

'Yes, sir?'

She listened as Roberts gave PC Peters his orders. He closed the door and left.

'I should've mentioned this earlier, but I had completely forgotten about it.'

With her expectations high, she turned and smiled at Mr Moore, as DI Roberts spoke.

'Hmm, I must say you have a very convenient memory.'

With bated breath, her eyes diverted towards the door as PC Peters returned with a see-through evidence bag. She could see it contained the business card, as PC Peters handed it to Roberts.

'That's it, that's the card John gave me.'

Relieved it was there, she watched him as he removed the card from the bag and looked at it.

'Mrs Saunders, would you be willing to sit down with one of our sketch artists and see if you can come up with some sort of description of Mr Jacobs? If he exists that is?'

Kate realised her life depended on it.

'Yes, of course John exists! I swear! Talk to the staff at the restaurant. There is an old photo of Jill and me in the side of my handbag. Please take it with you and show them. Someone will remember us, I'm sure of it.'

'You must find John. Like I said, he will tell you everything, I know he will.'

Roberts nodded at PC Peters, who left the room for a moment and returned a few minutes later with the photograph in another evidence bag.

They were both on holiday when the photograph was taken and they were standing at a bar sipping umbrella drinks.

'I must have had that picture for over ten years.'

Roberts studied it as she sank into her chair watching him. Kate was tired and felt thirty years older.

'Okay, we can circulate that around the restaurant, and don't worry, we will find him.'

Roberts stood up, causing his chair to screech across the floor. Kate flinched as it pierced her ears.

'I'm going to suspend the interview for a short while as I need to look into a few things.'

Kate watched him as he walked across to the

door, opened it and left the room. Optimistic, she turned her head and faced Mr Moore as he spoke.

'Come on, Kate. Chin up, you're doing ever so well. Let's stay positive.'

His words gave her a second wind.

'You're right. I'm stronger than this, and I'm telling the truth. That has to count for something, surely?'

They were interrupted as the door swung open. DI Roberts entered the room and restarted the tape recorder again.

'Now, you stated you gave this money to Jill Reynolds?'

She sighed.

'I have already told you all this. Yes, I gave the money to Jill.'

She glanced at Mr Moore as she sought assistance.

'Mrs Saunders has explained this to you already,' he said. 'She signed the paperwork at my office, left with the money and gave it to her friend to look after for her. It's not rocket science, Detective Inspector.'

Kate was impressed at his assertiveness.

'Well, we know your husband was a violent man. Maybe you never gave the money to Jill

Reynolds at all. Perhaps you paid someone to have him bumped off instead?'

She reeled back in her chair as Mr Moore intervened.

'Now, you're just clasping at straws. Just wasting bloody time when you could be out there finding evidence that clears my client's name and catching the real culprit, Inspector.'

She watched Roberts' face as his fury turned it into a giant red fireball.

'Oh, don't you worry, Mr Moore. If there is evidence to be found I can assure you we will find it. And in the meantime, I'm going to need you to stay here with your client a little bit longer while we continue our investigations further.' Kate silently caught Roberts' gaze as he made eye contact with her. 'Mrs Saunders, we will find Jonathan Jacobs or John boy bloody Walton whatever his name is, and we will bring him out of the shadows.'

Kate was terrified as he stormed out of the interview room and wondered what fate had in store for her as she anticipated his return once more.

CHAPTER 15

The Dalmatian spots of black hair dye were evident on the collar of the fluffy white robe when John emerged from the steamed-up bathroom. He sat down and picked up the rolled up fifty-pound note, held it to his nostril, and sniffed the perfect line of cocaine as he spoke to himself.

'Not bad gear, Mickey. Not bad at all for a fucking little street rat wanker like you.'

John raised his head and looked around the room at the endless dirty plates and cutlery. He walked across the room, picked up the phone and had ordered a steak from room service when he heard the knock on the door.

If that's Jill, I'm going to fucking well kill her, he thought.

Surprised at the second knock which came louder than the first one, he called out, 'Hold on! Give me a minute! I'll be right there.'

He glanced in the mirror, and finger-combed

his hair as he walked towards the door and opened it.

'Hello, Mr Chambers. I have a package for you that was delivered to reception this morning.'

The words 'Donna Keen' were highlighted on the gold name badge on her jacket that her long blonde hair almost covered. She reminded John of a young Pamela Anderson, with freckles.

'Oh, that's great! And what quick service … Donna. What a beautiful ambassador you are for this hotel.'

His robe dipped and exposed his chest. She smiled at him. Conscious it wasn't minimum wage, he took the package out of her hand.

'Thank you, Mr Chambers. We do our very best at the hotel to keep our guests happy, sir.'

John fixated on her pursed lips as she looked him up and down. He wanted her.

'Your best? I see. Well, you haven't disappointed me, that's for sure.'

He was aware she had noticed his premature erection as it poked through his robe. She twinkled in the doorway.

'I'm highly trained in customer service. If there is anything else I can help you with during your stay with us, just pick up the phone and call me at reception. You won't forget my name now?'

John was excited as she winked at him and rubbed her finger seductively over the name badge on her left breast.

'I definitely won't forget your name and I shall bear all of that in mind.'

She beamed one hundred and twenty watts of dental work at him as she made her way down the corridor. He eyed her shapely bottom, spellbound, as he closed the door.

'I shall definitely be calling you up again, very soon, darling, for some fun and games. I can guarantee you that.'

John sat down on the edge of the bed, overjoyed as he opened the envelope and pulled out his one-way exit strategy plan, dated for tomorrow. 'You fucking beauty.' He raised it to his mouth and kissed it. In a celebratory mood, he picked up the telephone and dialled room service.

'Hello. Could I get a bottle of champagne with that steak I ordered earlier? Oh, and just to let you know, I'll be checking out tomorrow night, so can you get my bill made up. Also, before I forget, could you ask Donna Keen to bring it up personally? Thank you, I have a huge tip for her.'

The smile spread across his face as he replaced the handset. Excited, he fantasised about her, determined he was going to give her the biggest, and best, she'd ever had in her entire life.

DC Webb parked the car outside the restaurant and switched off the engine. He turned his head and noticed the generated image of Jonathan Jacobs that was visible on DS Jones' tablet.

'He looks like a retro wide boy to me. I wouldn't buy a second-hand car off of him.'

Jones ignored him as he became more cynical.

'Could be anyone or no one. Who's to say she hasn't just made him up? Anyone could print off a business card and the number is probably for a burner phone.'

Remembering the photograph of Kate and Jill, he opened the glove compartment and removed it. He appraised it. 'I reckon, for what it's worth, Jill Reynolds is the cougar and Kate Saunders is the pussycat.'

Her train of thought interrupted, Jones looked at him.

'Bloody hell. Again, with the assumptions, Webb. You really are about as useful as a fart in a jam jar.'

Webb got out of the car onto the pavement as Jones caught up with him.

'Oh, shit in your hands and clap, why don't you?' said Jones.

Inside, it was busy. The lunchtime rush was in full swing as they made their way across the restaurant towards the bar. They introduced themselves to a young waitress as Webb held the photograph up in front of her.

'Could you tell us if you have seen these women in here before?'

The waitress took the photograph from his hand, and he watched her as she took a closer look at it.

'Oh, yeah. I remember them. The ginger one was really loud. A sort of cougar type. She ordered champagne and kept going on about how the other one could afford mussels dipped in gold or something like that.' He smirked at DS Jones, as he continued with the questions.

'How did they seem to you? Would you say they were good friends?'

She handed the photograph back in to his hand as she answered him.

'Well, to be honest, they were friendly, but like chalk and cheese. The other one seemed quiet. But then this guy joined them at their table and ordered more champagne. I remember him because he gave me a fifty-pound note and told me to keep the change when the bottle cost fifty quid. Bloody cheek.'

DS Jones showed her the generated image of Jonathan Jacobs on her tablet.

'Is this the man that was with them?'

They both watched her as she studied the image.

'Yes. That's him, the bloody tight arse. His hair is different though. It was more jet black, like it would run in the rain, do you know what I mean? My mate might have seen him too, hang on a minute.'

She summoned the other waitress with a hand gesture, who approached and looked at the generated image on the tablet.

'I remember him. He's a right sleaze. Always in here. I always caught him checking me out when he thought I wasn't looking.'

Unable to believe the stroke of luck. Webb double checked.

'You are a hundred percent certain that you recognise all three of them?'

In unison, they both answered him.

'Yes.'

Over the moon, they both thanked them for their time and left the restaurant. Buoyant, Webb was excited as they made their way back to the car and got in.

'Wow, that was brilliant! So, I reckon Jill Reynolds sets the trap and Jonathan Jacobs sits there like a praying mantis, waiting to pounce.'

Jones tutted, as she spoke to him.

'Webb, if you don't learn to wait, listen and absorb all the facts, you'll never move up the ranks.'

Pumped up, in a world of his own, Webb ignored her advice.

'What about police instincts and hunches? All the best cops run with their hunches.'

Jones shook her head as she interrupted him.

'On TV or in movies. Not in real life, you plank.'

Webb was deflated and as the crestfallen expression appeared across his face, Jones took pity on him.

'Look, Webb, I know you have a fire in your belly, but you have to look at all the pieces in a case. If you do things the wrong way around you'll end up embarrassing yourself, the force and me.' She punched him playfully on the shoulder. 'Believe me, Webb, you don't want to see a Welsh woman blush. It shows all my worst assets.' In spite of himself, he laughed.

'I know you're right. I think I get a bit carried away. I will try my best in future not to get ahead of myself, sergeant. Do you want me to call it in?'

Webb waited in anticipation.

'I'll call it in, Webb, while you drive. Let's get over to the Saunders house and see if uniform has turned up something. Fingers crossed it's our lucky day.'

The uniformed police officers were still present at Kate's house. As Webb stared at the photographs of Alan in the hallway, DS Jones walked down the staircase towards him, with a puzzled expression across her face.

'Well, there's nothing upstairs. I've been all over it and no sign of any money or anything out of the ordinary. Pretty boring really.'

Disappointed with the outcome, Webb said, 'There has to be something here, we're definitely missing something.'

Jones continued down the hallway into the kitchen, as he followed and caught up with her.

'Well, I'm going to concentrate on down here, and if there's a hiding place, I'm going to turn this bloody place inside out until I bloody well find it.'

Webb walked across the kitchen and opened all the cupboards above his head. He paused for a moment as he heard Jones' voice and looked at her.

'Webb, I'm going to check out the lounge while you're busy in here, okay?'

The curtains were closed in the living room, which prevented the paparazzi that had stood outside from getting their money shot. Jones opened them and as her eyes adjusted to the light, she called out as the noise from the kitchen escalated.

'Webb, keep it down will you! I can hear you in here. Do you have to make so much bloody racket?'

Undeterred, she scanned the living room. Her eyes fixated on the bright reflection off the picture that hung over the fireplace. She walked across, reached up and unstrung the image from the wall to inspect it.

'Webb! Webb! Get in here now, I think I've found something?'

He rushed into the living room. 'So, cheer me up, what have you found?'

She pointed to the top of the picture frame.

'What the bloody hell is that?'

Interested, he moved his head forward for a closer look.

'No. You've got to be kidding me, sergeant! Is that a camera?'

'That's precisely what it is, it shocked me as well.'

'Do you reckon the husband put it there? I mean, wasn't that his job, installing surveillance cameras?' Webb surveyed the room as he listened to her.

'Well, maybe there's more than one. Let's go to every room again and check the pictures. I'm going back upstairs to check the ones up there, you carry on down here.'

Within twenty minutes cameras from the kitchen, bedroom and lounge, along with telephone transmitters, were laid out across the kitchen table.

'Right, Webb, I'll give the guv'nor an update then let's get that locked door open. Uniform are bloody useless. They should've had it opened by now, so why don't you take a crack at it?'

In the interview room, Kate had been given a cup of tea. Not sure what it was, she inspected the grey coloured liquid and pushed it to one side. DI Roberts entered the room.

'Mrs Saunders, I have just been given an update from my detectives and they have found several cameras and listening devices installed in your home.'

His words hit her like a sledgehammer.

Unable to comprehend what he was saying she gasped, 'I don't know what you mean. What are you talking about? Who would do that?'

'Well, we're not sure at the moment. It's still ongoing. Did you have any idea you were being watched?'

She felt physically sick to the pit of her stomach.

'No, I didn't know I was being watched. Don't you think I would've said something? This is really creeping me out now.'

Her mind raced as she tried to compose herself.

'We will be sending everything we have found so far over to forensics for the necessary tests. Let's see what they turn up, shall we? Fingers crossed.'

Once again new hope appeared on the horizon.

'But that's good, isn't it? If there were cameras it will prove I didn't kill my husband?'

Her hopes were dashed as he shot her down

in flames once more.

'Not necessarily. That all depends if the cameras were on and running at the time your husband was murdered.'

She continued to grasp at straws. 'What about John? Did anything come out of the business card I gave you?'

Her lifeline slipped away as he shook his head.

'The email address was a dead end, along with the phone number. It looks like you're running out of luck. Maybe you might want to consider changing your story.'

DC Webb wasn't having much luck as he forced his body against the study door and tried to open it. DS Jones laughed as she dangled a set of keys in his face.

'You might want to try one of these before you do yourself an injury. I found them on a hook behind the kitchen door.'

Unimpressed, he growled at her and grabbed them out of her hand. He tried them all in the lock until he stumbled across the right one and opened the door.

'About bloody time. Why do people have so many keys on a keyring?'

The study was spotless out of respect for the high-tech equipment.

'Bloody hell, Jones, I'm impressed. He certainly has some expensive kit in here. This lot must have cost him a fortune.' They both orientated themselves with the room. Every surface was covered in an unbroken array of electronics.

'I got a feeling you might have been right about what you said in the car. This could definitely be our lucky day.'

She found the receiver hidden behind a stack of DVDs, tucked away in a false partition in the wall.

'Bingo! Take a look at this, Webb.'

The steady green light glowed on the box. Jones switched on one of the monitors that sat on the desktop.

'This has split screen views, Webb, probably from all the cameras we found. Our tech guys are going to have a right old party with this lot.'

Webb turned his attention to the endless stash of DVDs that were stored next to the receiver, unable to believe his eyes as he studied them.

'Bloody hell! I have DVDs dating back years here.'

Excited by their discovery, Jones pulled out

her mobile phone and faced him.

'I'm calling this in right now, then we can get this lot shipped back to the nick and see what we've got.'

Webb wasted no time as he started to put all the evidence into bags and label them, one by one.

'It's going to take for bloody ever to get through this lot. I wonder what's on them.'

She ended the call and replaced her mobile phone in her pocket as she answered him.

'Who knows what we will find on them, but if this leads to a result, then it'll all be bloody worth it, won't it?'

He smirked at her.

'I have got a feeling we're going to wrap this case up quicker than we thought.'

The last of the evidence bags had been removed from the study as Webb stood there and watched. Elated, he hoped there would be enough to nail Kate Saunders for good.

CHAPTER 16

Jill had woken up with a mouth like the Gobi Desert. Thirsty, she guzzled the bottled water and found her mobile phone. Laid out on the sofa, she pressed the redial button and belched out loud as John answered.

'Hello, baby, only me, have you booked those tickets yet?'

She could still hear the anger in his voice as he answered.

'What the fuck are you doing? You just can't be calling me up for the slightest thing. I told you this phone was for emergencies only.'

Jill held her foggy head in her hand and instantly regretted calling him.

'For fuck's sake! No need to shout at me! You're bloody touchy. Don't be mad just because I'm missing you. I want to come and see you.'

She forced herself up, picked up the bottle and gulped more of the water.

'How many more times do I have to fucking

tell you, the Old Bill will be watching. You really are acting like a stupid twat.'

Hydrated enough, she got up from the sofa and paced the room.

'I don't have to see you for long. How about thirty minutes? We can do a lot in half an hour. I'm bored and going out of my mind just sitting here.'

To her surprise, he knocked her back, shouting at her down the phone.

'Newsflash, you're already out of your fucking mind, bothering me for nothing. You think you've got it bad? I have to sit here, holed up in this hotel room drinking crap tea and eating soggy chips, and you want to fuck everything up for a quickie.'

She stood still for a moment, hugging herself.

'Poor baby.'

She heard the loud sigh down the receiver and changed tactics as she raised her voice and shouted back at him.

'I'm not the one fucking it up! I'm the one here under the hot lights mate, and don't you forget it.'

She composed herself as his tone changed.

'I know, but you have to grow up and be patient. Promise me you'll just chill out and stay off this phone and stay off the booze. It won't be long now. You know how much I love you. We're going to have such a good life together.'

She picked up the half-smoked cigarette from the ashtray and lit it. Reassured, she took a long drag on it.

'I will, I promise, but you better call me later or I might just show up at your hotel and knock on the bloody door. Bye.'

She tossed the mobile phone down the side of the sofa. As her eyes diverted towards the TV, she laughed. The regional news displayed Kate's house covered in crime scene tape and uniformed police.

'If only I could see your smug face. I bet you're not laughing now, Miss Fucking Money Bags.'

John picked up the glass of champagne and emptied it. As he lay back on the bed, he wondered what he was going to do about Jill. The thought was short-lived as he heard Donna's voice as she exited the bathroom.

'I hope you've left some of that champagne for me. I'm off duty now,' said Donna, seductively.

He watched Donna as she buttoned up her

blouse.

'Thanks for letting me use your shower. It's been a really long day, but I'd best get going.'

He stared at her, loosened his robe and spread his thighs.

'If you're off duty, why are you leaving so soon?'

His body ached, he wanted her so bad.

'Well, I had no reason to stay, until now.'

He surged forward and reached out. His wandering hand found its way up her skirt and grabbed her mound. Excited, he stroked his penis as it swelled in his other hand.

'How about me and you indulge in a little role play?'

She pushed hard against his hand and he watched her as she licked her lips.

'Why, what did you have in mind?'

He jumped up off the bed, and pinned her to the wall. John licked her lips along their length.

'I want you to go outside, wait for a couple of minutes, then knock on the door and pretend you're bringing me my tickets, okay?'

Donna complied and straightened her clothes. Giggling, she opened the door and exited the room.

Straight away, he pulled the walled side desk

into the centre of the room, and put on his shirt and trousers. He called out her name as he sat down behind it.

'Miss Keen, can you come in please?'

John was mesmerised by her surprised face as she entered the rearranged hotel room.

'Could you please put the tickets down on the desk?'

She walked towards him and pouted her lips at him. Excited, he felt himself get more aroused.

'Yes, sir, and is there anything else I can do for you today?'

He had already played this out in his head more than once.

'Can you take a look under the desk? I think I've lost a contact lens.'

She removed her high-heeled shoes one at a time, got down on her knees and crawled underneath the desk.

'Have you found it yet, Miss Keen?'

Bulging against his zipper, he bit his lip as he felt his strained cock.

'Yes sir, I think I've found it.'

She undid the zipper on his trousers and freed him with an experienced twist of the wrist. He looked down, open-mouthed, then grabbed her hair and forced himself inside, as she gagged.

'Take it all, you fucking bitch.'

He pushed her head away then pulled it hard against his shaft. He felt her teeth as they grazed his cock. He kicked back and stood up.

'Don't bite me, you dirty whore!'

John dragged her up from the floor by her hair as his penis throbbed. He pushed her face down across the desk.

'Now I'm going to show you, Donna, how to really service a customer.'

She was no match for him. After years in the prison gym he was fit—pure muscle with a six-pack to boot.

'How badly do you want my cock, Donna?'

He raised up her skirt and tugged at her delicate black lacy underwear. Lowering his face to her mound, he licked her and forced his tongue inside her, as she moaned.

'I'm going to give you something massive and extra hard.'

Unable to contain himself any longer, he raised his head and held her underwear aside. He positioned himself behind her and drove his penis into her.

'You enjoying that, Miss Keen? Is that the best you've ever had, or what?'

He loosened his grip on her hair, surprised as she turned around and opened her legs wide. He positioned himself as he drove into her again. She writhed against him, on top of the desk.

'You are making me so fucking hard.'

He pulled out, flipped her back on to her stomach and spread her cheeks apart. He raised his hand, grabbed his cock, and teased her strained clitoris with the tip as he rubbed his finger over her labia.

'You relax and enjoy yourself, baby, and take it all in.'

Her moans became cries as he slammed in to her again. He felt his testicles rub against her wet, erect clitoris. His rhythm accelerated. She stretched out rigid as her muscles gripped his cock like a victory kiss. He came inside her and shouted out, 'You dirty fucking whore! You whore!'

With one last arch of his body, John withdrew his wet cock, wiping it on her thigh and smacking her soundly on the arse. He pulled up his trousers and reaching into his pocket, he removed two fifty-pound notes.

'Well, darling, I don't want to insult you with a tip for all the services you were so keen to provide, but if you want it?'

He dangled the two fifty-pound notes in front of her face. She stood up, her legs wobbling as she straightened her skirt. He laughed out loud.

'Well, I don't usually do this sort of thing, but I'm saving for a new car.'

Disgusted by her reply, he crumpled the notes in his fist, raised his arm and laughed again, as he threw them over her head.

'That's okay. Pick them up on your way out then, darling.' He was delighted to see her face darken in a fury.

'What you playing at? Why would you do that?'

He pulled back his arm and slapped her hard across the face.

'Because I can. Now pick your fucking money up, take your customer service, and get the fuck out of my room, you slut.'

She bent down and retrieved the money. Enraged, he grabbed her in a headlock, frogmarched her towards the door, opened it and tossed her outside into the corridor.

'Now go and fuck a few more hotel guests, you dirty slag.'

The door slammed hard into her face. As he listened to her swearing at him from the corridor outside, he said to himself, 'She'll be lucky if she gets enough money for a fucking smart car, silly tart.'

The last box of DVDs had arrived in the incident room. As the three of them stood there gathered around a desk, DI Roberts shook his head. 'This doesn't make sense. None of it. All these years watching his own household.'

'I mean, if he didn't trust her, why not just divorce her like any other normal person?' said Webb.

Perplexed, Roberts stared at him.

'You'll never know what goes on in some people's minds, Webb, or behind closed doors for that matter.'

Webb shuddered.

'Remind me never to get married, guv.'

DS Jones sat in front of the computer and ignored the life lesson as the static images flickered across the screen.

'Well, well. Come and take a look at this. It looks like Alan Saunders wasn't just filming his wife, sir.'

He walked across the room as Webb caught up with him. The three of them, stuck like moths in hot wax, stared at the computer screen, shocked as Jill and Alan slapped bits together in full, sweaty colour.

'So, Jill Reynolds was having an affair with Alan Saunders. I wonder how long that had been going on.' She checked the file properties and leaned back in her chair, away from the detailed vision.

'Well sir, if this timestamp is anything to go by, this one was over a month ago.'

DI Roberts pondered for a moment as he turned to Webb.

'I want you to go through the whole bloody lot of these DVDs and when you're done, come and find me, okay?'

Webb surveyed the never-ending boxes of DVDs.

'Bloody hell. What all of them, guv?'

Roberts raised his eyebrows and dead-eyed him.

'Yes, bloody all of them, Webb. Jones, you're coming with me.'

Jones invited him to take her seat and reluctantly Webb plonked himself down as she squeezed his shoulder and giggled.

'Good luck with this lot.'

Pissed off, he gazed mournfully at the screen.

'Why do I get all the bloody crap jobs around here?'

Roberts raised his arm as he tipped an imaginary cap in his direction.

'Because you're the best man for the job. Now shut up, stop moaning and get on with it. Police work isn't all secret operations and arrests.'

Outside in the car park, he turned and faced DS Jones as he tossed her the car keys. 'Get a move on, Jones. You're driving today.'

'I take it we're paying Jill Reynolds another visit, sir?'

Roberts opened the door and got into the car, as she joined him.

'No, not yet, Jones. There's someone else I need to pay a visit to first.'

He belted up as she started the engine.

'Sir, so where am I driving to?'

Annoyed with all the questions, he snapped at her. 'Just bloody drive, Jones, will you, I'll direct.'

Penny Wheeler's house was a stone's throw from Kate's house. Hesitant as DS Jones pulled up outside and switched off the engine, he knew he had to speak to Kate's daughter, Sophie.

'I hate to do this to a little girl that has just lost her parents, but she could hold the key to all of this mess, so let's go and see what she has to say, shall we?'

They got out of the car and made their way up the path to the front door. Composed as he rang the doorbell, he could hear the sound of children playing as the door opened from within.

'Hello, can I help you?'

Penny Wheeler had mother written all over her and with three kids under nine, she was a survivalist.

'Hello, Mrs Penny Wheeler? I'm DI Roberts, and this is DS Jones. I take it you're looking after Kate Saunders' daughter, Sophie. Is that correct?'

He noticed the look of concern as it hit her face.

'Yes, that's right. I'm looking after Sophie. How is Kate? I mean Mrs Saunders. Can you let me know what's going on?'

He watched her, as she anxiously hovered in the doorway.

'Could we come in for a minute? The case is still ongoing, but we really need to have a quick chat with Sophie, with you present of course. If you could bring Sophie and meet us down at the station?'

Taken aback as her maternal instinct kicked in, she answered him.

'Well, as long as you don't upset her. She has been through enough. If we end it when I say so, then I suppose it would be okay. The children are upstairs playing. I'll tell Sophie to come down.'

She called out Sophie's name as she led them down the hallway and into the lounge. They both sat down on the sofa as Sophie ran into the room. Penny said, 'Sophie, these people are from the police and they want to ask you some questions at the police station but don't worry, I'll be there with you, okay?'

DI Roberts spoke to her like a kind uncle.

'Hello, Sophie. I'm sorry we have to take you away from your friends and games, but DS Jones, I mean Gwen, would really like your help, would that be alright?'

Nervously, out of his comfort zone, he watched Sophie as she stared at him, then turned her head. She looked at Penny Wheeler as she answered.

'Okay?'

DS Jones took the lead as Sophie sat down next to Penny Wheeler, holding her hand.

'Sophie, you're so brave.'

Roberts noticed her bottom lip trembled before she spoke.

'Please, can you tell me when I am going to see my Mummy again?'

Roberts was unable to give her a straight answer as DS Jones filled the gap.

'I'm sure it won't be too long, Sophie. Do you want to go back and play with the other children and we will see you shortly?'

Roberts acknowledged Penny Wheeler as Sophie ran from the room and they made their way into the hallway and out the front door. 'Well, thank you very much, Mrs Wheeler. We will see you very soon.'

DS Jones unlocked the car doors and they both got in. Roberts watched as Sophie reappeared. The little girl clung to Penny Wheeler's hip on the doorstep as they drove off.

Once back inside the station, Jones had set up the video for Sophie's interview in time for their arrival. As Roberts greeted them and got them seated, he started the video recorder.

'DS Jones, I mean Gwen, is just going to ask you a few questions. There's nothing to worry about, okay? There are no right or wrong answers, okay?'

DS Jones spoke softly to Sophie.

'Hello again, Sophie, I just wanted to ask you about your Mummy's friend, Jill Reynolds. I take it you know her well?

Sophie's eyes were open wide as they waited for her to answer.

'If you mean, Auntie Jill, then yes, I have known her since I was a little baby.'

Jones smiled at the small girl as she continued with the questions.

'That's great, Sophie. Can you remember the last time you spoke to or saw your Auntie Jill?'

'I see her all the time. She always rings Mummy, and they were talking for ages and ages on the phone the other day.'

Intrigued, DS Jones' ears pricked up.

'How do you know that, Sophie? Did Mummy tell you that she called her?'

'No, it's because I was in the living room, and I was calling Mummy to come into the living room because we were going to watch my new *Minions* DVD she had bought me that day.'

'Then what happened? Take your time, Sophie, there's no rush.'

Roberts studied her, relieved DS Jones was asking the questions and Sophie had settled into the rhythm of answering them.

'Well, Mummy was taking forever, so I went and listened at the kitchen door. I know I shouldn't have, am I in trouble?'

DS Jones smiled.

'No Sophie, you're not in any trouble, it's okay. Carry on.'

Sophie paused for a moment then continued.

'Well, I heard Mummy telling Auntie Jill that I had seen her in town that day, but she didn't mention the man. Mummy didn't see the man though, and I didn't know who he was.'

DS Jones, confused by her answer, let it slide.

'Okay, Sophie, now have a good think for me. When was the last time your Auntie Jill came to see your Mummy at home?'

Sophie tutted and rolled her eyes at her.

'I've already told you that. I see her all the time. Auntie Jill came around the other day and brought me some sweets which were horrible because they had peanuts in them, and I don't like peanuts.'

Amused by the child's lack of shyness, Roberts tapped DS Jones on the shoulder as he interrupted.

'Thank you so much, Sophie, you've done really well. Thank you, Mrs Wheeler, for your cooperation. PC Peters outside will show you both out.'

Once they had left the room DS Jones said, 'Well, sir, that was very interesting. What do you make of it all?'

He smiled as he turned his head towards DS Jones.

'Out of the mouth of babes, Jones.'

Amused, he watched her puzzled expression as it etched across her face.

'Well, Jones. Jill Reynolds has obviously been telling us porkies.'

She interrupted him.

'Well maybe she just didn't want us knowing about the affair with Mr Saunders? And what if Kate Saunders had found out about the affair? Doesn't that give her motive to kill him?'

He took stock for a moment.

'Maybe. All good thinking but let's check in on Webb and see if Mr Happy has turned up anything on those DVDs yet.'

The walk to the incident room was spent in silent contemplation of the possibilities, all of which were blown out of the water when they entered the incident room and were greeted by Webb.

'You'd better both come and take a look at this.'

The images had now been transferred on to a giant TV screen in the incident room.

'Sounds like you have made some progress,

Webb. Come on then, let's see it.'

The still shots on the screen were different images of Alan Saunders and Jill Reynolds.

'Well, boss, from what I have seen so far, it looks like they have both been at it for a good while—years in fact. We've got video evidence and even phone conversations.'

Roberts rubbed his hands together. He enjoyed it when a case gained momentum.

'Well, well. The plot thickens again. Good work, Webb.'

DC Webb interrupted him.

'Sorry, guv. But that's not all of it.'

Webb failed to keep the excitement out of his voice.

'Jill Reynolds has also been lying to us about when she last saw Kate Saunders, there is no doubt about that. There is footage showing her coming and going several times over the last few months, and one shows her there only last week.'

'Well, we have just been to see Mrs Saunders' daughter, Sophie. She told us Jill Reynolds was at the house last week and is always coming and going.'

Jones interrupted.

'So, it looks like Mrs Saunders was telling the

truth. Well, about that anyway.'

Webb raised his hand and shook his finger in Roberts' direction.

'But wait, I'm not done yet because there's more.'

Webb had made them wait as he savoured the moment.

'Far from being a secret agent, Alan Saunders also knew about the money. There is pillow talk between him and Reynolds, discussing how they are going to run off together and live the good life.' Shocked and disgusted, Roberts shook his head. 'Tut, tut! To think this is the wife's best friend? For Christ's sake. Who needs bloody enemies?'

DS Jones interrupted him.

'Well, this is how I see it, boss. Jill Reynolds kills the husband to set the wife up for murder so she can take all the money for herself.'

Not impressed, he looked at her.

'If only it were that simple, Jones.'

She pointed out her facts.

'But it all fits, guv. Reynolds became greedy.'

He noticed Webb as he grinned happily next to the computer screen. Webb said, 'Well, I have some more good news. The cameras at the house were running the night Alan Saunders was shot and we have the shooting on DVD.'

The room went silent for a moment as they stared at him. Roberts spoke.

'So was it Jill Reynolds?'

Webb teased them both as Roberts started to lose his patience.

'No! Not her.'

Pushed to his limit, Roberts could feel his blood pressure as it hit his red face.

Annoyed, Roberts slapped the palm of his hand down hard on the desk. 'Well, bloody well spit it out, Webb! Who the hell was it then?'

'Sorry sir, but I think we are going to have to rethink all of this because it wasn't Kate Saunders either. It was definitely a male.'

Hours of theories and speculation rushed out of the incident room.

'Get to the bloody point. A man? What bloody man?'

Roberts held his gaze, frowning at him.

'His silhouette was picked up by the only camera that was running, and that was the one in the lounge. It shows him entering and holding up the gun. Just as Mr Saunders stands up, it cuts out and we don't have any audio either.' Webb continued, 'Maybe Reynolds hired a hitman to do the job for her. She is definitely trying to do a bloody number on us, that's for sure.'

It was apparent Webb had developed a dislike for Jill Reynolds.

Roberts shouted at them both.

'Right, that's enough of all that nonsense! I want you both to get over to Jill Reynolds' house now and bring her bloody in. She's wasted enough of our bloody time. Then take the whole place apart, bit by bit, if you have to.'

Roberts was thankful as they left. He had never seen them move so quickly as they shot out of the incident room. He looked forward to his interview with Jill Reynolds.

CHAPTER 17

Her home was often ignored. Her life dedicated to pleasurable nights out, often aided by cheap vodka. She had managed to change into one of her garish tracksuits before she opened the front door, and was taken aback to see them both standing there with reinforcements in tow.

'Miss Jill Reynolds, we have a warrant to search your property. Please step aside.'

The two uniformed coppers pushed her aside as she tried to compose herself. She watched them run up the stairs into her flat.

'Hey! What the bloody hell do you think you're doing? How dare you do this. You can't just come barging in here like this.'

She continued to protest as DC Webb dangled a piece of paper in front of her face.

'Oh, I think you'll find we can, Miss Reynolds. Now please step aside and let us do our job.'

The loud banging of doors that echoed above her head and down the street brought out the owner from the pizza take-away next door, who was shouting at her in a foreign language. Jill swore at him as she made her way up the stairs, into her flat.

'This is a bloody joke. You can't do this, it's out of order.'

DC Webb reminded her of a Pitbull ready for a fight as he bared his teeth.

'No, Miss Reynolds. What is out of order is all the lies you have been telling us. Now where is the money, or do we have to turn this whole place inside out? It's your choice.'

Scared but defiant, she shouted at him.

'What bloody money? I really don't have a bloody clue what you are talking about.'

He shook his head, cold and deliberate.

'It's too late for more lies, Miss Reynolds. We have all the evidence. All those cosy pillow talks you had with Alan Saunders, you know … your best friend's husband? Have you no shame?'

Her bright orange tracksuit glowed in comparison to her wan complexion.

'I don't have the foggiest idea what you mean.'

She kept up the pretence as he laughed out loud.

'Let's put it this way, Miss Reynolds, apart

from your married boyfriend filming his wife's comings and goings, he liked to watch the homemade triple X-rated stuff also.'

The sound of her own heartbeat pulsated through her chest.

'I don't believe you, you're making all this up.'

Backed up against the wall, she took a deep breath as if braced for impact.

'Oh, you'd better believe me, and you will never guess who the main star was in his X-rated productions? It was you, Miss Reynolds, in full-colour HD quality.'

Her eyes diverted towards DS Jones as she stepped in with a polite tone.

'Well, it's like this. We would like you to come with us down to the station and answer a few more questions. We won't take up any more of your time than we need to, I promise.'

The effect of the courtesy relaxed Jill as she peeled her tangoed torso off the wall and whined, 'This is not on. I'm going to make a full complaint about this to your superiors. You see if I don't.'

The threat fell on deaf ears. Jill felt Webb's hard grip on her shoulder as she faced him.

'Well, let's go Miss Reynolds, and you can

make a full complaint when you get down to the station.'

Jill sat in the interview room next to the duty solicitor. DI Roberts entered the room and sat down opposite her. He noted who was present for the benefit of the tape as she made eye contact with him.

'Well, Miss Reynolds, at last we meet. I'm sure you won't mind me asking you a few more questions.'

Unimpressed, she was sullen and obstinate.

'Actually, it's Ms Reynolds to you, and I don't understand what the hell I'm doing here. I have done nothing wrong.'

She tried hard to keep calm.

'Lying to the police is a grave matter and a criminal offence, so let's see if you can give us the truth this time, shall we?'

She was intimidated by him as he leaned forward across the table and stared hard into her eyes.

'I have told the other two coppers, and I'm telling you, I don't know anything about a black holdall containing money.' She kept eye contact with him, as he reeled back in his chair.

'Black holdall? Who told you the money was

in a black holdall? Because I know it wasn't us.'

Lost for words, the colour drained fast from Jill's face.

'Now, where is it? We know Mrs Saunders gave it to you. Alan Saunders' house was rigged up with so many devices and cameras, it was like watching an episode of *Big Brother*.'

Not convinced, she refused to believe him.

'What do you mean, cameras?'

Her hands shook as she clasped them together.

'Did you have any idea at all what Mr Saunders did for a living?'

She didn't answer him.

'Well, he worked in surveillance. He installed cameras — that sort of thing. However, it seems Alan Saunders liked to take his work home with him and rigged his house up as well. Like my two officers told you earlier, we have everything captured on tape.'

Shocked, she held her head in her hands as she hunched her body over the table.

'What do you mean everything?' Her mind raced as she tried to think fast. He continued.

'Well, I can show you a DVD of yourself taking the holdall from the Saunders' house, amongst other things.'

Jill's curiosity piqued. She stared at him.

'Okay, okay. I did have it, but I don't have it any more, and that's the truth.'

He was uncertain whether to believe her. She didn't flinch as she looked him in the eyes.

'So, if you don't have it, then who does?'

She flexed her shoulders before she blurted it out.

'Alan took it. He said he would look after it and keep it safe.'

Jill was stunned as he banged his fist down so hard on the table it sent vibrations down her spine.

'Ha! What? A woman like you? And you just accepted that, did you? Are you telling me you let him walk away with the whole bloody lot? I don't think so.'

Her true colours shone through as her tone changed.

'He loved me more than her! Yes, Kate asked me to look after the money, and I did for a short while, but obviously Alan knew all about it. He promised me he would keep it somewhere safe, until …'

She stared into his face.

'Until what, Ms Reynolds?'

The floodgates opened as she forced out a few

tears.

'Until he left her and we started our new life together. But that bitch went and killed him, didn't she?'

She covered her eyes with her hand as she pretended to sob.

'Why do you think it was Mrs Saunders that killed her husband?'

She knew she had him hooked as he became more curious. Jill raised her head as she reeled him in.

'It's obvious, isn't it? She had all that money, their marriage was over and in the gutter. All she needed was a ticket out of there. Simple.'

She didn't flinch as she knotted her brows.

'So, you think Mrs Saunders is a smart woman? Well, I suppose you must do. Didn't you both attend the same university? But you dropped out, is that right?'

She conceded. 'So, what? She stayed on and I never, it's not a big deal. I suppose she is smart. Bloody hell, let's face it, she must be to have pulled this off.'

Worried, she watched his eyes as they narrowed.

'So, you think a smart woman, after years and years of abuse, would suddenly murder her husband after all that time, and expect to get away with it?'

Dubious of what to say next, she rolled her eyes at him.

'To put the record straight, Ms Reynolds, we have evidence that leads us to believe that Mrs Saunders didn't pull the trigger and kill her husband that night. In fact, it was somebody else, not a woman but a man.'

Her mouth formed an oval of concentration as the information filtered through. It hit Jill's brain.

'I don't understand what you're telling me. What man?'

Jill's eyes diverted towards the door as DC Webb poked his head around and called Roberts from the interview room.

'I'm sorry, but I'm suspending this interview. Please feel free to confer with the duty solicitor until further notice.'

Flabbergasted, she watched him as he made his way across the room, out of the door and into the corridor.

His tone was sharp as he stood face to face with DC Webb.

'What is it, Webb? It better be worth it, lad.'

Still psyched up in interrogation mode, he

noticed Webb's vague expression.

'I'm so sorry to interrupt you, but I'm afraid the full search at Reynolds' house turned up nothing. No bag, no money. In fact, we have been through her bank accounts, and to put it in a nutshell, she's skint, guv.'

Unfazed, Roberts said, 'I had a feeling you wouldn't find anything, Webb. Reynolds has told me she gave the money to Alan Saunders. Apparently, he was hanging on to it for their big getaway and a new life together.'

He watched Webb's puzzled face as the frown spread across his forehead.

'I'm sorry, Webb, but we're going to have to cut her loose for now. We have nothing on her.'

Disappointed with the outcome, Webb said, 'Bloody hell, boss, surely we can hold her a bit longer on something?'

Roberts sighed.

'I'm afraid not. All we have her for is having an affair with her best mate's old man. Even though she's not a loyal person and a bit of a tart, it's hardly a criminal offence, is it?'

Roberts knew Webb was as gutted as he was, as he interrupted him again.

'But, sir. I'm sure we can nick her for wasting police time?'

Roberts scratched his head hard, like he was infected with fleas.

'You have a point, Webb... I know, she's lied about a few things which we can't prove yet. But I reckon the odds are she knows this bloke. Call it a gut feeling, but I'd lay money on it.'

Frustrated, Webb watched him as he nodded his head in agreement.

Roberts continued, 'Listen, after she's released, I want you and DS Jones to follow her. Don't let her out of your bloody sight. I think she will cock-up somewhere along the line.' Filled with the new hope, Webb perked up. 'Right, you go and let Jones know what's happening, and I'll go and give the good news to Dame Maggie Smith in there.'

Once inside, Jill smiled to herself as she made her way up the stairs leading to her flat. She envisaged her name in lights. An award-winning actress who would give some of the greats a run for their money.

'What the fuck?'

Even at her worst, her housework hadn't got this bad. She waded her way through the carnage, relieved as she spotted a bottle of vodka underneath the sideboard and rescued it.

'Well, at least those bastards kept their priorities straight. Who'd have thought it?'

She opened the vodka and as she took several large gulps, she searched amongst the chaos for the mobile phone John had given her. Annoyed, she spoke to herself again as she pushed a pile of clothes off the sofa and sat down.

'Bloody hell, where the fuck is it?'

Jill searched down the back of the old broken sofa and her fingers touched it. Reaching out her arm, she grabbed it. She pressed the redial button, frustrated as her call went straight to his voicemail.

'Why are you not answering your bloody phone, you fool?'

She was on a redial rampage. Impatient as she punctuated her attempts with swigs of vodka, her temper intensified.

'Where are you, you … you fucker? Why don't you answer the fucking phone?'

After fifteen attempts to contact him, she conceded. Livid, she went to throw the mobile phone against the wall but stopped herself. Instead, she placed it in her pocket.

'Ha, so you think you're a fucking smart arse, John? Well, not this time, mate. I'm keeping this lovely little phone as it probably has your fingerprints all over it, you bastard. I'm going to find you.'

She brooded, raised the vodka bottle to her mouth and took another generous swig from the almost empty bottle. Undeterred, Jill pondered her next move as she continued to rant to herself. 'If you think I'm going to sit here in this shit hole while you're lording it up in a hotel with a tonne of cash, you can think on. Not answering my calls, ignoring me, you piece of shit.'

Fired up, she didn't bother to change her clothes as she stumbled towards the front door.

DC Webb was pumped as he sat outside in the unmarked police car and spoke to DS Jones.

'Stake-out.'

Unimpressed, she raised her eyebrows.

'What are you so excited about, Webb?'

Preoccupied as he opened the glove compartment and removed a sandwich along with an empty milk carton, he said, 'My first big stake-out. Why shouldn't I be excited? I'm ready for anything now.'

He noticed her perplexed expression, as she stared at him.

'You're worse than a child. What's the milk

carton for?'

He laughed.

'What do you think it's for? It's so I don't have to get out and leave the car if I need a slash.'

She reeled back.

'Let me tell you something now. If you whip anything out that is not a standard police issue, you will be walking with a limp and singing soprano for the rest of your life.'

Unsure if she was serious or not, he picked up the sandwich, opened it and took a bite as she sniffed the air.

'What the bloody hell have you got in that sandwich?'

He waved the sandwich in front of her face.

'It's egg mayonnaise, I think.'

Unrepentant and amused, he took another bite of the smelly sandwich as she gagged.

'Rule one. When in confined spaces, no smelly food that causes wind, or smells like it.'

He laughed again as she reached out and opened the window to waft the stench out.

'Well, some of us have been sifting through bloody DVDs all day and have not had time to eat. I had to take what was left in the vending machine.'

Jones interrupted him.

'Shut up, Webb, it looks like she's on the move.'

Focused on Jill as she made her way along the road, he tossed his sandwich onto the back seat as Jones started the car.

'Right, let's get to work, and get after her.' Webb excitedly rubbed both his sticky hands on his trousers as he spoke. 'I wonder where she's off to. She looks a bit unsteady on her feet, don't you think?'

They watched her as she staggered along the road and approached the bus stop.

'Bloody hell, look at her. Do you think she pissed?'

Patiently they both waited for the bus to arrive and watched Jill as she stumbled onto it.

Relieved they were on the move, Webb felt gleeful.

'Follow that bus, Jones.'

Unable to take his eyes off the bus, he peered ahead at each stop along the route, but she never got off until he clocked her on the pavement outside the hotel.

'Look, there she is. She's in a bit of a hurry. Quick, park up.'

Jones parked the car as Webb observed Jill.

She marched into the hotel, as they both exited the vehicle at the same time and followed her.

'Come on, Jones, let's not lose her.' Webb entered the hotel first as Jones caught up with him. He spotted Jill just as she disappeared inside one of the two lifts. The doors closed.

'She seems to know where she's bloody going. Quick, let's see what floor she's going to.'

Pumped, Webb charged over to the lift. He watched the illuminated floor numbers above the elevator light up, just as the second elevator arrived and the doors opened.

'Jones, grab that lift. She's stopped at the fourth floor. Let's go. C'mon c'mon...' he chanted as they both dashed into the lift and Jones hit the button.

The elevator doors opened just in time for them to see the flare of Jill's orange tracksuit as it disappeared around the corner. Jones whispered to him as they saw which room she went into.

'Webb, you go down to reception, see what you can find out about who's in that room, then give the DI an update. I'll stay here.'

Jill entered the hotel room.

John was in a good mood and celebrating. His bags packed and sipping champagne, he was taken aback as he heard the loud bang on the door and the sound of Jill's distinctive voice that bellowed after it.

'What the fuck? Shit, shit.'

Faster than a firecracker strapped to a cat's arse, he eyed the plane ticket on top of the suitcase on the floor, stretched out his leg and kicked them underneath the bed, out of sight.

'Hold your bloody horses. I'm coming.'

He made his way angrily across the room and opened the door. He grabbed her arm hard and yanked her inside as he slammed the door shut.

'Jill, what the fucking hell are you doing here? You're going to get us both nicked. You're a stupid cow. The Old Bill could be watching you.'

She noticed the bottle of champagne and made a beeline for it, picked it up and took a swig. Her eyes noticed the rolled up fifty-pound note sitting next to the line of cocaine.

'Where's your bloody phone? Why are you not answering? Have you shut it off? I've been calling you non-bloody stop.'

Pissed off that she had turned up, he tried to remain calm.

'Stop panicking. The battery must have died. Probably needs recharging or something. Calm down, will you.'

She grabbed the fifty-pound note and raised it to her nostril as she bent forward over the dusty mirror. He watched her as she inhaled the long white trail of coke.

'About bloody calm down. It's easy for you to say.'

He approached with caution as if she were a wild animal. Panicked, he noticed the corner of the plane ticket poking out from underneath the bed as Jill gulped more champagne.

'I don't think you need any more to drink. It looks like you've had enough. What the hell has happened to get you in this state?'

Jill held the champagne bottle at arm's length and paced the room as John tightened his robe around him.

'I'll tell you what's bloody happened. That stupid bastard Alan happened.'

John stood still as he eyed Jill, incoherent as she ranted.

'What the fuck are you talking about? You're talking bollocks.'

She plonked herself down on the bed as she continued.

'Do you know fucking Q from James Bond? The government snoop took his work home with him. He had his whole house rigged up with cameras—eyes in the fucking sky everywhere. That's what I'm talking about.'

He could feel the anger as it rose up from the pit of his stomach and hit his face.

'Tell me you're fucking joking with me.'

He stared at her as she made eye contact with him.

'Do I seriously look like I'm fucking joking? The police have everything on film, disc, tape or whatever. You should see the state of my place after they gave me a spin and took me down the nick.'

Shocked, he reeled back as he listened to her.

'What did you tell them? Did they mention me?'

John, not at all concerned about her ordeal, stared at her as she hesitated for a moment.

'Hmm, always about you, isn't it? Well no one knows about you, you're still fine and dandy. I told them I gave the money to Alan and they believed me, I think.'

He breathed a sigh of relief.

'Well, stop whining. Of course they believed you or they wouldn't have let you go.'

She leaned back on the bed as she started to wind down.

'Nah, they didn't have nothing on me. It's a

good thing I can think on my feet.'

John started to calm down. He changed his tone.

'I told you they would be on to you. It's all part of their game, baby. Anyway, the worst is over now so you can chill out.'

He was taken aback as she laughed out loud.

'That's what you think. They have the shooting on tape. They know it's a man so they know Kate never shot him.'

His face paled and his eyes darted from side to side. He replayed the night Alan was murdered in his head.

'For fuck's sake.'

His anger built as he stood over her and stared at the state of her.

'Listen to me, when you brought this job to me, you told me there were going to be no complications. There's no way I'm going back inside again for anyone, especially not you.'

He backhanded her hard across her face.

'You're a fucking idiot. You shouldn't even be here.'

He looked at her worried face as the red glow spread like wildfire across her cheek.

'John! What the hell did you do that for? I had to come here to warn you. It's not my fault you didn't answer your crappy phone, is it? I even had to get the bloody bus.'

His head was in turmoil. Enraged, he stared at her hard as he tried to think.

'How do you know the Old Bill never followed you here? I told you never to come here. Under no circumstances. But you never listen.'

She raised her hand and rubbed her smarting cheek, as she retorted, 'Oh please. Nobody followed me here. Give me some credit. I did go to university, remember.'

He laughed at her.

'Yeah, for one fucking year, and you spent most of that off your head.'

Deep in thought, he knew she had served her purpose. She had become a liability that he no longer wanted, or needed, in his life.

'Well at least I haven't spent it banged up in the nick like you.'

Jill, unsteady on her feet as she walked across the room, tripped and knocked the rolled up fifty-pound note straight off the night table and into to the bin.

'Don't think you're having any more of that coke, Jill. You're already shitfaced enough as it is.'

Jill surprised him as she bent down and reached into the bin. She stood up and held the sim card from his mobile phone between her fingers as she walked towards him.

'Just when did your phone run out of juice, you liar? Do you want to tell me what the fuck is going on here?'

Standing in front of her, he pushed her hard towards the bed but missed. Instead, she fell hard onto her hands and knees on the floor. 'Why do you have to make everything so fucking difficult? You never let up, do you?'

Furious, he noticed as she turned her head that she had spotted the plane ticket next to the suitcase.

Determined, Jill reached out her arm and pulled them both out from underneath the bed.

'One ticket. One single ticket. You bastard! You were going to go without me and leave me here with nothing, just the Old Bill all over me.'

His patience started to wear thin as he lied, 'Don't be stupid. There was a mix-up with the tickets. Reception is sorting it all out.'

He was alarmed as she reared up off the floor, reached out her arm and picked up the bottle of champagne.

'Oh, I bet there was. Do you think I'm fucking

stupid? I don't believe you would do this to me. All the years I have stood by you. I honestly thought you loved me.'

He snatched the bottle of champagne out of her hand as he raised his other hand and slapped her hard across the face again.

'Are you mad? Fuck you, Jill! You're fucking deluded.'

Jill changed her demeanour. Raising her hand to her face she smiled at him. 'What's wrong with you? I know you like it rough, but you're going too far now.' Her tone softened. 'Come on baby, don't be like this. You know I love you, even if that black dyed hair does make you look a little bit like a hustler.'

His stark, white face glared at her in contrast to the fresh dye job.

'You fucking what?'

He was infuriated as she laughed at him.

'Now you listen to me, John. Don't you forget I chose you for this bloody set-up. I could've pulled it off with Alan and run off with him, but I didn't because I loved you.'

He could feel the blood rise up inside him as it flooded into his cheeks.

'You chose me? Who do you think you are? Look at you! You're no oil painting are you, darling? Can you see what the fuck you are wearing? You look like a bottle of Lucozade in that get-up.'

Jill retorted fast.

'Fuck you, John. Fuck you!'

He laughed out loud.

'Fuck me! You did that enough times, and let me tell you something, you weren't much good at that. I would probably rate it a five out of ten, and that's being generous, you troll.'

Delighted he had rattled her, he watched as her face became enraged.

'Ha, is that right? Don't think for one second I won't take you down with me. You killed Alan, John! Not me.'

He gripped her shoulder hard as he pulled her towards him.

'Like they are going to believe a slut like you. They already know what a liar you are.'

She struggled to free herself as he tightened his grip. 'You think you have all the answers, but you don't. I'm not going to prison for this. If they nick me, I'm taking you down with me, Johnny boy.'

He laughed in her face as she forced his grip from her arm and broke free.

'I'll be out of here on a plane to Bangkok in a

few hours. I can't believe you thought I would take you with me. I was just treading water, baby.'

He felt the hot burn on his cheek as she reached out her arm and clawed his face.

'You fucking spiteful bitch.'

Outraged, he grabbed her by the throat. In a trance-like state he watched her eyes as they bulged from their sockets, adamant he was about to put this whore down for good.

CHAPTER 18

DI Roberts scribbled down Johnny Chambers in his notebook as he ended the call with Webb. Pleased as PC Peters entered the incident room, he said, 'Peters, get Mrs Saunders from the holding cells and stick her in interview room one, will you.'

PC Peters, a boy who hadn't grown into his years yet, stood up straight as he acknowledged him.

'Yes, guv. I'm on it.'

Roberts smirked as the pieces of the puzzle started to fall into place. He made his way out of the incident room towards interview room one and said to himself before he opened the door and entered, 'Johnny Chambers, your luck is about to bloody run out today, my friend.'

Roberts nodded at Kate and Mr Moore as he set down a cup of water on the table in front of her. Kate eyed him as he primed the recorder once again.

'So, Mrs Saunders, did you know your husband was having an affair with Jill Reynolds?'

She reeled back in her chair and her eyes widened.

'No. What? No, I think you've got that wrong. Jill, she knew how Alan treated me, she hated him.' Kate looked at Roberts warily.

'Well, we found years of film footage. He preserved everything.'

Her mouth felt dry and her hand shook as she picked up the cup of water.

Roberts continued, 'That's how we found out about the affair. He filmed them in bed together several times over the years.'

She stopped him in his tracks and banged the cup down hard on to the table.

'So, you're telling me that my husband put the cameras up in my home and he has been carrying on with my best friend for years? Why are you saying these things? That can't be true!' Kate tried to make sense of it all, as the tears trickled down her cheeks. 'Oh, my god! In my own home! In my bed! We've been friends for decades, how could they both do this to me?'

Her thoughts were interrupted as James Moore pushed a handkerchief into her hand.

Kate wiped her tear-soaked face.

'Well, from what we have seen and heard so far, your husband knew all about the money and he was planning on taking it and running off with her.'

She stared at him, confused.

'Well, why didn't they? I mean, I gave her the money, I told you that.'

Her mind raced fast as she waited for him to answer.

'We don't know why. That's what we are trying to find out. We believe there was somebody else involved.'

Kate was intrigued as Roberts flicked through the pages of his old notebook.

'Who?'

She forced herself upright in her chair as a flicker of hope appeared in her eyes.

'This man you met, Jonathan Jacobs. You told us Jill Reynolds was with you the first time you met him.'

He was starting to annoy her as he tapped his notebook with the top of his pen.

'Yes, it was the day I gave Jill the money. We went to her flat first to drop it off then she took me to the restaurant as I have already told you a hundred times.'

Curious, her eyes diverted to James Moore, then back to Roberts as he spoke.

'Yes, we have checked with the restaurant and they did remember you and Miss Reynolds. They also remembered this Jonathan that was with you. Only I'm afraid that's not his real name.'

She found it hard to register the information. Shocked, her jaw fell open.

'I don't understand what you're telling me. What do you mean it's not his real name?'

Kate felt the tremble run through her body as her legs shook, unsure whether she could deal with any more revelations.

'I'm just waiting for some more information to be sent over to me, but we are sure his name is Johnny Chambers. Have you heard that name before?'

Kate kept his gaze as she thought hard.

'No, I've never heard that name before. Why would he lie? John's a lovely man. The complete opposite to Alan — caring and considerate. That's what attracted me to him in the first place.'

Kate was in denial.

'Well if you knew he had a criminal record, would you still be attracted to him then?'

The bile rose to the back of her throat and as

she turned her head the vomit projected out of her mouth on to the floor as her world crashed down in front of her.

They were one fuse away from detonation. Jill, her clothes dishevelled, clenched her fists at her side as John held his hands away from his body like a gunfighter. He spat straight in her face.

'Surely you're not that stupid to think I was going to run off with a tart like you?'

In one swift motion, he gathered her hair in his hand as he frogmarched her, face first, towards the mirror and yanked her head backwards.

'I mean, when was the last time you actually looked into one of these? Or are they all shattered in your house?'

John watched in fascination as she gulped against the pressure on her neck.

'I fucking hate you! Let me go, you bastard!'

He mocked her as he laughed out loud. She spat back at him.

'Of course you do. You keep telling yourself that, bitch. I thought I'd got away from your needy, greedy drunk arse. But no, you have to turn up here.'

He pulled harder as he shook her head from

side to side, like she was a rag doll.

'You visiting me in the nick, telling me this was easy money. I actually listened to you and agreed, but what do I get? Sex with two cougars, and a voyeur with cameras.'

He looped his arm across her chest. As she struggled hard, he held her still.

'You are, what we call in my world, a fucking liability.'

He leaned his weight against her back as he crushed her against the mirror. Jill groaned aloud.

'If you don't … let me go, I'm going to scream this place down.'

He flattened her nose against the glass as he pushed her face into it harder.

'I don't know which one I feel sorry for the most. You or the desperate housewife of north London.'

He eased off the pressure as he pulled her head back from the mirror.

'I don't want to get nicked for slut abuse! Look at you. Take a good hard look at yourself. You look like something that has just washed up on Brighton beach and you want to try and fuck me over? Standing here, shouting the fucking odds at me.'

Despite himself, he felt the first pulse of an erection.

'You're a whore that tricks men.'

He hated himself for it. He rubbed his hard-on against her buttock and could feel the rush of adrenalin as she spoke.

'You're one sick bastard! You're getting off on this, aren't you?'

He hiked down her trousers and pants as he released his erection. He steered into her hard from behind as she moaned.

'Oh … you … bastard…'

He could feel her as she ground her hips back into his wild thrusts.

'You love it, don't you? Whore.'

The loud squeal signalled she was about to orgasm. Repulsed, John punched her hard in the back of the head as he pulled out of her. Jill slithered to the floor.

'You are nothing… If nothing had a piece of shit, then that would be you.'

His fist was still clenched as he stood over her and brandished the full extent of his erection.

'I have my own plans that don't include you. Do you hear that? You are collateral damage.' He laughed at the crumpled heap on the floor by his feet. 'Tart.'

Unable to put his erection back in to his trousers, he dragged her up from the floor and threw her face down on top of the bed.

'Don't hurt me no more, please. You can have all the money, I don't care about it anymore. Take it, just leave me alone.'

Holding her down with one hand, he leaned across her and picked up the steak knife from the side table, then held it against her throat as she struggled.

'This is all you're good for, you whore.'

He thrust his erection into her, hard, from behind. Overcome with power, John peaked quicker than he ever had before as he dominated her, then pulled up his trousers.

'Sit up, you bitch.'

He watched her as she turned around. Impatient, he stretched out his hand and pulled her up onto her feet and held the tip of the knife against her breastbone.

'One thrust and I'll be straight through your heart. You probably won't even bleed much.'

He felt untouchable as he watched the fear in her eyes.

'Please, John, don't hurt me. I'm sorry, please take the money, I won't say a word to anybody, I promise you.'

He mocked her.

'I won't say a word to anybody...'

John was in control. He watched as the beads of sweat formed on her forehead.

'No one threatens to take me down, especially an old scrubber like you. Who do you think you are?'

He pushed against the knife as the tip of it pierced the skin. Jill screamed.

'Please, Please! John, stop this. I won't mention you to anybody, honestly.'

He laughed in her face again.

'My mother, God rest her pickled soul, always said "never trust anyone who says honestly", and she was right. Like I'm going to listen to one word that comes out of your disgusting mouth.'

Jill gasped as he exerted more pressure on the knife. John smiled as the sea of crimson trickled down her tracksuit top.

Outside the hotel room, DS Jones and DC Webb had already sealed off the whole of the fourth floor. Webb, edgy, was ready for action as he turned to her.

'You're playing this very close, Jones. Shouldn't we get in there now?'

She turned her head towards him as she whispered.

'Not until the back-up arrive, Webb. Once they're here, I'll have them hang back until I give the order.'

He had never felt excited but frustrated at the same time.

'But what if he bloody kills her? Then what?'

He watched her as she rolled her eyes at him.

'Stop being so dramatic, Webb. I'm not going to let that happen.'

On full alert, he turned around and noticed the uniformed police officers as they made their way along the corridor towards them.

'Looks like the wait's over. The cavalry is here, sergeant.'

Kate had drained her second cup of water as PC Peters entered the interview room. She eyed him as he spoke to DI Roberts.

'Sorry to disturb you, guv, but you asked me to come straight in when I received the file you wanted.'

She watched as he handed it to DI Roberts, who opened it and scanned the contents.

'Cheers, Peters. You can go now.'

Roberts waited for PC Peters to leave the room, then pressed the button on the recording device.

'For the benefit of the tape, I am showing Mrs Saunders a photograph of Johnny Chambers. Mrs Saunders, is this the man you know as Jonathan Jacobs?'

Gobsmacked, she looked at the larger than life picture as he held it up in front of her face.

'I can't believe it. Yes, this is John … my John.'

She was transfixed, unable to take her eyes off the photograph.

'Mrs Saunders, are you one-hundred percent sure this is definitely him?'

She touched the photograph with her hand and traced the outline of his face with her finger.

'Yes, I'm totally sure, even though he looks a lot younger and his hair is brown, not black.' She watched as he placed the picture down on the table in front of her.

'Well, this confirms who we thought it was. He is very well-known to us and is extremely dangerous.'

Kate was dumbfounded and glared at him.

'But I never felt like I was in any danger around him, he was so kind and gentle.'

In a trance-like state, she looked up at him as he changed his tone.

'He got ten years for armed robbery and has not long been released from Bellmarsh Prison.

You don't get time like that for being gentle. Wake up, Mrs Saunders.'

Her head was in turmoil as she looked down at the photograph once more.

'He told me he was a stockbroker and worked in the City.' She looked at James Moore as she felt his hand gripping her shoulder.

'It's okay, Kate, take a breath.'

She placed her hand on top of his and patted it as Roberts continued.

'This is definitely not the sort of chap you want to bring home to meet your mother. He also has previous for extortion, kidnapping, drug dealing, prostitution – in fact, the list goes on.'

Angry, she pushed the photograph back across the table towards him.

'I feel such a fool. I actually believed everything he told me.'

She noticed his expression as it softened and wondered if he had become more assured of her.

'He is a very devious and clever man. He has been known to us for years but as Chambers, not Jacobs.'

She replayed the whole of the late relationship in her head over and over.

'But what did he want with me? I never told

him about any money. None of this makes sense.'

She sighed as Roberts tone was final.

'Well, the only way he could've found out is if someone else had told him.'

Her eyes widened as if someone had just switched on a light.

'So, do you think that John and Jill knew each other?'

Kate watched his eyes as they diverted from her gaze and looked at James Moore as she waited for him to answer her.

John's hand had started to cramp. He eased up on the pressure of the knife, watching the relief as it hit her eyes.

'Please, John. Please don't do this to me.'

Her voice was faint. He listened as she added a tone of desperation.

'What's the matter, Jill? You don't sound too mouthy anymore,' he said, laughing at her.

Jill's despair seemed to give her strength as he continued to laugh.

'John, you have the money now. You wouldn't have had it if I hadn't told you about Kate. Just take it all and go please. Don't hurt me any more, please, I'm begging you.'

The loud bang on the door shocked him as he heard the words he had dreaded. They echoed through the door as he reeled back.

'This is the police, open up.'

With a violent swing of her leg, Jill kneed him hard in his groin and as he doubled over, she screamed out at the top of her voice.

'Help me! Help me! He's trying to kill me.'

He composed himself fast as Jill raced to the door and opened it. John was wrestled to the ground, and handcuffed by DC Webb.

'You're a sick bastard. You're not going anywhere. Now get up!'

John felt Webb's hands on his shoulders as he was yanked up on to his feet, laughing as the paramedics inspected Jill's injuries while she gasped for breath.

'Look what you've done, you stupid fucking whore! Wait till I get my hands on you.'

Webb interrupted him as he marched him out the door.

'Going to be a long time before you get your hands on anyone pal, but I'm sure that where you're going they will be itching to get their hands on you, as you look so pretty.'

John was fuming as Webb pushed him towards the uniformed copper, who read him his rights.

Kate watched a uniformed police officer enter the room. Focused and confused, she watched as he approached Roberts, whispered in his ear, then turned around and left the room.

'Well, Mrs Saunders, you will be pleased to know we have now got Johnny Chambers in custody.'

She let out a big sigh of relief as she clutched at her chest.

'Oh, thank God for that. Does that mean I can go home soon?'

Kate's mind raced at the thought of seeing her daughter again. Overwhelmed and emotional, she couldn't hold back as she burst into tears.

'I'm afraid not, Mrs Saunders. We have to interview him first.'

Confused, her heart sank as she wiped away the tears.

'But I have to be with my daughter. She's lost her father and for all she knows, her mother is locked up in prison and never coming home again.'

She watched his face as it softened; he sympathised.

'I know this is hard but this is still an ongoing

investigation. However, the good news is that Jill Reynolds led us straight to him.'

She felt the trembles in her legs as her mood changed again.

'Really? So, they did know each other? I can't believe they have both done this to all of us. I thought it was an accident that I met John. How could she?'

Angry now, Kate could feel her face getting hot.

'I'm afraid, Mrs Saunders, you will need to go back to the cells while we interview them, but I will make sure someone gets you something to eat and drink, okay?'

She didn't respond but listened as Roberts walked across the room, opened the door and spoke to the uniformed officer stood outside.

'Take Mrs Saunders back to her cell and get her something to eat and drink. She's had a bit of a shock.'

She looked up at him as he spoke to her.

'Mrs Saunders, if you could come this way please?'

She stood up and followed the officer back to the cell. Kate felt the cold as she entered and sat down on the blue plastic mattress, unaware of her surroundings. Thoughts of Sophie flooded through her mind.

John sat next to the duty solicitor in the interview room, smirking at DC Webb. DS Jones sat opposite him as Webb started the recording device and spoke.

'You're a hard man to track down.'

Tipping back in his chair, John stretched his arms out, unconcerned.

'Is that right, officer?'

Her harsh Welsh tone took everyone by surprise as she interrupted.

'You've been a very busy boy, whoring around with the ladies in the area.'

Glad his reputation preceded him, he laughed out loud.

'Well not that busy, darling, as I never bumped into you. What a shame, we could've had so much fun.'

Without a knock, the interview door swung open as DI Roberts entered. Jones stated his presence for the benefit of the tape.

'Right, great work, you two. Go and get yourselves a cup of tea, I'll take it from here.'

John mimicked a sad face as he watched them leave the room and waved them goodbye.

'Now then, so many different names to

choose from. What should I call you?'

John was amused by the old-time copper as he tapped the page of his notebook with the tip of his pen.

'Well, you can call me Jonathan Jacobs.'

Roberts laughed out loud.

'Are you seriously sticking with that? We arrested you at your hotel, where you'd registered under your real name. Not the sharpest saw in the shed are you, Mr Chambers?'

Unfazed, John remained calm.

'I haven't got a clue what you're talking about.'

John watched Roberts as he shook his head.

'Oh, come on. I thought you were clever. Did you think we wouldn't find out who you were? Please give us some credit.'

Irritated by Roberts, John started to become indignant.

'I haven't done anything. This is harassment.'

John was surprised when Roberts gave out a loud chuckle.

'We've got you bang to rights. So many charges. It's going to take me all night to write them up. Just so you know, this was your last day as a free man, Mr Chambers.'

The smell of fear overtook John's senses as he scanned the small room.

'Now, Mr Chambers. I'm going to leave you here while I go and get a steak dinner, so you can have a good think about what you are going to tell me when I return. It had better be good.'

Freaked, John swung forward towards him in his chair.

'You can't just go and leave me here while you go on a jolly.'

Roberts got up, made his way towards the door and opened it.

'No rush, Mr Chambers. I've got all night and let's face it, you're not going anywhere for a long time. Don't worry, I won't be too long.'

John's mouth fell open, outraged, as the door banged shut behind Roberts.

CHAPTER 19

DI Roberts whistled into the police canteen and caught up with Webb and Jones, happy as he crept up behind Webb, who boasted about his latest arrest to anyone that would listen.

'Well done, Webb. Good work, lad.' He watched him almost jump out of his skin.

'Thanks, guv. Jill Reynolds took us straight to the hotel Chambers was holed up in. We recovered most of the money and a one-way plane ticket for Bangkok, leaving tonight.'

Roberts was intrigued as he listened to him. 'Rewind, Webb. What plane ticket?'

'Well, guv, it looked like Chambers was planning on doing a runner without Reynolds and that's what really pissed her off.'

Roberts raised his eyebrows as he mulled it over in his head.

'I bet it did. I'm on my way back to interview Chambers. I want both of you to go and talk to Reynolds.'

John was deep in thought as Roberts re-entered the interview room and restarted the recorder again.

'So, Mr Chambers. Let's start again at the very beginning, shall we?'

John's arms were locked against the table, taut with stress.

'I can't go back inside. Not again. This was all her idea. She came to see me in the nick.' John shifted in his chair, as he dead-eyed him.

'Go on. You've got my attention, Mr Chambers.'

John's tone sounded softer as he spoke.

'Jill, she told me about this friend of hers, Kate Saunders, and that her aunt had left her a lot of money.'

DI Roberts interjected.

'Did she tell you how much money?'

He thought about the question before he answered him.

'No, I don't think she knew how much it was at that point.'

Suspicious, Roberts stared at him as he started to write down notes in his little black book.

'Did you know about Miss Reynolds and Mr Saunders?'

He sighed.

'I'm a survivor. I've done what I've needed to get by, so has she. Yes, I knew about him, but I was doing a ten year stretch. I could hardly ask her to stay faithful for that length of time, could I?'

He wasn't bothered by the look of disgust that spread across Roberts' face.

'No, I don't suppose you could, Mr Chambers. So, what happened next?'

John relaxed and slouched back in his chair.

'Well, the next time she came to see me, she told me how much money the aunt had left Kate Saunders, but it had been put in a trust fund. However, there was also money in cash and Kate had asked Jill to look after it!' Entertained by what he had just told Roberts, he laughed out loud. 'I mean, her! Of all people she could've asked, she asked Jill! I wouldn't trust her to look after a cat.'

He remained calm as Roberts continued to encourage him.

'I bet she thought Christmas had come early. All that money just falling into her lap like that, and you stuck behind bars with your bum chums. You must have been seething.'

John cut his eyes at him.

'Shows you how much you know. I got parole and I told Jill I was getting out.'

John, distracted, started to pick the side of the table with his fingernails.

'So, I take it Ms Reynolds was pleased about your parole then?'

His eyes narrowed as he shook his head.

'No. She went fucking crazy. Said I should've told her sooner.'

John watched the confused expression on Roberts' face.

'I take it she doesn't like surprises then, Mr Chambers?'

John shrugged his shoulders.

'That's when she told me that Alan knew about the money and that he wanted them to run off together, to start a new life.' His confidence built as he continued. 'Jill didn't want him once she knew I was getting parole. She was only using him.' He was on a roll as he portrayed Jill as the shot caller. 'She had her eye on the prize. Have you seen the way she lives her life? She would put up with anything, or anyone, if it meant cash at the end of it.'

DI Roberts interrupted, 'So, the plan changed now that Mr Saunders became a complication.'

John leant forward in his chair, lifted his arms

and rested his elbows on the table.

'She said we had to get both of them out the way.'

Roberts sighed as he lifted his hand to his face and rubbed his forehead hard.

John continued, 'She told me Kate had made her the kid's legal guardian and if Alan was dead, we could frame Kate Saunders for it, get all the cash, plus the 2.8 million, and stick the kid in a boarding school.'

He paused as Roberts interrupted him again.

'That's quite a plan, Mr Chambers. I take it you were more than happy to go along with all this?'

Unsure of him, John thought hard about his next move.

'Jill said he knocked her about a lot and gave her a lot of verbal abuse and it would look like she had just lost the plot and killed the wanker.' John kept his eyes on Roberts as he scribbled away in his notebook.

'Let's back up a bit here, Mr Chambers, to your part in all this.' John listened as Roberts tried to put two and two together. 'So, Jill Reynolds asked you to seduce Mrs Saunders and string her along, is that correct?'

John nodded at Roberts and continued, 'Jill

said Kate was desperate. Her marriage and sex life had died years ago, plus she thought it would look better if people thought she was having an affair. Give her a motive for wanting him dead.'

Confident he had hooked him, he watched as Roberts looked up from his notebook.

'Well, how's that working out for you now, Mr Chambers?'

Shocked by Roberts' remark, he didn't answer him.

'Right, moving along now, Mr Chambers. How did you get into the Saunders' house?'

John smirked as he remembered the night in question.

'Well, Jill gave me her set of keys. Told me to go around the back and let myself in. Only I never needed them as the door was unlocked.'

Unable to finish his sentence, he watched as Roberts banged his pen down onto the table.

'So, you're telling me that all this was down to Jill Reynolds and you were just following her instructions? Let yourself into the house then shoot Mr Saunders?'

John stretched out his body, leant across the table as far as possible, and looked Roberts straight in the eye.

'No, I didn't shoot him. No, I couldn't go through with it.'

Roberts was irritated as he broke from his glare.

'You're going to have to do better than that, Mr Chambers. All that planning and you changed your mind at the last minute.'

John didn't flinch.

'It just all became too real, you know what I mean? I just couldn't do it.'

DI Roberts glanced up at the clock and slammed his notebook shut.

'Mr Chambers, did you shoot Alan Saunders?'

Unfazed, he answered him. 'No, I swear. I never shot anyone.'

Down the dingy corridor, in another interview room, Jill eyed her nervous solicitor, unimpressed. DC Webb started the tape recorder and noted who was present.

'Miss Reynolds, could you please tell us what happened on the evening in question, in your own time.'

She was precise and to the point as she spoke.

'I had to do what he said otherwise he would've killed me.'

'Are you saying this was all Mr Chambers'

idea, and if you didn't comply he was going to kill you? Is that correct?'

Once again, she didn't hesitate as she answered.

'That's exactly what I'm saying.'

She turned her head as she heard DS Jones speak in her Welsh accent.

'When did all this start, Miss Reynolds?'

She slumped back in her chair.

'When he was in prison. He sent me a visiting order so I went to see him. I told him all about Alan and that I was going to have a fresh start, and about the money.'

She stared at DS Jones as she carried on with the questions.

'Well, Miss Reynolds, why would you tell your old lover about the money if you wanted a fresh start?'

She gave out a half laugh.

'I suppose I wanted to make him jealous. Let him know how well I was doing without him. How was I to know he was up for parole? I thought we would be long gone by the time he got released from prison.'

DS Jones pointed out the obvious.

'But he got parole, didn't he, Miss Reynolds?'

Jill shifted in her chair with discomfort.

'Yes, after he let me run my mouth off. That's when he told me and that's when the threats started. He said he wanted a share of the cash and if I didn't cut him in, he would kill me.'

DC Webb interrupted.

'So, what was the plan? What did he want you to do?'

Jill made eye contact with him. Admiring his physique, she answered him.

'He told me to keep the affair going with Alan and make nice with Kate, then asked me to get him a set of keys cut to their house.'

DC Webb interrupted, raising his voice.

'Really? So, you just went along with all this did you, Miss Reynolds?'

'Of course I bloody did. You saw and heard what happened in that hotel room. John can go off like a rocket. So yes, I went along with it.'

She looked at them both as they continued to play good cop, bad cop. Jones retook the reins.

'What happened after that, Miss Reynolds?'

Jill sighed.

'John asked me to take Kate to this restaurant and I was to pretend I never knew him.'

She eyed Jones as she scrolled through the tablet that was on the table in front of her.

'Was that the day Kate Saunders handed over

the money to you?'

Jill paused for a moment.

'Yes, I think it was. We took it to my flat first, then went to the restaurant. It was a few days later when I noticed it was gone. I knew John had taken it, he had a key to my flat.'

Webb, to the point, worried her.

'Did you tell Mrs Saunders that the money had disappeared?'

She gave out an awkward laugh.

'Are you kidding me? Of course I didn't tell her. I didn't know what John was planning, I just did what John told me to do. Then I heard from Kate, who told me she was going to leave Alan, for John.'

Jill's eyes remained focused on Webb as he asked, 'I bet that upset you, didn't it?'

She rolled her eyes at him.

'For a split second, but now I know it was all part of his master plan. He wasn't happy with just the cash, he wanted to get his hands on the lot. Money is his god.'

She raised her eyebrows as Webb let out a big sigh. DS Jones intervened.

'When was the next time you heard from Mr Chambers?'

She raised her hand to her forehead as if she

were in deep thought.

'I didn't hear from him until after Alan had been shot. In fact, I only knew about it after you lot came knocking on my door.'

Webb was incredulous.

'So, Mr Chambers never told you he was going to kill Mr Saunders?'

Jill looked horrified, as she shook her head in disbelief. 'The last thing I thought he'd do is kill him. I had no part whatsoever in those plans.' She kept eye contact with him as he persevered.

'Then can you tell us both why you were in his hotel room, Miss Reynolds?'

She thought fast as her mind raced.

'He rang me after you lot pulled me in and told me to come to his hotel room if I knew what was good for me. Once I got there, he threatened me again, slapped me around and struck me with a knife.' She raised her arm to her throat, as she squeezed out the tears. 'Anyway, he told me if I ever mentioned his name to anyone he would kill me and blame the whole thing on me.'

She listened as DS Jones reasoned.

'What about the single ticket we found?'

Jill surged forward in her chair, placing both hands on the table in front of her.

'That bastard! That's when I got really

frightened. He was already setting me up to take the fall for all of it.'

She knew Webb wasn't convinced, as he interrupted once again.

'So, you're stating that Mr Chambers planned the whole thing from start to finish while banged up inside?'

She looked at DS Jones as she pleaded with her.

'Yes. Me and Alan were planning on taking the cash and running away together to start a new life, but that's all I'm guilty of, I swear. It's the truth.'

Jill stared hard at DS Jones, not convinced she believed her any more than Webb did.

'Why all the lies, Miss Reynolds? Why didn't you just tell us all this before, when we had you in here for questioning?'

Jill glanced at her duty solicitor for reassurance, but got none.

'Because I didn't want anybody to know about me and Alan. Especially Kate—she was my best friend. I was also in fear of my life from John.'

Jill was interrupted as Webb jumped in and got straight to the point.

'Miss Reynolds, did you plan, or have any

part in, the murder of Mr Alan Saunders?'

She lowered her voice as she answered him.

'No. I didn't have nothing to do with Alan's murder, and that's the truth.'

Jill was relieved as he stated the end of the interview for the benefit of the tape. She watched as they both stood up and left the room.

The next day, DS Jones caught up with DC Webb in the local café. Deep in thought, Webb stirred his hot black coffee and listened to Jones as she spoke to him.

'What a bloody mess this Saunders case is,' she said. He frowned as he lifted the spoon out of the hot mug set on the table. 'I mean, all their lies, deception and murder for money. Makes me wonder what goes on in some people's minds.'

His eyes widened and turned towards the waitress as she deposited the old-fashioned fry-up down on the table in front of him.

'I can't think about all this now. Do me a favour, let me get this down me first, I'm bloody starving.'

He reached for the pepper pot and as he seasoned his food, she tutted.

'It's the wife I tend to feel a bit sorry for. Her

husband and her best friend. Then just when she thinks she's found someone, she finds out it's been one big set-up and her husband ends up dead.'

DC Webb nodded in agreement as he took another mouthful of food, distracted by the sight of DI Roberts as he made his way towards them.

'I'd thought I'd find you two in here, stuffing your faces.'

He looked at DS Jones as she raised her cup.

'Just needed some decent caffeine, guv.'

Webb didn't look at him as he bolted down his food.

'What? You telling me you can't get that back at the nick, sergeant? Come on, my treat. Leave that, we've got work to do.'

They both jumped up in sync. As Roberts grabbed a sausage off his plate and made his way out of the café they both followed him.

Back inside the incident room, gathered around the large table, they held their vending machine coffees as Roberts spoke.

'So, to put it in a nutshell, Chambers is blaming Reynolds. Said she planned the whole thing. And she is blaming him. What a surprise.' Roberts winced as he raised his polystyrene cup and took a sip of the grey liquid.

'Do we have anything solid to go on?' said Webb. 'Don't we have Chambers for shooting Alan Saunders, guv?'

Unimpressed, Roberts said, 'No, we bloody don't. We have no prints, no DNA, and if you can remember that far back, Webb, we couldn't see who shot Alan Saunders on the video footage.'

He listened to the young hothead as he clutched at straws.

'What about the gloves and jacket we found in his car, sir?'

Roberts knew he was keen, but at the same time, he tested his patience. 'Well, we're going to need to keep our fingers crossed and hope forensics turn up something.'

The incident room door swung open, and in walked PC Peters. Roberts noticed he held a sheet of paper in his hand.

'Sir, the forensic report is back on the items we found in Mr Chambers' car.'

He grinned at Peters.

'Great, that was bloody good timing. Well done, Peters.'

Impressed as the uniformed rookie handed him the papers, he scanned them and dismissed him.

'Well, it looks like we have a bloody result.'

He looked up just as PC Peters was about to leave the room.

'Hang on, Peters. Go and fetch Chambers and his solicitor and stick them in interview room one, then hang around, will you?'

Ecstatic, he could see Jones and Webb were both on edge as he eyed them.

'What is it, sir?' said Jones. 'I take it from the look on your face it's good news?'

Unable to resist, DC Webb joined in.

'C'mon boss, you can't just leave us hanging like this.'

DI Roberts scanned the paper again as he opened the door and left the room. Webb's voice trailed behind him but he didn't reply.

'Sir! Where are you going? Sir? I can't believe he just did that? Oh, c'mon.'

Roberts arrived just as the uniformed copper had stationed himself outside the door of the interview room. Once inside, he started the tape recorder.

'To give you a fighting chance, Mr Chambers, I shall ask you this once. Are you sure there is nothing else you would like to tell me?'

Puzzled, John braced himself as his eyes searched the room for an answer.

'I have been more than honest with you. On my mother's grave, I have told you everything.'

Worried, John watched as Roberts waved a piece of paper in the air.

'Except for one thing, Mr Chambers. The night Mr Saunders was shot, you were in the house. We have that in black and white.' Roberts was unyielding.

'I told you I was there but I couldn't go through with it.' Scared and unsure of the evidence they had, he listened carefully.

'We've had the forensic report back on the jacket and gloves that were found inside your car, and they are positive for gunshot residue.' John's face dropped and his body shook. He felt like someone had cut his strings. 'We also found carpet fibres in the treads of your shoes from the Saunders' house.'

Desperate, John turned his head towards his solicitor and as he nodded at him, he spoke.

'Listen, I want to make a deal.'

Roberts, entertained by John's last-ditch attempt to save his arse, laughed out loud.

'I'm afraid that ship has already sailed. No chance of that now, Mr Chambers.'

John pleaded with him.

'You're not listening to me. She made me do

it. I'm telling you. She wasn't happy just having the cash, she wanted the lot.'

Roberts didn't listen. As he called out to the police officer standing outside the door, John continued to rant.

'Yes, Mr Chambers, save it for the courts. I've heard it all before. Now shut up, will you. Peters, escort our guest to his luxurious new room and bring Miss Reynolds back with you, there's a good lad.'

Dragged from his chair, John's voice escalated as it got closer to the door.

'Jill did this! Don't you see? I'm not guilty. We can make a deal! Watch out for her, you have no idea what she's like.'

His voice fell on deaf ears as Roberts looked across at the duty solicitor and spoke to him.

'You can leave now, sir, and, if you would be so kind, could you inform the other solicitor in the waiting room to come through. Thank you.'

He didn't have to wait long for them as they arrived together.

Jill was sullen as she folded herself into the chair opposite him. She examined the table as Roberts spoke.

'Miss Reynolds, we will be charging Mr Chambers with the murder of Alan Saunders.'

Her heart pulsated in her chest as she felt a glimmer of hope.

'Oh, that's good. Does that mean you are going to let me go home now?'

She felt her lack of maintenance showed as he looked her up and down.

'Oh, Miss Reynolds, you won't be going home for a very long time.'

Astounded, she sat back in her chair.

'Are you taking the piss? Why are you saying that? I don't understand. I didn't kill anyone.'

She noticed he was impassive.

'Miss Reynolds, we have a whole list of charges against you. Conspiracy to commit murder, fraud, deception... Shall I continue?'

She sat in silence as PC Peters knocked and entered the room.

'Your timing is bang on again, Peters. Take Miss Reynolds back to her cell.'

Frightened as he walked towards her, she gripped the edge of the table.

'I'm not going to be locked up for years in prison because of him. I haven't done anything.'

She felt the hand as it gripped her shoulder. He pulled her straight out of her seat and steered her towards the door as she struggled.

'You can't do this to me. I've told you! I've

done nothing wrong.'

Scared as she reached the door, she came face to face with Roberts, as he spoke.

'Oh, and I forgot to add the charge of wasting police time to the very long list.'

Jill was traumatised. She couldn't speak as she was led away to a cell. The thought of a concrete bed and a scratchy blanket for the foreseeable future filled her with dread.

Lunchtime had come around fast. Webb had ordered a ploughman's and two halves of lager, and then made his way across the room of their local boozer and joined Jones at a corner table.

'Here you go, sergeant. Get that down you. Better than a Welsh beer any day.' He handed her the drink as he sat down opposite her.

'It's not like the guvnor to ask us to meet him in here.'

Webb let out a half laugh as he built himself a sandwich.

'Well, enjoy it while you can. He'll be here any minute and I want to bloody eat something today.'

Webb was gobsmacked as he looked up. DI Roberts was standing in front of them both.

'Aw, guv, you've got to be kidding me. I've

only just ordered this.'

Amused, Roberts noticed the disheartened look on the lad's face as he grinned at him.

'Rest easy, Webb, you'll get to eat your lunch. Come on then, let me buy you both a drink. What are you having, same again?'

He watched Jones salute him as he walked off towards the bar.

'Cheers, guv.'

Suspicious, Webb wasted no time and took a large bite of the sandwich.

'Blimey, Webb. I think that's the first time he's ever bought me a bloody drink.'

He didn't answer her as he caught sight of him on his way back from the bar with the drinks. He chewed his food faster.

'Here we go then, you two. Enjoy.'

Roberts took an empty seat next to Webb and placed the drinks on to the table.

'Well, I say we have had a bloody great morning. A good result all round.' Happy, he picked up his glass and gulped back half of it.

'I'm just glad it's all bloody over, guv.'

Before Roberts answered, he placed his glass back down on to the table.

'Well, so am I. You've done a good job, well done.' Transfixed on the hungry copper next to him as he stuffed the oversized sandwich in to his mouth, Roberts continued. 'Amazing how Reynolds was still trying to wriggle out of it at the end. She and Chambers make for a pretty evil pair.'

He turned his attention to Jones as she nodded her head at him in agreement.

'Well, I was only saying to Webb this morning, it's Mrs Saunders you have to feel sorry for in all of this.'

He sighed.

'You're right, Jones. They both played her very well. Very well indeed.'

They were both taken aback as Webb spat out his words, along with his food.

'Evil pair of bastards. I hope the court throws the bloody book at them both.'

Jones interrupted.

'At least Mrs Saunders gets to go home to her daughter.'

Roberts concurred.

'Yes, just waiting on the paperwork and then we can cut her loose.'

Jones intervened.

'She'll be able to attend the funeral with her daughter now.'

DI Roberts frowned at her as he gripped his

glass. He drained the rest of the contents in one go before he answered.

'I'm not sure that's going to be much consolation after what she's been through. Never mind the fact that Alan Saunders doesn't warrant much mourning.'

Roberts was not the least bit surprised as Webb interrupted the conversation again.

'Mind you, she has all that cash to help her get over it. She can start again somewhere else, that's what I would probably do.'

Shocked by Webb's outburst, Roberts tutted.

'It was all that money that got her into this mess in the bloody first place, Webb.'

The ringtone of his mobile phone paused the conversation, as he answered it.

'Roberts here. Yes, that's right. Okay thanks for letting me know.'

He looked across at Webb's half-eaten food and smiled as he replaced his mobile phone inside his jacket pocket.

'All the paperwork has been completed. We can now go and release Mrs Saunders.'

DS Jones interrupted.

'Would you like me to go and sort it out sir, I don't mind?'

He thought for a moment before he answered

her.

'No, no, there's still reports to be typed up. Best get back to the station. Everyone on their feet. I'll deal with Mrs Saunders and both of you get started on those reports.'

Webb intervened as he held his sandwich inches away from his mouth.

'What, right now, sir?'

Straight-faced, Roberts raised his eyebrows and stared at him.

'Yes, right now, lad. That'll have to wait until later.'

Roberts was amused as Webb's ploughman's pyramid collapsed back on to his plate. He made his way towards the door and waited for them both to catch up with him.

Webb noticed Jones was unsympathetic as she let out a half laugh, teasing him.

'Look on the bright side, think of all the weight you've lost on this case.'

Pissed off, he answered, 'Yeah, who needs bloody Fat Fighters when Roberts is about?'

Standing at the door impatiently, Roberts shouted out to both of them.

'I can hear you, Webb. I'm not bloody deaf! Now get a move on, the pair of you.'

Tickled to see Webb jump out of his skin,

Roberts watched them as they chased after him.

Kate noticed Roberts seemed relaxed as he handed back her property. She thought he seemed genuinely happy to see her released.

'Well, Mrs Saunders, you're now free to go home.'

She showed no emotion.

'I just want to see my daughter.'

She lowered her head as she inspected her belongings, still in the clear evidence bags.

'I suppose that's understandable, given everything you've been through.'

She removed her handbag as she looked up at him.

'I still can't believe this has all happened. I keep thinking I'm going to wake up in a minute. Those two put me through a nightmare.'

He sighed.

'Well you have survived a terrible ordeal, but hopefully you will be able to rest easy knowing that those two will be behind bars for a very long time.'

Grateful for hearing that, she stared at him for a moment.

'I suppose so, Inspector, but it doesn't get away from the fact that my husband is still dead, and my daughter has been left without a father.'

She placed her handbag on her shoulder.

'Yes, I'm truly very sorry for your loss. It's tough to lose anyone under these circumstances.' She looked at his thoughtful expression. 'I'm told the funeral is next week.'

Her eyes widened as she composed herself. She buttoned up her coat. 'Yes, it is. Yet another ordeal, but at least I'm on my way home.'

She made her way towards the door, taken aback as he pushed past her and held it open for her.

'Just so you know, we have informed Penny Wheeler so she can let your daughter know that you're on your way home.'

She never spoke as she walked out of the police station into the fresh London breeze. Free, she took in a deep, sharp intake of breath as she smiled to herself.

CHAPTER 20

Kate was enraged when she arrived home. She noticed the shreds of crime scene tape still attached to the railings fluttering in the air.

'Why would they leave them on there? They have got to go.' She pulled them off and placed them in the rubbish bin. 'I don't want my Sophie bloody seeing that.'

Distracted, she could hear the telephone ring from inside her house as she removed her keys from inside her bag and opened the front door. She raced inside and answered it.

'Hello, Kate speaking.' She was relieved to hear the sound of Penny Wheeler's voice on the other end of the telephone.

'Hi Kate, I'm so pleased you're home. I shall bring Sophie round soon. She can't wait to see you.'

Kate smiled to herself as she dropped her bag to the floor.

'I have literally just walked in. Thank you,

Penny, for everything. Tell her I love her and I can't wait to see her too.'

She replaced the receiver and flipped on the light switch, knowing Sophie's arrival was imminent because Penny only lived around the corner.

'It's like nothing's happened. Everything is the same.'

She glanced up at the stairs and remembered her hidden photograph. Kate drew strength from it as she turned around to face the living room door and chanted to herself, 'The only way forward is through. The only way forward is through.'

She had dreaded this moment as she gripped the door handle. Cautious, she started to open it.

'Mummy! Mummy!'

The sound of Sophie's voice through the letterbox was enough to make her almost jump out of her skin, as she raced towards it.

'I'm here, Sophie.'

The sight of her daughter's face as she opened the door banished the ghost of Alan, as she enveloped her in a tight embrace.

'Oh, Mummy, I've missed you so much. To the moon and back.' She was lost to the world. Wrapped up in a universe that was a mother's love for a child. 'I love you more than chocolate, Mummy, and all my stuffed animals, and all my dolls.'

She beamed at her daughter. Happy now, she glanced behind at Penny standing there, her face emotional, watching the reunion.

'I have missed you so much, Mummy.'

Kate straightened up as she kept eye contact with Sophie and held on to her hand.

'Wow, what a lovely welcome, Sophie. You give the best hugs ever, my angel.' She smiled at her daughter.

'Mummy, you're not going to leave me alone again, are you?'

Saddened by her question, Kate noticed the tears as they streamed down Penny's cheeks.

'No, I'm never going to leave you again. Now why don't you take your things upstairs like the good girl you are, while I make Penny a nice cup of tea.'

Kate watched as Sophie climbed the stairs, followed by her pink rolling suitcase that disappeared out of sight behind her. Kate turned her attention towards Penny.

'Please, Penny, come in. Let me go and put the kettle on.' She made her way down the hallway as Penny followed behind and caught up with her. 'I can't thank you enough, Penny, for looking after Sophie. You've been amazing and as for all the cleaning that's been done, I'm amazed.'

She turned on the cold tap, picked up the kettle, filled it, and placed it on top of the stove.

'Well, Kate, it was the police who suggested I contacted some professional cleaners, but don't worry, I have paid them, it's the least I could do. I know you would've done the same for me.'

Kate removed the cups and sugar from the cupboard and placed them onto the kitchen table.

'I'm just so grateful, Penny, for everything you've done for us. I can't thank you enough.'

She embraced her friend.

'It's okay, Kate. It's fine, really.'

The embrace was interrupted as the kettle whistled. Kate removed it from the stove.

'Oh, Penny, I'm sorry. It's going to have to be a black tea, I'm afraid. I've not had a chance to get any milk.'

She stared at Penny, puzzled as the broad smile appeared across her face.

'I already thought of that, Kate. Check the fridge. I popped in this morning and got you a few essentials when the police rang me and told me you were being released.'

Grateful, Kate closed her eyes for a second, as she sighed.

'What would I do without you? You've thought of everything. Please take a seat, Penny.'

She took the milk from the fridge and joined her at the table.

'How are you feeling, Kate, now you're home?'

The vivid memory of the night Alan raped her flooded her brain and she quickly closed a lid on it, as she banished it from her mind.

'I think I'm still in shock. To say this has been one of the worst experiences of my life is an understatement.'

Touched, Kate looked up as she felt Penny's warm hand covering hers.

'I can't imagine what you've been through, and as for Jill! I have never liked her much but would never have thought her capable of anything like this. What she did is pure evil.'

Kate could feel the bile as it rose in her stomach. She could taste it in the back of her throat.

'I feel like such a fool. All those years and you think you know someone. I told her everything and she used it against me! Never mind the rest of it.'

She tried to compose herself as she made the tea.

'I'm so sorry about Alan. I know you never had an easy time of it but it's still a loss.'

Kate's mind wandered as her thoughts switched to Sophie.

'Thanks, Penny. Has Sophie mentioned him at all?' She gripped the cup hard as she raised it to her mouth and took a swig of the hot tea.

'I don't think it's registered yet. She hasn't mentioned anything to me. I can ask Megan if you like?'

Defiantly, she shook her head.

'Only if she mentions it and as you said, it's probably too soon. I'll have to keep my eye on her, especially with more grief to come.' She placed her cup down onto the table and twisted it, watching the tea as it swirled around inside as she daydreamed.

'Oh, of course, the funeral. When is it?'

Kate broke from her reverie as she answered her.

'Next week. My solicitor told me that Alan's brother Barry has arranged it all since he thought I'd be in prison.'

She noticed the concerned look on Penny's

face.

'Oh, I'm really sorry. After everything else, you still have to bury him.'

Kate let out a long sigh. 'I think I will go, but after everyone has left.' She fidgeted as she tried hard to keep it together.

'Well, if you don't want Sophie to go with you, I will always have her that day.'

Kate smiled as she looked across the table at Penny.

'Thanks, but I think it's important she comes with me, I think we both need some kind of closure. It's important, so we can move forward.' Leaning back in her chair, Kate watched Penny's sympathetic face.

'Maybe, when it's all over, you and Sophie should think about getting away for a bit. Spend some quality time together.'

Kate raised her eyebrows.

'I haven't really thought that far ahead yet, to be honest with you, although it doesn't sound like such a bad idea.'

She knew that was what she wanted to do, but didn't want to discuss it with Penny.

'No, I don't suppose you have, you poor thing. Well, if you ever need to talk, you only have to pick up the phone, you know that, right?'

Kate knew deep down in her heart that Penny was a reliable, kind person. 'You're a good friend, Penny. Knowing you were looking after Sophie was a huge weight off my mind, and I owe you so much for that.'

She watched Penny as she stood up.

'Well, I'm going to have to make a move. I've still got so much to do. I don't know where the time has gone today.'

Kate followed her out of the kitchen and down the hallway, stopping next to Penny by the front door.

'Now don't worry, Kate, you'll get through this. I know you will.'

Kate smiled as she reached out and opened the front door. She watched Penny as she made her way down the front steps.

'Thanks again, Penny. Don't forget to give the kids my love.'

The day of the funeral had come around fast and Kate stood in front of her bedroom mirror watching her reflection. As the flawless woman stared back at her, she called out, 'Sophie, are you ready yet? Come on, darling, we really need to get a move on.'

She continued to admire herself as she heard Sophie's voice behind.

'I'm ready, Mummy. How do I look?'

She took Sophie's hand, sat down on the bed and lifted her onto her lap.

'You look beautiful, my princess, like you always do.' She smiled at her daughter's shyness. 'Now listen to Mummy. Do you understand what's happening today?' She looked into Sophie's eyes as she waited for her to answer.

'Yes, Mummy. We're saying goodbye to Daddy because he's in heaven now.'

She nodded.

'That's right. Daddy is already in heaven, and we're just burying a box today.'

She felt Sophie's hands as the small child reached out her arms. She cupped her face.

'I know. Are you sad, Mummy?'

Taken aback by her daughter, she hugged her close.

'Everyone gets sad at funerals, baby. It will get better though, I promise.'

A car horn beeped twice and Sophie jumped up off of her lap. Kate watched her as she ran across to the bedroom window.

'That's our taxi, Mummy.'

Sophie raced out of the bedroom and pounded down the stairs. Kate stood up and followed her.

'Put your coat on, Sophie, there's a good girl.'

Nervous, Kate grabbed her bag off the coat stand as she opened the front door, and glanced across at the two suitcases sitting in the hallway. She buttoned up Sophie's coat.

'I think we're all set. Just the suitcases now. Sophie, you go and wait by the car while Mummy fetches the cases and locks up.'

She gripped the handles and pulled the suitcases behind her down the path. Once outside the gate, she relinquished them to the driver.

'Sophie, come on, get in to the car, darling. We've got a hectic day today.'

The driver put both cases into the boot of the car. Distracted, Kate noticed the Jamaican woman watching them from her window across the road as the driver pulled away from the house.

'It's only five minutes in the taxi. Not far, Sophie.'

The long driveway inside the cemetery passed many headstones and seemed to last forever. Sophie said, 'There's a lot of daddies in here,

Mummy.'

Sophie's puzzled face made Kate smile.

'No, sweetie. They're not all daddies. There are mummies, nannies, grandads, even children. Everyone dies at some point.'

Sophie frowned and Kate could almost read her daughter's thoughts as she looked at her small face.

'What, even you, Mummy?'

Kate gave out a half laugh.

'I'm not going anywhere for a long time yet, thank you very much. I want to be here for your wedding.'

Kate was amused as Sophie screwed up her face.

'I'm never getting married, Mummy. I'm going to live with you forever and ever.'

Her daughter was the one person who could break and heal her heart.

'Well, that's okay then, isn't it, my angel?'

The car stopped near to the graveside. Kate looked out of the window and noticed the many wreaths of flowers stacked next to it.

'Okay, Sophie, we're here now.'

She opened the door, got out and held it open for Sophie.

'Mummy, there are so many graves. What do

all the words say on them?'

Kate shuddered.

'They say the names of the people who have passed away and their age —' Sophie interrupted her before she finished her sentence.

'Can I stay here for a bit and read some please, Mummy.'

Her words stopped her in her tracks.

'Okay, just for a minute, but you will have to come over and say goodbye to Daddy soon.'

She waited for her to answer as Sophie sidled over to a nearby headstone.

'Okay, Mummy.'

The anger in her chest burned deep inside Kate as she approached Alan's grave. She knew she had so much she wanted to say to him.

CHAPTER 21

Kate bent down and as she plucked a rose from an arrangement, she stared at Alan's grave while she twirled it between her fingers.

'I thought I'd wait until everyone had gone before I acted like the doting widow. I wasn't sure how good a performance I'd manage with everyone watching me.' She let out a half laugh. 'I mean, I might have broken out into a little song and dance. It's hard to keep in character when you feel so bloody happy.'

She reached out her hand and dusted off a tombstone next to Alan's grave. Kate sat down and continued.

'Your brother Barry did a good job. This really is a lovely spot. Mind you, too good for a bastard like you.' Frustrated, she crossed her legs, swinging her foot back and forth. 'All those years I put up with you. Then I find out that you've been sleeping with that whore, and you thought I never knew.'

She cast her mind back to that dreadful day she found out.

'I can remember it like yesterday. The day I let myself into your study and found your disgusting DVDs.'

She had watched him on a screen, naked on top of someone as he shifted around. The woman's hair spread like a fiery sunset and exposed her best friend, Jill.

'I felt sick to the pit of my stomach as I sorted through them all.'

She took in a deep, sharp breath.

'Mind you, the recent ones were good. The ones where you were planning to leave me and run off with that back-stabbing bitch, and your daughter's inheritance. You must have thought Christmas had come early when she told you about the money.'

The last shred of loyalty she'd had to either of them had dropped away that day.

'You thought you had it made, didn't you? A bit on the side and a fortune into the bargain.' She shook her head. 'Jill didn't want you, Alan, she wanted you dead. I heard her on one of your tapes, plotting and planning with John on the phone, in my own kitchen. Can you believe that? Only I didn't know who he was at the time.'

Kate tutted. 'Anyway, I thought it best to delete that part of the tape recording. I mean, I didn't want you hearing that now, did I?'

Her thoughts switched to John.

'I never forgot his voice, then I heard it again the day I met John in that restaurant, with Jill.'

She looked across at Sophie. When Sophie waved at her, she waved back.

'But it was when I was in town with Sophie and she spotted John and Jill together — that was when I could see the whole picture, while all of you were blinded by the money and scheming behind my back!' She cocked her head to the side and raised her hand to her ear. She pretended to listen out. 'What was that you just said, Alan? Did you just call me a fucking bitch?'

She threw her head back as she laughed again.

'You deserved everything you got, the way you treated me and your daughter. You were a vile, disgusting, vulgar human being.'

She could feel her heart as it pounded through her chest.

'All I had to do was play along, sit back and let them kill you. After hearing John and Jill on the phone, I knew they were planning on running away together and after they killed you, they were going to try and set me up for your murder. However, I was one step ahead of all of you. Because I knew about all the surveillance you had set up through the house, didn't I?'

Kate had never felt so betrayed in her entire life when she realised what was going on.

'You had the audacity to call me a stupid fucking bitch. Really?! When I managed to take all three of you down, single-handed. I got rid of you: my violent drunk of a husband; my jealous, greedy whore of a best friend, Jill; and John, the lying, murdering conman.'

Kate smiled.

'Now that's what I call fucking justice, but I doubt the police would see it like that. But they never saw all the beatings I took from you on a daily basis, did they?'

Kate's eyes welled up as she remembered all the pain and suffering Alan had inflicted on her.

'I might still have the scars, and you might have ground me down for a while, but once I'd hit bottom, I knew I had to fight back. The only way was up. I wasn't going to let the three of you destroy me.'

She raised her shaking hand as she pointed her finger towards his grave.

'I will never forgive you, for turning our

daughter into a bloody nervous wreck. She is scared for life because of you, but I'm going to make sure I fix her. I rue the day I ever set eyes on you.'

Kate stood up, brushing down her skirt. She composed herself and looked down over his grave.

'Do you like my new look, Alan? It's very nice, isn't it? Probably a lot nicer than what your bit-on-the-side whore, Jill, will be wearing for the next fifteen or twenty years.'

Kate stretched out her leg and prodded the fresh soil with her shoe.

'I will sleep so much better now, knowing you are six feet under. It's a shame the dirt is so soft, or I would've danced on your grave.'

The tug on her skirt dragged her out of her séance as she turned around and looked down into the eyes of her daughter.

'Come on, Mummy, he can't hurt you anymore.'

She stretched out her hand and handed Sophie the rose.

'No, Sophie. Nobody is going to hurt us ever again, I can promise you that.'

She looked at Sophie as she jammed her nose into the top of the flower.

'This flower smells like a weed, Mummy.'

Kate thought even that was too good for Alan as she stared at the flower.

'It's time to say goodbye to Daddy, Sophie.'

Relieved at the closure, she reached out and felt for Sophie's hand as she led her to the graveside.

'Now, just throw the flower on the top of the earth and say goodbye to him.'

Sophie, dry-eyed, launched the flower onto the heap of soil as Kate watched her.

'Bye bye, Daddy.'

Kate drew Sophie close towards her as they headed back towards the taxi.

'Mummy, are we really going on holiday right now?'

Sophie opened the car door as she preceded Kate into the back seat.

'How many more times? Yes, the tickets and passports are in my bag.'

Worried as she reached into her bag, Kate double-checked again as she caught the driver's attention, in the rear-view mirror.

'Could you take us to the airport now please?'

Kate never looked out of the window as they drove out of the cemetery. She didn't want to look back, committed now to her only daughter's future.

'I can't believe we are really going, Mummy, I'm so excited.' Kate laughed.

'Well you better believe it, Sophie, and if you like it that much, we can stay forever.' She watched as her little girl's face lit up.

'You are the best mummy in the world. I love you so much.'

Happy, Kate pulled her close, hugging her tight.

'I love you too, Sophie, and don't you ever forget that.' She flinched as Sophie playfully prodded her side.

'But I love you more. Remember, Mummy? To the moon and back.'

Kate closed her eyes and threw her head back.

'Oh no, here we go. We're not playing that game again.'

The taxi turned onto the main road. Kate was thankful it was over, it had been a bittersweet experience for both of them.

DI Roberts was feeling somewhat caged, back in the privacy of his own office, when he heard the knock on the door.

'Yes, come in.'

Surrounded by his medals, he was polishing

them. Roberts still yearned for action. Caught off guard, Webb sprinted into his office.

'Steady on, lad! What's the rush?'

Astonished by his urgency, Roberts watched the beads of sweat run down the side of Webb's face.

'Boss, it's the Saunders case.'

Uninterested, he rolled his eyes at him.

'That's all done and dusted. Chambers and Reynolds are both banged up, Mrs Saunders got her money back. Case closed, full stop.'

Roberts became concerned as Webb retreated backwards, beckoning him with his hand.

'Nope, I don't believe it is. You need to come with me and see what Jones has found.'

Intrigued, Roberts got up out of his chair. 'I can't imagine she has found anything that is going to change our result.'

Roberts made his way across the room towards the door as he listened to Webb.

'I think this might change everything, boss.'

No time was wasted as he made his way into the incident room. He spotted Jones, who greeted them both with a nod as Roberts raised his voice.

'Would someone like to tell me what the hell is going on here?'

His eyes turned towards her as she touched her computer screen. It displayed two sets of fingerprints.

'Well sir, when we processed the computer and discs, we found one set of fingerprints.'

Impatient, he interrupted her.

'Yes, Jones, we know all that. They came back a match for Alan Saunders.'

He glanced at Webb, who stood next to him.

'Well, forensics, on closer inspection, found another set of prints on the edges of the discs.'

He waited for her to go on.

'Get to the point, Jones, before I grow a beard. Who did they belong to?'

Roberts was shocked as Webb blurted it out.

'Kate Saunders.'

Baffled, Roberts reeled back.

'So, that means Kate Saunders knew about the bloody cameras and what her husband had been up to on those tapes all along?' Roberts looked at the computer screen as Jones displayed all the discs Kate Saunders' fingerprints had been found on.

'Yes sir, you're right. Kate Saunders knew her husband was at it with Reynolds and they were planning on running off with her money.'

Deep in thought and livid, Roberts' mind

raced. 'She probably knew a lot more than that.'

Webb excitedly interrupted him. 'Looks like she was playing the lot of them. Even us, guv.'

Roberts could feel the angry burn on his face, as it reddened.

'Yes, I bloody get it, Webb! Would've flaming helped if we had known all this before. Why the bloody hell didn't forensics give us this earlier? Talk about a cock-up.'

He stared across at Jones as she explained.

'They've had some problems in the lab with equipment, so had a bit of a backlog, guv.'

Roberts rubbed the top of his head with his knuckles.

'A bloody problem in the lab! Someone's head is going to roll for this. I can't believe this has happened. Kate flaming Saunders deserves a flaming Oscar for playing the victim.'

Roberts looked towards DS Jones. He thought she looked miles away.

'Pull yourself together, girl. Enough thinking, let's sort this bloody mess out.'

He noticed Webb smiling wide. Roberts thought it would crack his face.

'Right, you can drive, lad. Now let's go.'

Roberts tossed his car keys towards Webb and they both followed him outside into the carpark.

'That's one bloody thing you learn in this business: The truth is like wine. It changes with time.'

The rain fell hard as he raced across and opened the car door. Roberts got in, followed by Jones as Webb revved the engine.

'Let's get a move on, lad.'

He looked out through the rain-streaked windows. As Webb pulled away fast, he jolted back in his seat.

DS Jones piped up, 'I actually felt sorry for her, guv. She was the ultimate victim. Beaten by her husband, betrayed by her best friend and widowed by her lover.'

Optimistic, Roberts' years of experience in the police force surfaced.

'Don't let this eat you both up. Look upon it as a learning curve. One you'll never forget. Anyway, let's not get too carried away until we hear what Kate Saunders has to say for herself.'

He turned his head towards the pumped-up boy racer as he joined the conversation.

'I'm going to look her in the eye, and drill her until …'

Concerned for his safety, he calmed him down as they approached the house.

'Let's all take a deep breath, shall we, and

start with a conversation first before we do anything else.'

Thankful as Webb parked the car, Roberts opened the door and got out. They both followed him onto the pavement and Roberts cautioned them again.

'Right. I don't want anybody running their mouth off, is that clear? If anyone is going to arrest Kate Saunders it's going to be me. Understood?'

He watched them both as they nodded at him in sync.

'Webb, ring the doorbell, will you, before we get soaked by this blasted rain.'

Roberts surveyed the street. Webb shouted out to him from the doorstep.

'Nobody's home, guv.'

Preoccupied, Roberts didn't answer him as the house on the opposite side of the road caught his eye.

'We've got ourselves a watcher. Get over there and see if they know anything, Jones. Fingers crossed they're the neighbourhood watch. Those curtain twitchers don't miss a trick.'

The houses were grimmer on the other side of the road, Jones noticed as she made her way towards her target of inquiry. She knocked on the front door and didn't have to wait long as it opened from within.

'Hello, can I help you?'

She stared at the forty-plus Jamaican woman as she reached into her pocket to pull out her warrant card and show it to her.

'Hello, I'm Detective Sergeant Jones and I was wondering whether I could ask you a few questions, Mrs …?'

She noticed she was well-dressed, in a quirky kind of sense, as she answered her.

'It's Miss Kalisha Khad, and you'll be wanting to ask me about her who lives across the road?'

Amazed by the woman's sharpness, she said, 'If you mean Mrs Saunders, then yes. Have you by any chance seen her today?'

'Well, I saw a black car early this morning. I think it might have been a taxi. Then she and her daughter got in and drove off. I think, in fact, I'm sure it was her husband's funeral today.' Jones didn't interrupt her as she continued. 'Terrible thing it was. He was murdered, you know? Of, course you know. You probably saw him. They said on the news and in the newspapers, it was a gunshot that killed him. Was it a gunshot? Did you catch them? That woman, her with the big orange hair, was always there. Did you talk to her? I did tell the police in the uniforms about her already, after it happened, you know.'

Bamboozled by the barrage of questions, Jones cautiously retreated, annoyed that they never got the memo from uniform.

'Okay, okay. Thank you very much for all your help. It's much appreciated.'

Jones turned around quickly as she heard the woman's voice again.

'Mind you, something odd happened this morning as well. She loaded two large suitcases into the car before they drove off. I mean, who takes luggage to a funeral? I bet she won't be having any nine-nights for him either. That's what us Jamaicans call a wake, you know.'

Jones, confused, watched her as she kissed her teeth and disappeared back into her house.

Inside the car, Roberts felt hopeful as Jones opened the car door and joined them both.

'Sir, she told me it was Alan Saunders' funeral today.'

Roberts raised his eyebrows. 'Well, that's where she is then, obviously.'

Deep in thought, he contemplated their next move as her voice interrupted him.

'The neighbour told me that when the taxi arrived, the driver put two large suitcases into the boot. But she said that was hours ago. You were right about her being nosey, she didn't stop talking.'

Angered by the information, Roberts raised his voice as he spoke.

'She's doing a runner. So, where the bloody hell is she going? Someone must know something.'

The dense cloud of thought inside the car was lifted as he heard DC Webb's voice.

'What about the daughter's friend, Megan Wheeler? Her mother, Penny Wheeler, might know something. What do you think, sir?'

Impressed that Webb had, for once, contributed a good idea to a conversation, even though he had already thought of that, he praised him.

'Good thinking, Webb. What you waiting for, lad? Drive on, Webb.'

The four hundred yards around the corner to her house wasn't worth the drive as Webb pulled up outside.

'Okay you two, I want you to let me handle this. Is that clear?'

Standing on the doorstep, Roberts rang the

doorbell. Impatient, as he lifted his arm to ring it for the second time, Penny Wheeler opened the door.

'Hello, Mrs Wheeler. You probably remember me, DI Roberts? I'm so sorry to bother you again, but we are trying to get hold of Mrs Saunders. I hope you don't mind if I ask you a few questions?'

She seemed a lot more relaxed than the last time they had met.

'Of course I remember you, Inspector. I'm glad it's under different circumstances. How can I be of help?'

He remained calm and casual as he spoke to her.

'Well, I have tried ringing Mrs Saunders, unsuccessfully, and I can't seem to get any reply at her home address either. Do you happen to know if she's gone away anywhere—a holiday, maybe?'

He watched her standing on the doorstep as she nodded her head towards him.

'Well, you do know it was Alan's funeral today?'

He acted surprised.

'Oh really, I wasn't aware of that fact.'

He kept eye contact with her as she

continued.

'Alan's brother had arranged it all and Kate thought it best not to go. But she told me that she and Sophie were going to pay their respects afterwards then have some time away together. In fact, it was me who suggested it to her.'

He leaned in closer to her as he spoke.

'Probably just what they needed. Have they gone somewhere nice?'

She rolled her eyes towards him.

'Nice? Amazing more like. They've gone to Florida. I think they're flying from Gatwick Airport. I'm a bit jealous if truth be told, all that lovely hot weather, but if anyone deserves a holiday they do.'

Roberts forced a smile.

'How wonderful. Florida. I bet they go to Disneyland.'

She laughed as she answered him.

'That's exactly where they've gone. I mean, where else would a little girl want to go for a couple of weeks?'

His ears pricked up as he listened to her.

'Are you sure they are going for two weeks, Mrs Wheeler?'

He noticed her concerned face as she tensed up.

'Yes, I'm sure. Why, is there some sort of problem?'

Happy he had got what he came for, his tone changed. 'No, nothing to worry about. Just need to sort out some paperwork she forgot to sign. I suppose she's contacted the school, what with taking her daughter away in term time?'

She answered him abruptly as he eyed her.

'I'm afraid I can't answer that. You're going to have to take that up with Kate or the school.'

He reached into his pocket and pulled out a card. He handed it to her.

'Well, if you hear from her, please call me day or night. My number's on the back.'

His mind raced as he turned around and made his way back towards the car. Penny Wheeler called out to him.

'Mr Roberts, if it's not important, I'm sure Kate will contact you after she and Sophie have had a much-needed holiday.'

He stared at her as she closed the door. Roused from his reverie, he opened the car door as Webb spoke to him.

'What's next, boss? What did she say? Where do we go from here?'

Worried that time wasn't on their side, he gave them their orders.

'Webb, we're taking a trip to Gatwick Airport, so put your foot down. Let's go. Jones, I want you to get on the blower and contact the daughter's school, find out if she's told them the same story as Mrs Wheeler.'

The shops and office buildings flew past as his head whirled. Frustrated, Roberts listened to the tail end of Jones conversation over the sound of the noisy traffic.

'Well, Jones, don't keep us guessing. What did the school have to say?' He drummed his fingers on the dashboard as he waited for her to answer him.

'Well, you're not going to like this, sir. Mrs Saunders informed the school over two weeks ago.'

The realisation crept deep inside his mind.

'So, she bloody well planned this holiday before Alan Saunders was shot dead?' He turned his head around and stared at Jones as she continued.

'No sir, not about a holiday. Kate Saunders informed the school she was removing her daughter for good and moving to Florida. In fact, they told me she had already enrolled her daughter in a school there.'

Livid, he slammed the palm of his hand down

on the dashboard.

'Well, it's obvious she had this planned all along. She has taken us for complete bloody idiots. Did they mention anything else?' Bitter, he listened to her.

'They just said they would miss her and her daughter as they were hoping Mrs Saunders would have a change of heart and return to her old job at the school, after her husband's death.'

Intrigued, he spun his head around fast as he spoke to her.

'So, she worked there, before, at the school? Doing what, Jones?'

Her Welsh lilt softened as she spoke.

'She was head of the drama department. She's also a trained actress.'

He threw his head back as he laughed out loud.

'Now, why doesn't that bloody well surprise me? She could give Dame Judi Dench a run for her money. She seems to have thought of everything.'

Transfixed on the road ahead, he watched Webb as he overtook a slower vehicle. Pissed off she had slipped through his net once, he was adamant it wasn't about to happen again.

Sophie had started to get impatient inside the taxi as it raced along the motorway. Kate had tried hard to keep her occupied.

'Mummy, I'm really bored. Are we nearly there yet?'

In a daydream, Kate was happy at the distance she had put between herself and the nightmare she had left behind, as she answered her.

'Stop fretting, Sophie. It won't be long now, sweetheart.'

The movement of the taxi along the road made Kate feel tired and as she closed her eyes for a moment, she heard Sophie's voice again.

'Mummy, will we have time to look around all the shops at the airport?'

She opened her eyes and looked at Sophie's, whose eyes were as wide as on Christmas morning.

'Not really, Sophie. We're running a little late and we don't want to miss our flight, do we?'

Kate checked her watch and calculated how long it would be before they boarded the aircraft.

'Oh Mummy. I wanted to look at all the toys in the shops.'

Kate was disheartened as she watched her

daughter's smile vanish from her face.

'Don't worry, Sophie, they sell toys on the plane and if you're a good girl, I shall buy you one. Also, after we land I will buy you another one from a shop. How's about that?'

Relieved she had brought the smile back to her daughter's face, she closed her eyes again and rested them as they drew closer towards the airport.

Roberts wasn't a happy bunny as he raised his voice and yelled at DC Webb.

'How long is this going to take, Webb? For heaven's sake put your bloody foot down, lad.' Frustrated by the heavy traffic, Roberts yearned for a police siren as he listened to Webb whine.

'There's nothing I can bloody do, sir. The traffic is feeding in from both sides. I wish we had taken a squad car, guv. All I have is a horn and high beam. Not exactly the same thing as having a blue flashing siren.'

Roberts took in a deep breath, as he churned over the situation in his head.

'Well, the only way to look at this positively is that if we're stuck in this traffic, fingers crossed, she's stuck in it also. Jones, dig out Kate Saunders' mobile number and keep trying it.'

With Sophie fast asleep, Kate downloaded the boarding passes to her new mobile phone. Startled as her old phone rang out, Kate saw Penny Wheeler's name flash across the screen.

'Hello, Penny, are you okay?' Kate's curiosity was aroused as to why Penny had called her.

'Are you at the airport yet, Kate?'

The worry in Penny's voice transmitted itself to her through the receiver.

'Nearly, Penny, why, what's wrong?'

Kate was concerned as Penny sounded flustered and spoke fast.

'Well, I'm not sure. I didn't know whether to call you or not, but I thought I better had, only the police showed up on my doorstep.'

Kate glanced up at the driver, who seemed preoccupied with the music on the radio, as she answered her in a whisper.

'Really, what did they want?'

Her heart raced as Sophie stirred in her sleep. Kate's eyes diverted towards her.

'Well it was all a bit cloak and dagger really. The one in charge, that DI Roberts, said they needed to speak with you, and that they had called you on the phone and been round to your house but couldn't get hold of you.'

Kate tried hard to control the tremor in her voice as she spoke.

'It's probably nothing, Penny. I will give them a call.'

She took in a deep breath as Penny continued.

'Well, I told them that you would call them when you got back from your holiday. They even asked me if you had informed the school you were going away in term time. I mean, you'd think they'd have better things to do.'

Rattled, Kate could feel her whole body as it shook.

'You told them I was going on holiday? Did you tell them where I was going?'

Kate was panicked now. She stared out of the window and turned her head around, glancing behind her at the traffic.

'Yes. I told them you and Sophie were going to the cemetery and then going to Gatwick to catch a flight to Florida for a couple of weeks.'

She almost dropped the mobile phone as Sophie stirred again in her lap.

'Okay, Penny, thanks so much for letting me know. Give a kiss to the kids for me, and I'll look forward to telling you about Florida when I get back.'

She cut the call as she glanced up again at the

driver. Kate stared at the back of his head and willed him to drive faster. Her phone rang out again as she said to herself, 'Shit.'

She stared at the phone which displayed an unknown number, unsure what to do. She composed herself, picked it up and answered it.

'Hello, Kate speaking.'

She clenched her fist as she recognised the voice on the other end of the phone.

'Hello, Mrs Saunders, it's DS Jones. So sorry to disturb you. How are you?'

Her blood ran cold as she looked down at Sophie still asleep.

'I'm fine, DS Jones. What can I do for you?'

She felt like someone had their hands around her throat as she struggled to control her breathing.

'It's just to let you know, we've released all of your husband's possessions and they're ready for you to pick up. When could you come and get them?'

She gritted her teeth as she tried to mask the sigh.

'Well, I'm going on holiday, so you could drop them round at Mrs Wheeler's, or I can collect them when I get back.'

She could feel the dryness in her mouth as she

waited for DS Jones to reply.

'How lovely. Are you going somewhere nice?'

She scrunched her eyes up as she spoke.

'Just a package deal to Florida. I promised my daughter I'd take her to Disney.'

Kate tried to gauge her tone but her Welsh accent was unreadable as she listened to her voice.

'That's fine, Mrs Saunders. I'll look forward to seeing you soon. Goodbye.'

Without a thought, she opened the window and tossed the mobile phone out of it, relieved as the last part of her past left her shaky hand.

Roberts turned and looked at Webb, unimpressed as his language intensified at the blocked traffic. 'Is there something wrong with you, Webb? Stop yelling at the bloody traffic when DS Jones is trying to make a bloody phone call.' Roberts slapped him on the back of his head. 'Do you know what operational silence actually means? No, I thought not. Now shut up.'

He looked at Jones as she interrupted.

'Well, I was surprised she answered the call, sir, but she's definitely lying. I can hear it in her voice, even though she told me exactly what she told Mrs Wheeler.'

Roberts eyed Webb as he jumped on board the bandwagon, crowing, 'Old news, sergeant. Tell us something we don't know. She knows we're on to her. I wouldn't put anything past that woman. Hey, boss, nearly there. I can see the airport.'

Reassured as he sat upright in his seat, Roberts peered ahead through the windscreen and noticed a low flying aircraft as he spotted the airport terminal buildings.

The taxi halted outside the terminal building as the driver deposited their luggage onto a baggage trolley. She leaned forward and whispered into Sophie's ear.

'Come on, sleepy head, we're here now. Time to wake up.' Kate watched her as she sat up. She grabbed Sophie's hand as they disembarked the taxi.

'I'm so excited, Mummy, but I'm still sleepy.'

Kate watched her wide-eyed as she yawned.

'Hold on to the side of the trolley as I push it and look for our check-in desk, there's a good girl.'

The illuminated boards inside the terminal building flashed the gate numbers and check-in desks. Without hesitation, she managed to find the right one and checked in their luggage.

Kate still felt uneasy and could feel her heart as it pulsated in her chest.

'Right c'mon, we need to get a move on, Sophie, or we're going to miss our flight.'

Sophie clung onto her hand as Kate hauled her through passport control, into duty-free.

'Mummy, Mummy.'

Kate looked down at her.

'Mummy, I need to go to the toilet right now. I need to pee.'

Sophie hopped up and down.

'Can't you hold it a bit longer, until we get on the aeroplane?' Sophie whined at her. 'Okay Sophie, come on then, but you must be really quick.'

She veered away from the main concourse into the toilets. Sophie, ahead of her, dived into a cubicle as Kate waited for her by the hand basins.

'Sophie, come on. Hurry up please, sweetheart.'

Relieved when Sophie emerged out of the cubicle, she turned on the tap. Sophie washed her hands as she spoke.

'Mummy, are you okay? Are you sad about

Daddy still?'

Kate looked into her eyes as she stretched out her arm and dried her hands with a paper towel.

'No, baby. Well, maybe I'm a little sad, but we haven't got time to talk about it now because we really need to get to the departure gate and get on that aeroplane, okay? Are you ready to move fast?'

Kate watched the smile surface on her pale face.

'I'm ready to run as fast as a cheetah, Mummy.'

She grabbed Sophie's hand again, as they left the toilets. Kate raced her towards the departure gate.

DC Webb parked the car. DI Roberts and DS Jones got out fast and raced inside the terminal building.

'Stay alert, Jones, and keep your eyes open. Kate Saunders could be anywhere.'

Standing at the departure boards Roberts scanned it as it refreshed and blinked. Webb caught up with them.

'No point looking at the board sir, checked it already. The flight isn't up on the board yet.'

On a mission, Roberts raised his voice as he

barked his orders at them.

'Doesn't mean she's not here. Come on, follow me.'

Roberts raced towards the baggage check-in desks. Irritated, he halted, stuck in a river of passengers. He surveyed the area as he shouted at them again.

'Right, this is no good, we need to split up. Jones, you search the food court area. Webb, you take customs. Meet me back here in ten minutes.'

They scattered into the crowds of travellers.

Ten minutes came around quick. Roberts noticed Webb's unhappy face as he approached him.

'I take it by the look on your face, you got no joy.'

Webb shook his head from side to side.

'I have spoken to airport security, guv. I have also circulated her photograph but no one I have spoken to has seen them.'

Roberts turned around fast as he heard DS Jones' voice behind him.

'No luck, guv. Maybe we're too late.'

Distracted, he noticed three airport ground staff, reached into his pocket, pulled out his warrant card and flashed it in front of their faces.

'I'm DI Roberts. I need to know if we have

missed the flight to Florida SFB Airport.'

He listened as a rugged man, whose name tag branded him as Andy, said, 'No sir, you haven't missed the flight. In fact, you're really early.'

He reached into his pocket again, removed a photograph of Kate Saunders and held it up in front of them.

'Have you seen this woman? She's travelling with a young girl. It's imperative that we find her and stop her from boarding that flight.'

Roberts felt frustrated as they shook their heads, and listened to a smaller man standing in the group.

'No, we haven't seen them, but we have only just started our shift. Sorry, but check-in for the Florida flight is not for hours yet.'

Roberts' patience had started to wear thin. 'What are you talking about? What time is the bloody flight to Florida?'

'The next flight is six o'clock tomorrow morning.'

Still angry, he was confused by their revelation.

'Really! Are you bloody sure about that?'

He listened as the man branded Andy answered him.

'Yes sir, I'm positive. There are no flights out

of this airport to Florida until six o'clock tomorrow morning. Now, if there is nothing else, we need to get back to work.'

Roberts, his lips pursed like he had kissed a lemon, felt the rush of blood flow into his cheeks. Jones intervened. 'Bloody hell, guv. It looks like she's taken us for yet another ride.'

His brow furrowed as he pulled back his leg and kicked a nearby dustbin. He had been duped again. He clenched his fists, adamant he was going to make it his lifelong goal to find her.

Kate nervously looked around the airport as she and Sophie sat at the end departure gate. Impatient, she waited for the flight to be called. 'Mummy, are we getting on yet?'

Transfixed on a young mother as she strapped her wayward child in to a buggy, Kate remembered Sophie at that age, as she answered her.

'Not long now, my princess. We just have to wait for them to call out our flight, then we will be able to board the aeroplane.'

She took in the panorama of the hundreds of faces as she looked for three in particular. Kate shuddered as Sophie spoke to her.

'I can't wait to see him; do they call him the

same name in the country we're going to, Mummy?'

Kate, relieved as she heard the announcement over the PA system, stayed silent.

'Welcome to Heathrow Airport. Could all passengers on flight number two six three zero travelling to Venezuela, please board now at gate number fifteen.'

She took in a deep breath and let out a sigh. Kate looked at Sophie, smiled and spoke to her.

'That's us, Sophie. Come on, let's go.'

Kate stood up and felt the tug on her sleeve as Sophie pulled her back.

'Mummy, are you still cross with me about what happened to Daddy?' Kate, taken aback, froze as Sophie continued, 'I only came back home that night for my gloves and teddy.'

Kate recalled the night in question, when she had rewound the video footage the night Alan had been murdered. Kate, shocked, had watched Sophie as she put on one of her gloves in the hallway. She heard Alan's voice as he cried out in pain and looked into the lounge. Kate was surprised by Sophie's actions: as she picked up the loaded gun it went off in her hand. Panicked, she dropped the gun and her other glove in the hallway as she fled scene.

'No, Sophie, I'm not cross.'

Kate, heartbroken, had deleted any evidence of Sophie's presence the night she arrived a few minutes after John. Leaving only him in the frame on the video footage, Kate threw herself across Alan's now lifeless body.

'Listen to me, Sophie. Promise me you will never mention this again to anybody. It was an accident and we're going to leave it all behind us now, okay? This is a fresh start for both of us. Now let's go and get on this aeroplane.'

Kate still questioned the events that happened that night. Still paranoid, she looked around the airport one last time before they boarded their flight. Unable to shake the image of Sophie from her mind, she wondered to herself whether it really was just an accident.

THE END

AUTHOR BIOGRAPHY

Suzanne Seddon was born in 1968 in Islington, London. After leaving school she had many interesting jobs, from swimming teacher to air hostess, and was able to travel the globe. Now a single mum to her teenage daughter Poppy-willow, Suzanne spends her days writing and has written several articles for magazines and newspapers.

Growing up, Suzanne experienced mental abuse and physical abuse within her own family which strongly influenced her when she wrote her first play, *A Fool's Circle*, when she attended the famous Anna Scher Theatre. Suzanne, however, was not content to leave it there and decided to go ahead and transform her play into a novel.

Not one to shy away from exciting challenges, she also wrote, acted, directed, cast and produced a trailer for the book around her hometown in Islington with the support of local businesses, who recognised the drive and importance of Suzanne and her work.

Suzanne is a passionate writer and she is determined to be heard so that the issue of domestic abuse is raised amongst the public's consciousness, empowering others to speak out. She wants those who suffer at the hands of another to have their voices heard, loud and clear.

Publisher's Author Page:
https://www.wallacepublishing.co.uk/suzanne-seddon.html
Amazon Link:
https://www.amazon.co.uk/Fools-Circle-Suzanne-Seddon/dp/1999613635/ref=sr_1_1?ie=UTF8&qid=1548460249&sr=8-1&keywords=Suzanne+Seddon

Facebook: https://www.facebook.com/afoolscircle
Twitter: https://twitter.com/afoolscircle
Instagram: https://insta-stalker.com/profile/suzseddon/
Twitter (Personal)
https://twitter.com/suzseddon?lang=en

USEFUL CONTACTS

If you are in need of help, please don't feel alone. I have put together a list of wonderful organisations that can give you the support you need in breaking that vicious circle.

Refuge
0808 2000 247
helpline@refuge.org.uk

Woman's Trust
0207 034 0303
office@womanstrust.org.uk

NSPCC
0808 800 5000
help@nspcc.org.uk

Victim Support

0808 168 9111
supportline@victimsupport.org.uk

Solace Women's
Aid 0808 801 0305
rapecrisis@solacewomensaid.org

Men's Advice Line
0808 801 0327
info@mensadviceline.org.uk

Mind
0300 123 3393
info@mind.org.uk